SHERRY**ASHWORTH**

Sherry Ashworth was born in London. She started writing in 1989, and now has a total of eight adult novels and three young adult novels under her belt, including *Disconnected*, her first book for Collins. She lives in Manchester with her husband and two teenage daughters. All of her books are set partly or wholly in the North.

By the same author

Disconnected

BLINDED BY THE LIGHT

SHERRY**ASHWORTH**

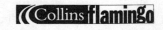

An imprint of HarperCollins*Publishers*

First published in Great Britain by CollinsFlamingo 2003

CollinsFlamingo is an imprint of HarperCollins*Publishers* Ltd,
77-85 Fulham Palace Road, Hammersmith, London W6 8JB

The HarperCollins website address is
www.**fire**and**water**.com

1 3 5 7 9 8 6 4 2

Text copyright © Sherry Ashworth 2003

The author asserts the moral right to be identified as the author of this work.

ISBN 0 00 712336 1

Printed and bound in England by Clays Ltd, St Ives plc

Thanks to Linda Kerr, Robyn Ashworth, Jonathan Abel

*****

For Greg and John

PART ONE

THE JOURNEY

BODIES RECOVERED

The bodies of Matthew Chalmers, 20, and Trevor Norrington-Smith, 21, were recovered today from Hoy Sound.

The young men, together with another friend, Colin Rendall, were students at Cambridge University, holidaying in Orkney. The accident occurred on Saturday evening, when the three men took a boat out for a midnight row. Rendall managed to stay afloat until he was picked up by Angus Middleton, 66, a retired fisherman, who had witnessed the capsizing from his bedroom window. Rendall was flown to Aberdeen, where he is recovering in hospital with his father by his bedside.

Police are refusing to comment on how the accident could have happened. The inquest will take place in Kirkwall after Easter.

1.

From The Preface, Rendall's Book of Prayers

The pain and struggle ceased. I was travelling without effort, moving towards the Light. Where there had been terror, there was now beauty, and peace beyond all understanding. An angel swathed in brightness stood by a table. On it was the Book. White pages, whiter words, thousands upon thousands of them. In essence they said, be free, be pure, do not despair of Perfection. The Book remained inscribed in my head and heart. My purpose was clear.

Didn't feel like talking to anyone. I was pissed off, to tell you the truth. I'd been on my own since two o'clock when Phil had to go to band practice and left me in the middle of campus.

"Great seeing you, Joe," he'd said, thumping me in the ribs. I thumped him back even harder. We grinned at each other.

"The sixty or sixty-one'll take you near the station," he'd said. "Come up again. Any time, like."

"Sure," I said. I thought, I might, but then again, I might not. I slung my overnight bag over my shoulders and set out for the bus stop.

Hell, it wasn't Phil's fault. If all had gone according to plan I wouldn't have been in Birmingham, or even in England for that matter. I would have been in a village in Kenya digging, or teaching kids, or doing some other GAP voluntary work. But just after my A2s, my throat swelled up like a balloon. I lay in bed for weeks – glandular fever.

At first I was too ill to care. Life was just Mum changing damp sheets, pain, nightmarish dreams. Then I was as weak as a baby. When Tasha came to see me she looked taken aback. I date the end of our relationship from that moment. But who could blame her? I was hardly sex on legs. I couldn't even struggle on to my legs for that matter. Tasha shoved some flowers down by my bed, pecked me on the cheek, and stressed a bit about her forthcoming results.

But it was OK in the end. She got her place at Oxford, went up in October and was mesmerised by the whole experience. She sent me a couple of emails about the college and how cool it was, the amazing people she'd met, the course being harder than she thought, more about the amazing people and parties, and then there was the email which started, *I don't know how to tell you this*... You can guess the rest.

To tell you the truth, I wasn't really gutted. I saw it coming. But put together with the fact that I had to cancel the overseas stuff because I still wasn't a hundred per cent, and all my mates were off at uni, and I was living at home, it was a bit of a bummer. OK, I *was* gutted. Tasha and I had been going out for ten months, which was a long time for me. And I liked having a girlfriend. The weird thing is, even when you're close to your mates, as I was – as I am – you don't talk to them in the same way as you do a girl. You say stuff to her you wouldn't say to anyone else. You *do* things, too, but that's another story.

But please don't get the impression I was a loser. That's never been the case, which was why being at a loose end that November was getting me down. I wasn't used to it. As soon as I was well, I got myself some work – nights in a pub pulling pints and lugging crates around, and weekends in Electric Avenue selling geeks the latest PC, PlayStation and Dreamcast games. So I wasn't short of cash. Or invitations. Dave, Rich and Phil all asked me to stay, and I took Phil up on it. So I spent two nights on his floor, both times in a drunken stupor. It was good, kind of.

But like I said, he had to go to band practice, and I made my own way back to Birmingham New Street.

Nowhere is more depressing than a railway station on a Sunday afternoon. There's a kind of sour, dusty smell. People look fed up; they stand around eating junk food and swigging Coke. Their luggage makes them look like refugees. But you can't help feeling that where they're going to might be worse than where they're coming from. You feel yourself becoming more trashy by the minute, sidling up to the newsstand and reading all the tabloid headlines about scandalous celebrity love lives – as if I gave a toss about which plastic bimbo went to bed with which braindead footballer. I'm tempted to buy the paper anyway – something to read, innit? But then again, I'm almost out of cash and I might want a coffee on the train.

I feel myself getting depressed and I don't like it. It's not me. I've had this a few times since the glandular fever, a sort of heaviness washing over me. I fight it by walking up and down the platform, reading the ads for frothy paperbacks for women with boring lives. I look down the line to see if the train's coming. Gotta keep moving. The train should be here any minute now. And sure enough there's a dot in the distance that grows into the front of an engine and, yes, it gets bigger and is arriving at my platform.

So I'm moving through the carriages to find my reserved seat, taking involuntary snapshots of people's faces: Chinese guy reading a paper, couple of chubby pensioners with sandwiches in plastic bags, good-looking girl staring sullenly out of the window, fat bloke asleep with his mouth hanging open. I finally reach my seat and discover I'm on my own; mine is the window seat and the other three seats are empty, having only reservation tickets sitting on the top of them like shrunken hats. I get my Walkman and phone out of my bag and settle down. I glance at my mobile and want someone to text me. And with a jolt and a lurch the train moves forward.

I reckon it'll take about two hours to get to Manchester, more if there's works on the line, which there usually are. The guard announces all the stops, and then another voice takes over to talk about the buffet. When I was a kid I used to like train journeys, but this one feels like another form of waiting, which is all I ever seem to be doing at the moment. Waiting for texts, for phone calls, for next year when I start uni, for something – anything – to happen. Even when I go out to try to make something happen, nothing happens. Or I drink too much and forget what happened. I feel that slide into depression again and stop it by trying to remember the joke Phil's mate told which had us falling about. Then I look out of the window, through the smears and grime. The train stops and starts. I see embankments with rubbish strewn down them, scrubby old plants. And then we pull up in Wolverhampton. And wait. And move again.

It comes as a shock when I realise the couple moving along the carriage in my direction are going to come and sit opposite me. But they check their tickets and acknowledge to each other that this is the right place. I sort of watch them. They can't be much older than me. Girl has brown hair in bunches, a good figure, jeans, white sweatshirt. Bloke looks thin; he's wearing a denim jacket over a white T-shirt, cream combats. Students? They don't look seedy enough. I wonder if they're an item but they don't make body contact – I get the weird impression they must be brother and sister. She gives me a shy smile and he nods in a friendly way. But like I said before, I don't feel like talking to anyone.

So off we go. I try to go back to my previous stupor, but the presence of the couple opposite stops me. It's hard sitting with someone and not interacting – it seems rude. But there's two of them and only one of me, so I won't make the first move. She's pretty, the girl, brown eyes, heavy lids, well-defined lips – a thoughtful face. I can see her as a singer in a folk band in the sixties, say. The bloke is harder to place. He has to be a student – maybe the sporty type? Nah, he's too skinny for that. But what's intriguing me is their total ease with each other, and I can't reconcile it with the read-out I'm getting that they aren't a couple.

Yet they can't be brother and sister because they're being nice to each other. I have a sister – Gemma – who irritates the hell out of me. And even when we're getting on, I'm always taking the mick, because that's what you do with sisters. Sure, this couple opposite could be platonic friends, but I have my doubts. I don't believe in platonic friendship. Take Tasha; she wants to be friends – *I can't stand the thought of losing your friendship, Joe!* Like you should have thought of that before you split with me. It was your choice, Tash. I don't reckon a bloke and a girl can be friends without sex coming into it somehow. Unless, of course, you don't fancy the girl one iota. But then, she might fancy you. Which is worse in a way.

And so I was drifting off again when the bloke spoke to me.

"Are you going to Manchester?" he asked.

I started. "Yeah, yeah."

"Us too." His voice, his body language all gave away that he wanted to talk. So I couldn't see that I had a choice.

"We're running late," I said.

The girl joined in now. "Yeah. Half an hour, they said at Wolverhampton. We've been staying with friends from the university there."

"Yeah, I was with a mate from Birmingham."

"Are you a student too?" she asked.

"Will be. Next year. It's my gap year," I said. Weird how it's easier to talk about yourself to strangers. I could feel my earlier reluctance to speak dissolving. I liked the way this girl was taking an interest in me.

"Cool," she said. "What are your plans?"

I explained about the glandular fever and how I was earning money so I could travel – backpack, maybe – in the spring. I didn't tell her that I seemed to be spending most of it on clothes and CDs and booze.

"Where are you thinking of going?" the bloke asked. He had bleached hair, wore glasses with thin black frames.

"Maybe Thailand, or India. I haven't really looked into it yet."

The girl smiled. "Nick's been to India."

I looked interested. I was, a bit. "Backpacking?"

"No. Teaching," he said. "I was involved with a scheme that sent classroom assistants to Indian schools. I lived there for six months."

I was impressed, and jealous, too. But this bloke – Nick – he didn't seem as if he wanted to go on about it. I appreciated that. Still, I was curious.

"Did you live with Indians, like?"

"I had lodgings in a house and shared a room with one of the other assistants. A lot of the Indian families gave us hospitality. India changes you – you look at the world differently afterwards."

"You mean, coming to terms with the poverty and that?"

"Yeah," Nick nodded. "That, and just comparing other cultures. And it makes you appreciate different things about living here."

"Like what?" I asked.

Nick paused before he answered, as if my question had made him think.

"The freedom to move about," he said, which wasn't what I was expecting. I found myself cheering up. It put me in a better mood to be able to talk about something not to do with my life.

"Have you travelled?" I asked the girl.

She shook her head deprecatingly. Yeah, she was pretty. Not my type, but pretty.

"I've not had the chance yet. I did my art foundation course last year and I'm hoping to go on to college next year, but right now I'm getting some cash together."

"Sounds familiar," I said.

We all smiled, as if it was us three against the world, cash-strapped and just travelling. It was great, finding people to talk to like this, people I could relate to. I revelled in my luck at actually sitting opposite this couple, rather than a Palm-Pilot-obsessed man-in-a-suit, or a family with noisy kids. And weirdly, the sun made a last effort to brighten up the late afternoon sky. Fields rushed by on both sides.

"So you live in Manchester too?" I asked them.

Nick answered. "Not in Manchester exactly. Just outside Todmorden. West Yorkshire."

"Yeah – I know it well."

"We share a house there."

"Like, together?" I mumbled. I was fishing to see if they were boyfriend and girlfriend.

The girl laughed. "Not together in the way you mean! There are a few of us. We're renting an old farmhouse."

"Nice one!" That sounded great to me.

"What about you? I'm Kate, by the way." The name suited her. It was fresh and wholesome. And by now my tongue had loosened. My earlier blues had lifted completely. Words were coming easily.

"I still live with my parents – no choice, if I'm going to get some funds together. I probably wouldn't mind if I'd planned to stay at home, but I imagined myself somewhere completely different. But I'm not complaining – they stay out of my hair. But it's *their* place, know what I mean?"

Kate nodded vehemently. Nick asked if I wanted anything from the buffet. I thanked him and asked for a coffee. I offered him the money but he was adamant in refusing it. This left me and Kate.

"I bet you have lots of friends, though?" she asked.

"Yeah, but they're all at uni. Not all of them," I corrected myself "but the crowd I went around with last year have all gone."

"Your school friends, you mean?"

"Yeah, mainly."

"Which A2s did you take?"

"Maths, Politics, Economics. Actually, I've got a place to study law next year. At Bristol." I said this to impress her. She seemed the sort to fall for that. She was, too. She raised her eyebrows and smiled.

"Why law?"

"Well, I got fed up with all of my A2s. I couldn't see myself studying any one of them exclusively. And even though I know law doesn't guarantee you a job, it must improve your chances. But I don't see myself as one of those city lawyers raking it in through extortionate fees."

Kate was nodding, as if she emphatically agreed with me.

"I'd like to get involved with legal aid," I continued, "helping the sort of people who find themselves outside the system. What appeals to me is representing people who can't represent themselves."

At that point Nick came back with drinks – a coffee for me, a fruit juice for Kate and a bottle of water for him.

"Nick – he wants to be – you haven't told us your name yet!"

"Joe. Joe Woods," I said.

"Joe's going to be a lawyer."

"But as I was saying to Kate, not at the business end. With the underprivileged." This was a kind of reverse boasting. It was true, everything I said, but I hoped they would see me as a nice guy. I wanted to create a good impression, and so I selected the things about me that I felt would go down well. Doesn't everybody do that?

"But a lot of the people I was at college with were studying for a good job, pure and simple," Nick said, unscrewing his bottle of water. "It was all about money."

"I know what you mean. But that pisses me off. Like, it's a pretty meaningless world if you're only looking after number one. To me, job satisfaction isn't just about your salary, but about feeling you've done good."

"Oh, I so agree with you!" Kate said.

"Are you religious? A Christian, or something?" Nick asked.

It was a fair question. I was painting myself as a bit of an altruist.

"Religious? Me? I can't get my head round any of that stuff. It seems to me every religion asks you to believe things that can't be true."

Nick nodded. "Without ever giving you any proof."

"Yeah – that's right. I mean, I wouldn't knock other people's belief because it comforts them. But to me, thinking there's a God is like kids believing in Father Christmas. It would be nice if it was true. But it ain't." I thought I sounded rather cynical so I backtracked a bit. "Don't get me wrong – I'm not knocking morality – just Church and that."

Kate nodded enthusiastically again. It was amazing to meet someone who agreed with me so much. I liked her. I also liked the way both of them were listening to me. It gave me the confidence to carry on spouting, hoping I'd hit on something else that built me up in their eyes.

"And school assemblies – what an exercise in hypocrisy! All those people singing hymns and not one person believing in any of it. Even the Head. Especially the Head."

Kate laughed.

"It was the same where I was," Nick reflected.

I took the lid off my coffee as it had cooled down. "What do you do?" I asked him.

"Freelance web design, working from home."

It was my turn to be impressed. Kate interrupted.

"But I was interested in what you were saying. That you think people need to believe in something."

"Yeah, that's right. For some people it's God, for others a football team. Or hero worship."

"Hero worship?"

I was mouthing off now, but I didn't care. Kate and Nick were a good audience. I rabbited about Gemma and her bedroom full of pop stars, and how growing up was about smashing idols. How unbelief was maturity. How the world was a tough place and exploited by people who want to sell you stuff. I admitted I wore Nike trainers and Gap jeans, but only in an ironic way. Kate laughed again. We discussed how difficult it was to know where products came from these days, how hard it was to be an ethical consumer. Crewe. Macclesfield. We talked about music and films. We complained about the latest Hollywood blockbuster. I remembered the joke Phil's mate told, and Nick was nearly crying with laughter. Stockport. The journey was nearly at an end. I had this crazy idea of suggesting we go for a drink, but something stopped me. What if they didn't want to?

We pulled into Piccadilly. It turned out they were taking the tram to Victoria, so I went with them. We stood by the doors, chatting, as the tram rattled through a Manchester temporarily closed for business. Market Street was dead.

"You ought to come up and see us," Nick said, as the tram clattered into Victoria.

"Yeah!" Kate said. "We're having a get-together next Saturday. Can you get up to Todmorden?"

"Sure," I said. "I reckon I can borrow the car."

Kate's face lit up. I wondered for a moment if she fancied me, and I was flattered. Nick busily wrote some details on a scrap of paper – the address, some rough directions, a phone number.

"It'll be a good night," he said. "Give yourself a break and get some country air."

I smiled as I knew that was a joke. Todmorden was hardly the country. They got out and waved goodbye, and as the tram moved out of the station I watched them walk in the direction of the trains.

I found myself a seat now and settled down, smiling. It had been a good journey after all. Nick and Kate were sound. They were interesting, good listeners, a bit more to them than a lot of people I met. We *talked,* rather than just messed around. I wondered why. Perhaps it was because neither of them was fresh out of school. They were more mature – and they seemed to like me. OK, so I was flattered. Who wouldn't be?

I tried to imagine what their house would be like, and speculated who their other housemates might be. If I had too much to drink, would they let me kip on the floor? Did they do weed?

Then I thought, would I actually have the courage to go all the way to Todmorden? I would have, if I had my mates with me. Alone, it seemed more difficult. What if I was to turn up and they'd forgotten who I was? I'd have to think about it and decide what to do. Whatever, it was good to have the option. I looked at the piece of paper Nick had given me. I had somewhere to go next Saturday night. Things were looking up.

2.

From Rendall's Parables: The Tale of the Traveller

A Traveller is lost in a Wilderness. Despairing of ever finding his way out, he builds himself a shelter, a garden and a maze, in which he wanders endlessly. How can he be freed? By a journey towards the source of the Light.

⟨⟨◉⟩⟩

It was a pretty average sort of week. Monday I slept in late, did a bit of cleaning otherwise Mum would hit the roof, emailed some friends, but said nothing about Kate and Nick to anyone, not even Phil. I read a bit, watched MTV. Last year I would have killed to be able to do nothing like this all day; now I feel like life is a head-to-head game with boredom.

Tuesday – much the same, except I went into Manchester and looked round the shops. I was getting low again. Sometimes Manchester strikes me as the best place to live – home of United, Oasis, Coronation Street – even when you meet people from other places and they take the rise out of you for your northern accent. At night, down Deansgate, the clubs in the village, girls walking down the middle of the road mad for it, you feel there's nowhere else you'd rather be. But other times, when the sky is loaded with grey rain clouds and the smell of burger stalls hangs around and makes you sick, you wonder. All the shops are the same – HMV,

Virgin, Our Price; Next, Top Shop, Burton; JD Sports, JJB Sports – you're supposed to have all this choice but you can never find anything you want. I get to thinking that life never delivers. I have this feeling on some days that anything's possible, that round the next corner *it* will happen – whatever *it* is – that there's a prize waiting for me, and me alone. But I haven't found it yet and I reckon that maybe I never will. That's Manchester melancholy for you.

Wednesday was better because I had a shift at the Red King. It gave some focus to my day. Since I was working late, I had to sleep in, didn't I? I began to think about whether to go to Todmorden at the weekend. I even got as far as asking my dad if I could have the car, and to my amazement he said yes. But by now I was feeling nervous. Sunday seemed a long time ago and maybe Nick was just being polite. A lot of people find it hard to say a plain goodbye and kid you with *I'll ring you, speak soon.* Crap like that. I know, I've done it often enough. I reckoned, if something else came up, I'd give Todmorden a miss. Nick and Kate's address was in the drawer by the computer. Lower Fold Farm, Lumbutts, near Todmorden.

There was fun and games that evening. Dad came home and opened the telephone bill.

"Bloody hell!" he shouted.

Mum, Gemma and I were in the lounge watching TV. I saw Gemma go dead still. Mum just raised her eyebrows. Dad came storming in, talking to us as if we were skiving employees.

"It's over a hundred pounds this month. I just don't credit it! What's this? Eight pounds seventy-two to a mobile number? Which of you made that call?"

I saw Mum tapping her foot in irritation at Dad's bad temper. Meanwhile Gemma's eyes were glued to the local news. I felt it would be disloyal of me to say the call wasn't mine (it wasn't), so I just shrugged and grinned at my dad.

Well, as they say, the best form of defence is attack, and Gemma was no slouch as a military strategist. She suddenly bounced up from the sofa.

"Why are you all staring at me? You think it's me, don't you?" (It was.) "I get blamed for everything in this family! It's so unfair! Other people use the phone, you know."

"Fiona?" my dad said, passing the buck. It killed me how Dad never had the guts to tell Gemma off. He always went through my mum.

"Was it you?" Mum asked Gemma.

"That's not the POINT, is it!"

I just kept my mouth shut. Dad ranted on.

"I just don't understand why you have to be on the phone all the time. Absolute waste of money. Next time, you pay me back."

"Like I have my own private income," muttered Gemma.

So Dad marched upstairs, tail between his legs. Gemma sighed expressively and settled down in front of the TV. I couldn't tell whether she was bothered or not. She's quite good at cutting out the things she doesn't want to hear. This didn't include her mobile, which announced the arrival of another text. She's all right, really, my sister, but she's just typically fifteen – into boys, friends, gossip, all the girlie stuff. I tease her sometimes about being such a clone until she loses her rag, but she makes sure we're never bad friends for too long, as she fancies most of my mates.

I went into the kitchen to get a coffee before work and Mum followed me out, as I thought she would.

"Your father," she said, shaking her head. "Why does he have to come home and stir it up? I find it difficult enough to manage Gemma as it is."

"He'll have forgotten about it by the time he comes downstairs," I said.

Mum just grumbled. She tends to use me as a sympathetic ear. When my GAP plans fell through she told me she was only too pleased to have me at home for another year, and she meant it. She once said I was her safety valve, whatever that meant. I'm certainly a bit of a go-between in the family. Mum moans about Dad, Dad moans about Mum, Gemma moans about both of them, and they both moan about Gemma. Welcome to the Woods family.

Not that any of this was serious. Life in our house was much better than a lot of the families I knew. It was more that I'd outgrown them, which was natural. I was pleased to get to the Red King that night, even though there was a darts match on and we never stopped. So the next day I was shattered – I still wasn't back to pre-glandular fever fitness levels. Then the pub again in the evening. And so on. And then it was Saturday.

It was slack at Electric Avenue and I did more than my fair share of staring into space. I'd decided more or less not to go to Todmorden. It just seemed too much effort. I thought I'd have an early night instead, gather my strength.

Kevin, the deputy manager, sidled over. He wasn't much older than me, and because of that, he liked to throw his weight around, in my direction.

"Have you brought out the new Golf Tournament?"

I nodded.

"Got to keep you busy," he said, only half joking. He was dressed in a flashy suit and his hair was brittle with gel. His eyes darted about the shop and were held by some girl who'd come in and was hunting through the GameBoy games. He nudged me conspiratorially. Kevin was pretty disgusting. He'd relay to the shop floor exactly what he got up to every weekend. Not that any of us wanted to know. When a bloke came into the store and put a proprietorial arm around the girl's waist, Kevin looked away.

"Not my type," he said. "No bum."

I made no comment. I might think things about girls, but I don't normally say them. Most of the time.

"So," Kevin carried on. "What are you up to this weekend?"

"My little secret," I said, trying to sound as careless as possible.

"Come on! Who is she?"

"Girl I met last week coming back from Birmingham," I lied.

"You're a fast worker," Kevin said.

I felt a shit for lying but pleased the lie took effect. And then I thought, what the hell, I might as well make the most of it.

"Yeah, an artist. Lives out in West Yorkshire. I'm going out to her place." I sounded cool. I liked how I sounded. Of course, I knew this meant I would never go to Todmorden now. But I wasn't going to go, anyway.

"An artist, eh? So what are you going to do? Model for her? A Life class?" Kevin sniggered.

I laughed as if to dismiss his insinuations but concede nevertheless that there might be something in them. Yeah, all right,

I was right down there at his level. But it felt good to impress, even a shit like Kevin. And the lying didn't bother me. Everybody lies, even when they don't mean to. Then some punters drifted in and we separated.

Business picked up, and I didn't have any more time to think, except about what would make good Christmas presents and the new features of the latest Tomb Raider. Before I knew it, it was six o'clock, and Kevin was pulling down the grille at the front of the shop. Surprisingly, I didn't feel too tired. I waved goodbye to everyone and sauntered to the bus stop.

Waiting for the bus, my mood began to spiral downwards again, perhaps because I was alone. Being with other people lifts me, makes me act OK, even if I don't feel OK. By myself, reality bites. The reality was that I had nothing to do and it was Saturday night. Even Gemma was out with her mates, and when I got home she'd be prancing around asking me if she should wear her pink top, or the black one, and which trousers. I'd spend the night up in my room or in front of the box with my aged parents. If my luck was really in, Dad would buy in a four-pack of lager. Great.

Lower Fold Farm, Lumbutts, near Todmorden. I'd drive down the M62 to Milnrow, then go on through Walsden. I was pretty sure that Lumbutts was on the moors, a bit further down than Walsden. It would be interesting to see the farm. Not that I would see much in the dark. Stupid idea. Maybe there were some films on Sky. The bus came.

It was weird – for the first time in ages I had some energy. I wanted to go out. I wanted to go into town with my mates, only they were scattered all over England, in different campus bars at different universities. You can't go clubbing by yourself.

And then I had my brainwave. Stu was still around. He'd failed all his A2s and was retaking them at a local college. I got out my mobile and texted him. My luck was in. He was at home, no plans, but no money either. I texted him back. I told him about a party I knew in Tod, that I had a sort of invite to. He said he was up for it. I said I'd pick him up on my way, as he lived in Rochdale. Sorted. Even if the party was a disaster, we could have a drink or two instead.

Now I'd decided to go to Todmorden, I realised it was what I'd wanted to do all along. Because Kate and Nick were new people, they were different. Everyone was meeting new people now except for me. I wanted to have an adventure too. I wanted to start living. So I got home, reminded Dad he said I could have the car, listened to the lecture about not drinking and driving, changed into some jeans and a sweatshirt, shovelled down the dinner Mum had made, told Gemma the pink top looked better than the black. And I was in the car, stereo playing loud. I was moving, life was moving again. At last. This was more like it.

Because the music was playing so loud I didn't hear my mobile the first couple of times. I was already driving through Rochdale and it was in between tracks before I heard the ring. I pulled over to answer. It was Stu.

He sounded like death. Apparently he'd just spent the last hour or so throwing up. Either a stomach bug, he said, or something he'd eaten. Either way, he was going to have to cancel on me. I said that it was OK, and wished him better. He said he'd ring in a few days.

So much for my Saturday night.

Then I realised I had two choices. Either I turned the car around and went home, or carried on to Todmorden. Neither appealed. But just then, going back home seemed the worse of the two alternatives. I'd been vegetating all week, and as much as I love my parents, they aren't exactly stimulating company. Going to Tod was risking the fact Nick and Kate wouldn't remember me, or would have changed their minds about seeing me. But on the other hand, if it was a party, I could just blend with the crowd. It dawned on me I'd never gone to a party or club by myself before. That made me smile. I teased Gemma often enough about being a pack animal, and here I was, hesitating about going to a party just because I was on my own.

That decided me. I started the engine again and drove on. I saw an off-licence and pulled in, leaving the car to get some Bacardi Breezers – I didn't want to arrive empty-handed. I was feeling better already. The roads were clear, and just as I had remembered, the way to Lumbutts was clearly signposted just outside Walsden. I put the car in second as I took several steep corners past stone-built cottages teetering on the side of the road. I crawled along, as the road was narrow. On my left the whole of Todmorden was laid out, a sprinkling of yellow lights. On my right, dark masses of hills.

Eventually the road levelled out and I was up in the moors. I guessed I must be near the Pennine Way, but it was too dark to see much. It occurred to me then I might not find it easy to locate Lower Fold Farm. So I slowed right down, checking to see no one was behind me. The road was completely empty. I was the only idiot up here on a Saturday night.

In fact Lower Fold Farm was easy to find. There was a large

painted board on my right announcing it. A rough track between two gateposts led to it. I turned in carefully and was relieved to see lights were blazing from the windows. The car bounced along the track and I tried to make out the size of the farm. There was the main house, painted white, several stone outbuildings and a grey-looking caravan. A rusty Transit van and a scooter were parked outside. I was too curious to be nervous now. I left the car by the side of what looked like an old barn, locked it and made my way to the front of the house. Too late to turn back. It seemed quiet for a party. What if I'd got the wrong day? I banged on the door.

Nick opened it and seemed to recognise me immediately.

"It's Joe!" he shouted. There were footsteps and Kate appeared, her hair flowing loose.

"I knew you'd come," she said, smiling.

3

From Rendall's Laws Governing Purity: Abstinence

White Ones, and those aspiring to be White Ones, should refrain from those substances and impure actions which cloud the vision. You shall not imbibe alcohol or caffeine; neither smoke tobacco, nor use any artificial substances – legal or illegal – to alter your consciousness. You shall not gamble nor overeat. You should not fix your mind on worldly success, nor love another as much as you learn to love the Light. Purity leads to enlightenment. I have spoken.

Funny how as soon as you cross the threshold of a new place you yourself become different. The place exerts an influence. Like I'm different collecting empties at the Red King from the way I am at Electric Avenue. Different again when I'm with my mates. With Kate and Nick I was different once more, and I liked this new me.

They ushered me into the house, made me feel welcome immediately. They said they'd been talking about me and felt they should have stressed more strongly that they had meant the invitation for tonight. I was flattered I'd made such an impression on them. In my fantasies, people sought me out. Now it was happening for real.

I don't know what I expected their house to be like. In fact it was a rambling old farmhouse and the centre of activity was a large kitchen. That was where they took me. In the middle of it was a wooden table laid out with food and drink, and around the table a few people were seated, late teens, early twenties. More people were standing around. Naturally they all turned to see who I was. Then some people made a space for me at the table, although I wasn't ready to sit down yet. I put my Bacardi Breezers down on the table and hoped that would be the sign for someone to offer me a drink. I know Dad had lectured me about drinking and driving, but one drink now would help me relax, and I'd stay long enough for it to have time to wear off.

Then Nick came over, holding a bottle opener.

"Do you want one of those?" he smiled, indicating the Bacardi Breezers I'd brought with me.

I did. I drank it straight from the bottle. I suggested he have one but he shook his head ruefully.

We were joined by Kate and a bloke about my age. Then a slightly older man came up to us as well. Instinctively I straightened, stood to attention. Some people have that effect on you.

The younger bloke turned out to be called Will.

"This is Fletcher," Kate said, smiling at the older one. "I told you about Joe, Fletcher. He's the person Nick and I met on our way back from Wolverhampton. Fletcher's the tenant of the farm, Joe. We're all responsible to him."

I gave him the once over. He was tall, cool blue eyes, rather intense. He wore a white kaftan and I immediately had him down as one of those ex-hippie types who are into ecology and tree-saving and that. He seemed friendly enough, though.

It turned out Will ran a charity shop in Hebden Bridge, and Fletcher was the tenant of the farm. He grew stuff in the adjoining land and looked after the place. Will seemed more normal. He grinned quite a lot, out of shyness, I reckon. His head was shaved; he wore a white football shirt with the name of some bloke I didn't recognise on the back. They asked me quite a bit about myself, and as the Bacardi took effect, I found myself more and more ready to answer.

Quite an adult party, I thought, looking around me during the lull in conversation. It was all talk, no music. Maybe this was just a warm-up session. The other thing I noticed was, I was the only person who seemed to be drinking. There were jugs of fruit juice on the table, and bottles of water, but that was it. The food was mainly dips, hummus, vegetable sticks and hunks of bread. The lack of alcohol puzzled me, and I wondered whether this was because they did something else. This was just the sort of place you could grow your own. I looked around the kitchen. Sure enough there were things growing in pots, but nothing that looked to me like cannabis.

It's a bit weird being the only person drinking. You feel like you're undressed in a room full of clothed people. Still, that didn't stop me helping myself to another bottle. I looked around the room again, and saw Kate talking to a girl. She was stunning. Shorter than me, with loose blonde hair and dark eyes. Kate noticed my repeated glances in their direction, and brought the girl over.

"This is Bea," she said.

"B?" I said, puzzled.

"Beatrice," the girl explained. "Which is a bit of an embarrassment, so I get everyone to call me Bea."

I was going to say something stupid like, to be or not to be, but luckily I stopped myself in time. I grinned at her. I could see now that her eyes were brown, contrasting dramatically with her fair hair. Kate didn't seem to be there any more. I asked Bea whether she lived on the farm.

"No," she said. "But I'm going to. They said I could move in during the week."

I nodded. "So where do you live now?"

"In Rochdale," she said. "With a sort of friend. I'm studying at the college. But I sing too."

This was getting better and better. I definitely fancied her and she looked around my age. I had a good feeling about tonight. I gestured in the direction of the Bacardi Breezers and asked her if she wanted one. She shook her head. Then she smiled at me impishly.

"Why are you drinking it?"

I shrugged. "It's a party, innit?"

"So?"

"Well, everybody else…" My voice trailed away. I was the only person drinking. I tried to defend my position.

"Well, OK. It relaxes me, makes me feel good. What's wrong with that?"

"Do you need alcohol to make you feel good?"

"No, I don't need it, but I choose to have it, which is different."

"But you said before it relaxes you, which means you were

feeling tense when you came in here. It sounds as if you're using alcohol as the solution to a problem. So it's a necessity."

"OK. So I walked into a place I've never been before. Of course I feel on edge. Drink isn't a necessity, but it helps. And I like it."

This was different. This was not normally how I chatted up girls. But somehow this argument was fun. We were sparring, sparking off each other. It was more meaningful than the usual crap. I swigged down a mouthful of Bacardi as a challenge. Bea laughed.

"I don't drink," she said. "I can feel good without it. As I do right now."

I wasn't sure what she meant. Was she flirting with me? I hoped so. I had to admit she seemed much more relaxed than I did, but then she knew these people. There was something about her, too, that was centred and peaceful. I'd not met any girl quite like her before. Tasha had been like me, a bit mad, a bit of a piss artist. Bea was completely different.

"Let's forget about us," she said. "Think of other people. It's Saturday night. The pubs are full. Hundreds and hundreds of thousands of people all over the country are getting wasted. If you were a Martian and came down here and looked, you'd think we had a problem."

"Drinking's just a recreation, like football," I said. "Or music."

"Music is harmony and order," she said. "Drinking leads to disorder, fighting, illness. Even football is controlled. Drinking leads deliberately to a lack of control. People are giving themselves permission to do things they wouldn't otherwise do, not if they had their judgement intact."

This was strong. I realised then she may have had hidden reasons for speaking the way she did. What if her father was a drunk, say? What if she'd suffered from other people's drunkenness? I back-pedalled a bit.

"Sure. I'll concede that in some cases, drinking controls the drinker. But most people enjoy drink as much as they do a walk, a concert, ice cream, whatever. Alcohol is a naturally occurring substance." I knew that was illogical, but that was the drink talking.

Bea shook her head and her hair moved in ripples. "Men brew beer and distil whisky. It ain't natural," she said.

Then we were interrupted. A bloke came over to us with a guitar and asked Bea if she was ready to sing. She eagerly agreed and left me. There was a general exodus into another room and Kate swept me up and took me with her there. I picked up the third bottle on my way.

The room we arrived in now had a low beamed roof, and cushions and beanbags were scattered around it, some creamy leather, others a grubby white corduroy. There were plants, more than you would normally see in a house, and a poster of the planet Earth. I noticed the faint smell of incense and watched while some people lit candles. I reckoned I was right about the hippie thing. I imagined myself laughing about these people to Phil on the phone tomorrow.

Anyway, we gathered round, and the guy with the guitar played a few chords. It sounded as if it was going to be some kind of folk music. Definitely not my scene. Then Bea began to sing and I changed my mind.

Her voice was liquid and golden. The song she sang wasn't folk; it was simple, like a hymn, almost. The words were strange and sounded old-fashioned, like Shakespeare, though it wasn't Shakespeare.

They are all gone into the world of Light!
And I alone sit lingering here;
Their very memory is fair and bright,
And my sad thoughts doth clear.

It glows and glitters in my cloudy breast
Like stars upon some gloomy grove,
Or those faint beams in which this hill is drest,
After the Sun's remove...

Another thing alcohol does for you is make you appreciate music more. Bea gave the words such significance that they seemed true to me. I related to them. They made me think of this night, the moors, the feeling of being left alone. She sang with a rich melancholy that sent shivers through me. Candlelight flickered, shadows played on the ceiling, there was complete stillness as we were all held spellbound by her voice.

At the end of the song, there was silence. Then a ripple of applause. My clapping was the loudest of all and I regretted my enthusiasm immediately, as everyone looked round and smiled. Then there was more guitar music. I drank quickly, then. This time because something had moved in me that I couldn't put a name to. I felt different, spaced out, kind of emotional. Bea came and sat by my side.

"Nice one," I said to her.

"Thank you." She paused for a little. "I set it to music myself. It's a metaphysical poem."

"Come again?"

"Metaphysical. Seventeenth century. The poet was called Henry Vaughan. Metaphysical means beyond the physical, beyond our everyday experience."

I thought to myself, that was how I felt. Metaphysical. I didn't say that, though. I wondered if I could reach out and take Bea's hand, but I noticed no one else in the room was touching, even people who looked like couples. That inhibited me. You don't like to stand out from the crowd. It was enough that she was sitting by my side.

"Who are all these people?" I asked her.

"I suppose you'd call them a kind of commune. They have a vision about the way they want to live."

"They're not religious nuts?"

"Oh, no. Not in the conventional sense. Fletcher runs the place; Nick, Will and some other guys live here. So do Kate, Layla and Auriel. For now. But there are more of them that just visit."

"Why?"

"For enlightenment," she answered.

"What do you mean, enlight—"

People were making hushing sounds. Someone else started to sing, a bloke. It seemed rude to carry on talking, so I stopped. I took a closer look at the people around me now. At first glance, they looked dead ordinary. A few ugly blokes, a rather chubby girl in a white dress that made her look like a bridesmaid, faces you might see anywhere. But on closer examination they did look different. And then it dawned on me why. Everyone seemed remarkably happy. Most people look fed up seventy-five per cent of the time. These guys gave the impression that here was where they most wanted to be. I wasn't jealous exactly, but I decided I'd go and get the last Bacardi.

Back in the kitchen two people I hadn't been introduced to were sitting in a corner talking intently. They both said hi to me. I took the last bottle and thought I ought not to drink it as I wouldn't be fit to drive home. But then – what the hell! I opened the bottle and gulped some down. I felt unsettled and alone. I wanted Bea to come back but perversely I didn't want to fetch her.

There were stirrings from the other room and people started to drift back. Bea and Kate were among them. They came over and I saw Kate glance at my drink.

"How did you get here tonight?" she asked.

"I drove," I said.

"You can't drive back."

This was true.

Kate then invited me to stay the night. "We've lots of room," she said.

Well, why not, I thought. I was still sober enough to ring my parents and let them know I wouldn't be back until the morning, assuring them I was fine. Dad told me to make sure I returned the car by eleven. It was weird and uncomfortable hearing their voices. They sounded so ordinary. I was glad to end the call and put my mobile back in my pocket.

"Come on," Bea said. "I'll take you on a tour."

She reached out for my hand now and I let her lead me out into the hall. She pointed to a staircase. "The offices are up there. And Fletcher's quarters. A bathroom too." She took me back into the room where the singing had been. Now I could see a sort of conservatory adjoined it, roughly built, with wooden benches ranged around inside.

"That's the Gathering Place," she said. She opened the door and I followed her in. It was cold and damp in there. The floor was uneven stone. We went through another door and were outside. The slap of the wind sobered me up.

"Here's where the lads sleep," she said, pointing to a stone-built barn. "There'll be a bed in there for you."

Shit. I had hoped for something else, but never mind.

We went back inside the house and I finished my drink. There were fewer people about now. We sat by the table in the kitchen and I helped myself to some of the food. It was late but I was suddenly wide awake. I wanted to talk.

"Tell me about yourself, Bea," I said.

"No. I'm more interested in you, Joe. And your ideas. Like – are you happy?"

"I'm happy sitting here talking to you."

"Are you generally happy?"

"Sometimes."

"What is happiness?" she asked me, her voice teasing.

I began to formulate an answer but then realised this was a hard question. I struggled a bit. "Erm... happiness is when things are going right."

Bea looked reflective. "For me, happiness is knowing that you're exactly where you're meant to be. Here. Now."

For some reason, her happiness seemed better than mine. I wanted it.

"Joe, has it occurred to you that most of the time life is empty? That we fill it with trivia, which become obsessions?"

I thought of the computer games I played, of the trashy TV I watched, renting out videos I didn't like. I didn't say anything. She continued.

"We're just here, we have this life, we don't know what to do with it. Each of us makes up our own reason for being here. Listen. It's like Rendall's Tale of the Traveller, the way he builds himself his shelter." She paused. "Sorry, you don't know Rendall's Parables. I'll lend you the Book some day. You remind me of the Traveller."

I liked that. I am a traveller. It sounded like something vaguely sci-fi. The thought made me smile and Bea smiled back.

"Come on, Joe. What's the purpose of your life?"

It was turning out to be an impossible question. I hesitated. He who hesitates is lost. I shrugged.

"So you really don't know," she said.

"Does it matter?"

"It matters. Because if the purpose of life doesn't matter, then nothing matters."

"Do you know the purpose of your life?" I asked her.

"Yes" she said simply.

Her face seemed to light up as she said that. Like a Madonna. It stopped me doing what I was going to do next, which was to try to kiss her. But it was weird. Not kissing her was almost better than kissing her. Wanting to was more exquisite than doing it. Imagining it was beautiful.

We sat in silence for a while. I couldn't believe all this was happening to me. Then Bea took me back out to the barn where the blokes slept. She handed me over to Will, who set me up with a sleeping bag in a kind of dormitory with wooden panels between the beds, giving some sort of privacy. A few people were already asleep.

Of course I didn't sleep for ages. I was just thinking, where am I? Who are these people? I was a bit scared they were born-again Christians, but there had been no mention of Jesus. No crucifixes anywhere, nothing. No attempt had been made to brainwash me. Bea made me think, and think deep, but what was wrong with that? Maybe we all need to think a little more. Maybe I do.

It was true that sometimes I did ask myself what it was all about. Because when you come to think of it, life is incredibly strange. To think that all I can ever know or feel is my consciousness, and yet all the other millions of people on this planet have their own consciousness which I'll never experience. I don't know whether I believe in God. I don't know if I believe in life after death. Though I can't imagine just being nothing. It occurred to me that what Bea said was right in a way. If there was nothing, if life had no purpose, then I might as well go out and rob and cheat and steal, because it didn't matter. But I do believe in a basic sort of morality, so it follows I believe life must have some purpose. But what?

Thinking like that can do your head in. It makes you feel spaced out. I liked lying there just thinking in the dark. I wondered if Bea was thinking, and whether she was thinking about me. I wondered what she thought the purpose of her life was, what it would be like to have a purpose.

Imagine if you woke up every morning with something important to do, that you loved doing. If you knew what you had to do. If you were certain. Like Bea.

4.
From Rendall's Book of Prayers: The Morning Service

I ask for the power of the Light to enter my body and soul and make me a force for good. May it be my lot to achieve Perfection. I promise to remain pure, true and strong. I will stay by the fountain of Light. I ask all here present to witness these vows this morning. May it be my lot to achieve Perfection. May it be your lot to achieve Perfection. To the One, to the Light – salaam, shalom, peace. Peace be with you.

After I'd drifted back to consciousness in the morning, I lay awake listening for sounds. There were none. I got the feeling I was alone. I checked my watch, discovered it was eight o'clock and guessed the other guys must have gone to breakfast leaving me to sleep. Quickly I got up, threw on my clothes from the night before and stepped into the centre of the dormitory. It was deserted. I saw some bathroom facilities at one end and got myself presentable.

Then I went outside. It was a fresh day. The wind stung my face and blew my hair around. I could see the moorland clearly now, steep hills rising on one side, on the other the distant road and a criss-cross pattern of dry-stone walls. I felt apart from my normal life. I made my way to the farmhouse where I presumed people were having breakfast. I was sure there'd be something left for me.

When I got there, the kitchen was empty, scrubbed clean. I

frowned in puzzlement. I stood there for a while, undecided, then resolved to check out the living room. As I entered I saw people coming towards me from out of the conservatory, which Bea had called the Gathering Place. They were all dressed in white. It gave me quite a shock. Blokes in white jeans and white sweatshirts, the girls in long white skirts and dresses. Bea glided over towards me, her face radiant, like an angel.

"We've just finished our morning meeting," she said, and kissed me on the cheek, as my mother might. Other people shook my hand warmly. It was difficult not to be drawn into such good feeling. I followed them into breakfast, where two of the blokes began to get some food together.

"I could kill for a coffee," I confided to Bea.

She smiled teasingly. "Coffee? It's a drug too, you know."

"Yeah, well, it's only caffeine."

But there was no coffee. It was back to the fruit juice and herbal teas. In fact the fresh orange juice I had was very welcome. I forgot about the coffee as I listened to people talk. Some of the blokes were discussing football, which surprised me. Some girls were laughing as if they were sharing a private joke. Fletcher came and sat by me so I was flanked by him and Bea.

"Did you have a good night?" he asked.

I said I did and thanked him for his hospitality.

"You can stay any time," he said. He cut himself a slice of bread from what looked like a home-made loaf. "What do you think of us?"

I was a bit taken aback by his question, but well-mannered enough to come out with all the right platitudes.

"Everyone's been great. I really enjoyed the party."

"No. What do you think of us? In fact. The truth."

Did he want me to criticise them? Or was he doing what Gemma does when she says, do I really look fat in these jeans? Honestly?

But this wasn't Gemma. As a novelty, I decided to tell him the truth.

"You all seem weird to me. I was pretty spooked when I saw you all in white. Like, who are you? Bea hasn't explained properly."

Fletcher smiled as if I'd got the right answer. He obviously liked plain speaking.

"We are the White Ones. We're a group of people from different religious and non-religious traditions who have come to understand the nature of life. We live together so we can follow our own practices. For our own good, and for the ultimate good of the world."

There was no answer to that.

Fletcher questioned me further. "How do you feel about that?"

I carried on being honest. "Well, I'm half-inclined to make fun of you and write you off as a pack of weirdos. But also a bit curious to know what you're about."

I quite enjoyed talking like this. It was good not having to be polite. And Fletcher seemed unbothered by my straight talking.

"The choice is yours. Leave this morning and never come back, if you like. Or return and find out more." He helped himself to more bread, then looked me straight in the eyes. "We think you'd fit in."

I felt Bea nudge me under the table.

"Thanks," I said. Then Fletcher turned and spoke to someone on his left.

"What was all that about?" I asked Bea.

"It's an invitation," she said. "He thinks you have something. And we're not a bunch of freaks. We don't conform, but then, what's so great about conforming when you look at the rest of the world?"

This was true. I could feel my perceptions slowly shifting. It was a novel and not unpleasant experience. Meanwhile a niggling voice in my head reminded me of my promise to return the car to my dad before eleven. I explained to Bea that I had to go. To my pleasure, she looked a little crestfallen.

"Here," she said. "Take my mobile number."

I did, readily, and gave her mine. She chatted on, explaining that she was a kind of novice and had only been coming to Lower Fold Farm for the past six weeks. But it had changed her life. Maybe, she said, she would have the chance to tell me more one day. I said I'd love to see her again. She went with me out to where I'd left the car. Someone had tied a white ribbon around the windscreen wipers. We both laughed as I removed it, and put it in my pocket.

The wind lifted and tossed Bea's hair around.

"See you, Joe," she said.

"Ciao."

We didn't touch. I got in the car and turned the key in the ignition. Soon I was bumping down the track to the main road. And driving down to Todmorden.

It was lucky the roads were quiet as my mind wasn't really on my driving. I just didn't know what to make of everyone I'd met. I wanted to write them off as a load of nutters, but something stopped me. Who was I to say what was right and normal, and what wasn't? And think of Bea – she wasn't bullshitting. She believed everything she said to me, and she was no airhead. Also she was gorgeous, and gorgeous people weren't so desperate that they had to go and associate with a bunch of freaks. Kate and Nick too, they weren't sad. In fact the people I had met at the farm were better in some way than lots of the people in my life. I thought of Kevin and some of the idiots who hang out at the Red King. It was all bloody confusing.

Home seemed different when I got there. I managed to throw the keys to Dad so they sailed over the top of the Sunday paper he was reading and landed in his lap. He muttered his thanks. Gemma was in the sitting room watching TV, painting her nails. Mum was doing something in the kitchen. It all seemed so one-dimensional after the farm. And meaningless. Stereotypes. Doing what they were programmed to do.

I hated Sundays, anyway. When I was at school I spent Sundays sleeping in, maybe going over to the park to kick a ball around, then putting off doing schoolwork, then doing it late at night. It was a nothing day, the blood had been sucked out of it by the fact that Monday came after. Monday, Tuesday, Wednesday, Thursday, Friday. The working days. You get more and more tired. Then suddenly it's Saturday and if you haven't got anything on in the evening, you're sunk. And you go out and have your first drink and there's colour back in the world. And that was last year, when things seemed to be going my way. This Sunday, I lay on my bed and listened to some CDs. I got more and more depressed. I kept thinking about Bea and the farm. I wondered what they were doing up there now. I certainly wasn't using my time any better than they could be.

But I cheered up. I went with Dad to B&Q to get some wood and saw all the Christmas trees and decorations. That made me feel good. I always enjoyed Christmas – not for religious reasons, but the parties, the presents, the turkey, everyone letting their hair down. But today I was aware of how it was all mass-produced – forests of trees cut down to be sold at B&Q and supermarkets and garden centres, tacky tinsel and lights, cash registers ringing. To pretend for a moment that this had anything to do with religion was a joke. I tried to say something to my dad.

"Why do you think people are so into Christmas?"

"Yep," he said. "Gets worse every year. Christmas comes earlier and earlier. And it's all about the money."

"Is that all?"

"Christmas isn't a Christian festival," he said. "It's pagan in origin and it's pagan now. An excuse for letting go for a while."

"But if it's pagan," I carried on, "then there must be a basic human need for a winter festival."

"You'd think they'd have enough assistants around at this time of year!" he said. "Christ! We've looked everywhere for extension sockets. And there's never anyone you can ask." Dad gave an exaggerated sigh. He was always on a short fuse. Mum moaned about him, said he was hell to live with and was his own worst enemy. He needed to calm down and take life as it came. She was partly right.

Later on that evening I said to Mum, "Do you believe in God?"

She looked as embarrassed as if I'd asked her about sex.

"Well, I suppose I believe in something," she said. "But it's hard to say, really. I don't believe in organised religion. Look at the wars it's caused."

I had my mobile in my pocket in case Bea rang. Gemma mooched into the kitchen and opened every cupboard and the fridge on her personal quest – for something to eat.

"There's never anything in the house!" she whinged.

"Gemma," I said to her. "What is the purpose of your life?"

"Sod off!" she said.

"Language!" warned Mum.

The Woods family. Home of the great philosophers. I thought about sending Bea a text, something non-committal, like, had a great night. I decided to do that later. I watched TV, and decided there was nothing worth watching. I said to everyone I was going to bed early and I lay on my bed, thinking.

The White Ones. They didn't drink or, presumably, do drugs. They wore white and lived apart. So they weren't hippies, or Christians. They seemed normal, but clearly they weren't. Bea talked about a book they had. They had gatherings. Fletcher invited me back. If I went back, I'd see Bea again.

Nah, I thought. The whole setup is too weird. I'd be better off asking for extra hours at Electric Avenue, getting some cash together and travelling.

The Traveller. That's me.

I smiled to myself. I wouldn't go back. It was a cool adventure for a Saturday night, but I lived in the real world. Crappy as it was.

My phone rang. A message. *Thinking of you. Sleep well. Peace and Perfection. Bea.*

My fingers pressed out a reply. *And to you. Ive been thinking of you. Lets meet.*

Her: *When?*

Me: *Soon. Name a day.*

Her: *Come to the farm whenever.*

Me: *C u there.*

Yesss! She sent me a message first. She was keen. A smile spread over my face. And then I asked myself what I was pleased about. Mainly, that Bea was interested and I would get to see her again. But also that I had an excuse for going back. Because the truth was, the part of me that dismissed Fletcher and co. was the part of me that judged by appearances. I needed to investigate the whole thing more. It would be an experiment. I could go back and see what made them tick. It would be interesting to find out what they believed, what Bea thought the purpose of her life was. If what they said was stupid, then I was free to walk away. If, however, there was something in it, and something there for me...

It would be daft not to go and check them out.

5.

From Rendall's Parables: The Tale of the Hungry Child

Once in a distant land there was a child, who, despite his mother's warning, wandered out of the garden and into the field. Entranced by the blue skies and distant hills, he strayed. Soon he was hungry. In the distance, he saw a farm and made his way there. He entered the dairy and found a jug of milk, from which he drank greedily. But was it his to take?

When Mike rang from the Red King to say I wasn't needed on Wednesday, I took it as a sign. I'd go up to Lower Fold Farm instead, and see Bea. That is, if I could have the car. Dad grumbled a bit when I asked him and made me cough up for the petrol, but finally agreed. Then he asked me what on earth I was doing visiting friends on a farm? It was November, for Christ's sake. And who were these people, anyway?

I smiled, fairly nonchalantly. I explained about my meeting with Nick and Kate on the train, editing it neatly. I mentioned Nick had done voluntary work in India and that Kate was an artist. The farm, I told him, was just a house where they lived with some friends. I told Dad about Bea too, confessing I liked her. That went down well. His mouth curled in a half-smile. He thought he'd uncovered the motivation for my sudden interest in farms. The questioning stopped and I was half-relieved.

And so Wednesday night saw me on the way to Lumbutts again. I'd made a bit of an effort with my appearance with Bea in mind. I couldn't decide between my navy or fawn sweater, but went for the fawn in the end – dressed in dark colours, I'd be very conspicuous. It felt good to be going back to the farm. I had no fixed idea of what I wanted to happen, past the fact that Bea would be there – I knew that, as we'd been texting each other. She asked me to arrive before seven. At this rate, I was going to be early. Nearly all the traffic lights seemed to turn to green as they saw me coming.

This time I knew exactly where I was going and found the farm with no difficulty at all. Having spent a night there made it familiar to me. I guided the car carefully over the bumpy track to the farmhouse and parked it by a wall. There was the sense of rain in the air. I rapped loudly on the door. Fletcher answered.

"Joe," he said, seeming pleased.

It's nice to be wanted.

Bea came out from the kitchen and her face brightened when she saw me.

"You're in time for our Evening Service!" she announced.

"Come and join us," Fletcher added. "As an observer."

An evening service? It sounded suspiciously like church. I had a sinking feeling and wondered what I'd got myself into. But, hey, I was free to go afterwards. I might as well sit it out. So I put on a brave smile and followed Bea to the Gathering Place, where quite a few people had already assembled. There was Kate, who rose to her feet to greet me, smiling fit to burst. There were others I recognised, and who recognised me. They all said, "Peace!"

I muttered back, "Peace," since it seemed the right thing to do. I sat down on a bench where there was room for Bea to sit next to me. She did. I found that I was swallowing nervously.

I always feel edgy in religious services. Not that I've had experience of many. As a kid I'd been to church on some occasions, then we sort of stopped going. I'd been to weddings, and a couple of funerals. And countless school assemblies. It had always struck me that the point about religious services wasn't worshipping God as much as getting it right. Finding the right hymn number, singing neither too softly nor loudly, sitting and standing at the right times. Oh, and being quiet. And letting someone, like a vicar, or the Head, talk nonsense at you, feel-good stuff that you knew neither they nor anybody else would practise. And you just stood there waiting for it all to finish and thinking of something totally different.

This time, I was just very embarrassed. I didn't know what to do with myself. It suddenly occurred to me that my legs were too long, as the bench was low and I had to try to position them out of people's way. I didn't know what to do with my hands and found I was clenching my fists. And my scalp was itchy, so I tried to scratch it without anyone noticing. Then Fletcher came in and started handing round some pamphlets. They'd obviously done the rounds, and looked the worse for wear. I took one from the pile that was handed to me and passed the rest along.

The door opened once more and two of the blokes came in, carefully carrying one of those plastic baby bath things, half-full of water. They placed it in the middle of the circle. I watched the water level move back and forth, then settle. As it settled, conversation stopped. Bea squeezed my hand and I hoped she hadn't noticed how hot and sweaty my palm was. Kate went round lighting candles, and when she had finished, someone switched off the light. The room was lit by flickering flames and dancing shadows played on the floor. Some people began to hum a tune. It sounded vaguely Eastern. The refrain was simple and I could have easily joined in had I wanted to. I heard Bea take up the melody, then the person on my other side. I found myself swaying slightly in time to the tune. I was the only person not humming. I tried to look as if I was humming, then found I was emitting a sort of noise. Oh, what the hell. I joined in. It was just some communal singing. We weren't sacrificing goats or anything.

We all hummed for some time. Then slowly people dropped out until there was silence. Fletcher's voice broke it.

"O, source of Light," he intoned. "We are grateful for having reached the end of one more day. We offer thanks for those moments of illumination we have experienced and confess shame at the incursions of Darkness we have allowed. As the diurnal shadow envelops us, we affirm our commitment to the One Light, to Truth, to Goodness, to Peace, to Perfection. We approach the night confident that the day will follow, as the Kingdom of Light always surpasses in strength the Kingdom of Dark. We are glad that we are one day nearer you and yearn for the last night, when we can enter fully into the World of everlasting Day. We pray that we will be worthy of it. We work that we will be worthy of it. Our purity reflects our desire."

Everyone murmured, "Our purity reflects our desire."

Fletcher read some more prayers. I was trying to follow the gist of it, which seemed to be about light and darkness. I didn't hear him mention God, which was a relief. I also noticed there was none of that 'thee' or 'thou' stuff. It was all in modern English. But the strangest thing was that absolutely everyone was paying attention. People were either following in the pamphlet or watching Fletcher and listening. There was depth and seriousness in their eyes. It made me feel kind of inferior.

Then Fletcher stopped and there was more silence. I was getting used to this silence now. It had a quality all of its own, like a white noise, like a silken veil held close to your skin. It exerted a gentle pressure on me, on everyone. Then a bloke I couldn't put a name to got up from the bench, went over to the bath of water and knelt by it. He immersed his hands in the water and began to wash them, and spoke as he did so.

"I, Chris Taylor, swore aloud when I was cut up on the roundabout this afternoon."

"We trust you will be forgiven," came a few voices.

The guy continued to wash his hands for a few moments longer, then shook them over the bath. Without drying them, he went back to his seat. His place was taken by Nick, who also began to wash his hands.

"I, Nick Lewis, failed my ASD today. I deplore my weakness."

"We trust you will be forgiven," came the response.

Nick didn't look too well, I thought. I wondered if he'd been eating properly, and what that ASD was. That is, if I'd heard it right. But now was hardly the time to ask. Somebody came to help Nick up from where he'd been kneeling over the bath of water. At the same time a girl left the benches and came to the water. She was quite striking to look at, with high cheekbones, masses of reddish, curly hair, a good figure, but slightly gawky – or maybe she was just moving in a nervous way.

"I, Auriel Beaven, permitted malicious gossip to be spoken in my presence. I didn't have the courage to stop the backbiting – it was about my line manager at work – because it was true. I happen to know my boss does those things that her colleagues accused her of. So I wasn't sure whether to agree with the truth or stop the bad feeling."

She seemed really upset.

"I regret my confusion," she continued, "and ask for clarity of mind and purpose in the future. And when I washed the floor today, I accidentally made a dirty smudge afterwards, when I was carrying out the water, and didn't go back to clean it. For this I am truly sorry."

"We trust you will be forgiven," Fletcher muttered.

"And I had unlawful thoughts. I wanted to eat today, I wanted more than my fair share and looked enviously at the portions of others. I've vowed to give up all food containing sugar, but I doubt my own intentions. For this may I be forgiven."

"You *will* be forgiven," Fletcher said, this time loudly. Auriel flinched, and, trembling, returned to her seat. Well, I thought, there's always one weirdo in the pack.

One by one, more White Ones came to the bath to wash their hands and confess their wrongdoings. I was fascinated, hoping someone had done something really juicy. Then Bea left my side.

"I, Beatrice Rossi, have allowed my mind to become clouded by an obsessive thought. I have prayed for that which is not permissible. I acknowledge my weakness of dwelling too much on thoughts which are bad for me. I thank the Light for the help it has given me in the past and know it will continue to do so in the future."

"We trust you will be forgiven."

It looked quite beautiful, everyone kneeling by the bath, washing their hands. I wondered if I ought to join them, although Fletcher did say I was there as an observer, so perhaps I'd better not. I asked myself what I had done that day that, theoretically, I could confess. God, it was hard to know where to begin! It depends on what you count as a sin really, and what you would say was natural. Like, your body makes certain demands, so what can you do? Is that a sin? Or leaving the washing-up for Mum and Gemma because I just couldn't be arsed. Or thinking what a plonker Kevin is? Was my dislike of him a sin?

Then the humming started again. One by one people retreated from the bath. The two blokes who had carried in the water lifted the bath again, and Fletcher opened a door that led outside. Everyone rose and massed around the door. The candles flickered at the rush of cold air. The water was carried out to a drain and tipped into it. Fletcher's voice rose above the humming.

"As the water returns to the earth we ask that our Darknesses of spirit, thought and action return to their source, and we can move on unencumbered to the path of Light."

More silence except for the sound of gurgling water. Then everyone began to hug each other, murmuring something.

Bea hugged me. "Peace and Perfection," she said.

I said it back. Then a bloke hugged me. We exchanged the greeting of Peace and Perfection. I think I was hugged five or six times. It was like a match when you score a goal. These were hugs of friendship, of being on the same side. Sure, it was odd, but kind of nice.

Then everyone chanted, "I believe in truth, in purity, in wholeness. I believe in goodness, in right, in light. I ask for the power of the Light to enter my body and soul... May it be my lot to achieve Perfection... I will stay by the fountain of Light... May it be my lot to achieve Perfection. May it be your lot to achieve Perfection. To the One, to the Light – salaam, shalom, peace. Peace be with you."

Then they – we – let go of each other's hands and kissed our fingertips. Bea turned to me and placed her kissed fingertips on my lips, lightly. The tingle travelled from my lips to every part of me. Weird. But good.

We sat again. I looked round at everyone. They didn't seem so strange any more. Because we'd all taken part in something I felt connected to them. And yet. *And yet.* The truth was, I envied them. They had something I wanted – I couldn't have put it better than that. Yes. I wanted whatever it was they had.

6.
Rendall's Parables: The Tale of the Brothers

In a distant land dwelt a young man who loved his village. Every day, accompanied by his two younger brothers, he walked through its streets, greeting its inhabitants. Yet those that lived in the village reviled him; they spoke of him and his brothers as mad.

The day came when a bird settled on his shoulder, singing him a song of freedom and light. It sang of a land far away where all those he met would greet him with love and acceptance. So the bird led the young men from the village through the barren lands out to sea. Here was a boat packed with provisions, and the young man and his brothers set sail.

They sailed for a year and a day. One night the sky darkened and there was a storm of perilous magnitude. The sky crashed above them and the seas crashed around them. Despite the efforts of the young man, his brothers perished in the storm.

Soon after that time the young man arrived at the place the bird had promised. And in the morning he arose, went to his new home, and knew that he was loved. And he donned his white garb, and dwelt among his brethren.

So I kept going up to the farm, attending some Services, watching, talking. When my old mates came back from uni, I wriggled out of seeing them, except for Phil, who insisted we go out to the pub. I offered to drive so I didn't have to drink. In fact it wasn't too bad. The only mention I made of the White Ones was of Bea. I just talked about this girl I was seeing. Phil was only slightly interested as he was full of himself and just wanted to tell me what he'd been up to. That suited me. I didn't want to say a lot about Bea either. I wasn't quite certain what to do about her. Because she was training to be a White One, I had to bide my time and see how she wanted to conduct the relationship. To tell you the truth, I was a bit lost. In my other life, in the real world, I'd usually snog a girl first, then decide if I wanted to see her again. And I might or I might not. If I did, I'd suggest a film or something, and see if I could talk to her. And if I could, if I found I both fancied and liked her, then I'd go for it. Because a relationship with a girl was like a double thing, mental and physical.

With Bea it was different. I definitely knew I fancied her, and I was pretty sure she fancied me. I caught her looking at me in a certain way. But apart from the odd squeeze of her hand, a peck on the cheek, or the sensation of her thigh pressed close to mine when we sat on a bench together, there had been nothing. Nothing physical. Instead I found myself pouring out the story of my life. She had interesting comments to make about my mates and family. I told her about Tasha too. She said some partings were inevitable, were meant to be. I found myself getting closer to Bea, but we'd never kissed, nobody acknowledged us as an item – heck, even *we* didn't acknowledge ourselves as an item. Yet we were one, I was sure of it. But I didn't want to press the point, in case she said something negative. So we drifted on, getting closer, not saying or doing anything. I thought about her most of the time, dreamed about her, thought of her as my girlfriend but couldn't say she was. There was no one else on the farm she spent as much time with as me.

But don't think I only got involved with the White Ones because of Bea. There was more to it than that. Like, when I went to the farm, everyone around me was happy. You don't realise how miserable most people are. At work, at home, at school, everyone has long faces. If you're in a good mood, people think you're clowning around. I read once that some bloke said most people lead lives of quiet desperation. That's true. Except on the farm. There, people communicated, smiled, opened up. I liked it, pure and simple.

And I admired them for giving up things – the way they didn't drink or smoke or do drugs. That took some willpower, willpower most people didn't have. I reckon their belief system helped them. Personally, I didn't know what to make of that part of it. For me, going to their Services and joining in with their rituals was like playing a virtual reality game. Like when I was a kid and you'd play aliens or whatever and you'd really BE an intrepid space commander for half an hour or so, and then your mum would call you in and you'd drop it. So while I was attending their Services I kind of believed it all, but I knew really that I didn't. Or so I thought.

Then my mum started asking me questions, like who my new friends were, that sort of thing. I almost told her the truth but luckily stopped myself. My parents *might* have understood what good the White Ones were doing me, but then again, they were more likely to ask awkward questions and then pick an argument. So I told them Nick, Kate, Bea and Fletcher were living in a commune, that they were mainly artists, were into wholefood, the alternative living thing. I said quite a few of them worked outside the commune, too. I made more of my individual friendships with them, especially Bea. I lied and said she was my girlfriend. When Mum asked do they take drugs, I answered with complete honesty, no way! When she said, if you have a girlfriend, you must be responsible, I said, we're not sleeping together. Then she asked, you're not thinking of going up there to live, are you? That was harder. I can see the attraction of their way of life, I replied, but I like my home comforts too much. Mum seemed satisfied, and anyway, she was totally stressed out about Christmas.

Just before Christmas was the one night I'll always remember. It began just like an average evening – me at the farm, watching Auriel dish out a rather watery but over-spiced chickpea stew. I was quite happy not to have too much of it. I was glad that Nick was able to join us. I knew he suffered bouts of ill-health, but he was looking slightly better tonight. Kate was there, Fletcher, and Bea. The Evening Service had been about an hour ago – it was pitch-black outside now – but the kitchen was warm and it was great to be all together like that.

"Do you like it?" Auriel asked. She meant the stew.

"Sure," I said.

"You don't. I can tell. You're eating it too slowly, Joe."

I shovelled in a few mouthfuls and grinned at her. I'd already got to know Auriel quite well. She was the neurotic one, always needing reassurance. But she wasn't on anti-depressants any more, Bea had told me. Before the White Ones, Auriel had had some kind of mental problem. Her family were talking about having her sectioned. Then she met Kate. Living here had straightened her out. Well, almost. But the White Ones tolerated odd behaviour – it was only on the outside that unusual behaviour was classified as mental illness. Auriel lived happily here, and Bea said her parents even came to visit her from time to time.

"Eat some more, Nick," Auriel cajoled.

Nick moved his spoon around the plate and then attempted a mouthful. He never had much of an appetite. Will meanwhile shovelled his food down. He used to be a soldier, I'd learned. He was a straightforward kind of guy, loyal, no nonsense – the most ordinary person you could think of. He'd come from a group of White Ones in Scotland – because I'd learned there were groups everywhere. Not that they advertised themselves. They didn't seek to convert, but just wanted to live according to their principles.

Fletcher said to Nick, "You look better." Then he turned to me. "When Nick was in India, Joe, he picked up a parasitical infection. He's not completely cured yet. We're all focusing on his recovery, and Nick's doing what he can to overcome it. It's a matter of boosting his immune system."

"Yes," Nick said. "The mental and physical are linked."

I nodded vigorously. "Like when I had glandular fever – it was after my exams, when I was exhausted."

"Yes," Nick continued, looking flushed. "But your body also expresses its spiritual lack of balance in an external fashion."

"Come again?" I said.

"Illness isn't random – it seizes on a weakness, a fifth column in your system. Tackling illness is as much about spiritual discipline as medicine. Rendall shrunk a tumour through a full SD vigil."

That was interesting. Rendall, I knew, was the Father of the White Ones. SD was sensory deprivation. However, White Ones mainly practised Alternate Sense Deprivation – ASD – as a spiritual discipline. I'd seen them do it, wearing blindfolds, stuffing their ears, covering their skin. They did without one sense each day. But full SD! I wondered what that would be like.

Before I had a chance to ask, Bea spoke. "I only wish I'd met the White Ones when my mother was ill."

I saw Auriel reach out to hold Bea's hand and I wished I'd thought of doing that. Bea had told me her mother had died of cancer, around two years ago. We were all sombre for a moment.

Then Fletcher said, "She is with the Light."

Bea looked at him gratefully. Just then she looked so vulnerable and lost I wanted to hold her tight to me and show her that someone loved her. But instead I had to satisfy myself with being part of the group.

Still, when the meal, such as it was, had finished, I asked Bea if we could have some time alone. She looked a little unsure and I noticed how her eyes sought Fletcher's.

He answered my question. "Later," he said. "There's some things I'd like to talk to Joe about."

It was a friendly suggestion, and I was made to feel as if there wasn't enough of me to spread around. So later I followed Fletcher up to his quarters. Nick came too, leaning on Will's arm for support.

I'd not been to Fletcher's room before. We walked up the stairs and along a corridor into a large living/bedroom with a door leading off, presumably to a private bathroom. There was a fireplace with a three-bar electric fire standing in it, a bed with a faded patchwork bedspread, a desk with books, papers, and an anglepoise lamp. In one corner there was a rail with a few items of clothing hanging down. There was a poster on the wall of that mushroom-effect explosion you associate with nuclear bombs. Quite striking, when you looked at it. The floor was just polished floorboards scattered with cheap rugs. The effect was fairly Spartan, but also comfortable, the kind of place you wouldn't mind spending time in.

Fletcher sat on the floor, cross-legged, his back against his bed. Nick sat by him on the bed, like a sort of bodyguard. Uncertain what to do, I followed Will and sat on the floor, below the poster, my back against the wall, my legs stuck out. I had this feeling that the guys had something important to say to me and my first thought was that I'd done something wrong. I felt a bit fidgety. Or maybe they were going to say that I'd spent enough time with them and they wanted me out. Why was it I always expected the worst?

"So," Fletcher began. "How's it going?"

"Fine," I said, a bit nervous.

"Have you got any questions?"

Why is it your mind always goes blank when people ask you that?

"Questions about what?" I parried.

"Us. The Light. Anything. We've seen you getting more and more involved and thought it was time."

"Time for what?"

"Time for you to be honest. Why are you here, what do you want, what do you want from us?"

With Fletcher, you always told the truth. He had no truck with lies.

"I like you all as people," I said, "and I'm interested in what you do here. It gives me something to do with my time."

Whenever I spoke like that, completely honest, I felt kind of naked, or as if I'd crept out from behind a bush and a sniper had me in his targets. Fletcher rested his chin on his hand and thought about what I'd said.

"It gives you something to do with your time. Most people don't think about how they spend their time. They're just led by their desires, towards food, sex, material possessions. Thinking is what separates White Ones from the rest."

I was flattered by what he said.

"I admire the fact you're prepared to be different," I said, "and I admire your principles. But what I can't get my head round is your belief system. Tell me if I'm right. You believe in the forces of Light and Darkness. That Light is Good and Good is Light and you have to be one with the Light by living as purely as you can. And then when you die you sort of merge with the Light. And you fight the forces of Darkness. Like the Jedi," I kidded.

But Fletcher didn't look amused. "That's only a very crude description," he said.

"There's much more to it than that," Nick agreed.

Fletcher looked me in the eyes. "There are countless religions and superstitions all over the world, but in fundamentals they're all very similar. There's this belief in a divinity – God, Allah, Yahweh. And before the so-called discovery of God, people still saw the forces of nature at play, and still had the need to believe in something. What people call God is just their way of naming the incomprehensible."

I went along with all of that. "Like Father Christmas," I added, trying to be a good student. "He's just a symbol."

Fletcher nodded but didn't really seem to hear me. "We would never deny anyone's concept of God. But what we know is that there is a force for Good. That this Life is not all there is. And that there is a reason why we're here."

It intrigued me, the way he sounded so definite. He had a certain power, Fletcher. He had a compelling presence. When he talked, you listened. You were only aware of him in the room. His voice was slower than most people's and his eyes held you.

"Before Creation, there was just bliss. It existed beyond time and space in a unity of thought and emotion. Then a vast explosion occurred. Matter was formed, and antimatter. Matter is what our world is made of; antimatter is pure evil. It causes bad thoughts and propagates illness. All living things in our world have a yearning to return to the time that was. We can return to that time, but only through self-purification – achieved through self-control – keeping our bodies pure, total honesty, confession and working towards an end to hypocrisy and corruption in the world around us.

"That might not be achieved in one lifetime. Those among us who are full of evil – those who commit murder without reason, those drugged with power, enter oblivion when they die. It's as if they never were. Their names are blotted out. But those with sparks of goodness are given the chance to return and start again. White Ones are people who have already lived a few lives and have reached the next stage of their journey. They are ready to achieve total self-purification and the rules for them are stricter than for the rest of mankind. We are in training. We accept that others may live indulgent lives; we don't have that choice. We work towards Perfection.

"Our goal is to achieve Perfection. When we do, we will merge with the Light. At that time, we will still have our individual consciousnesses. These enable us to re-enter the world as immortals. These immortal beings are called Perfects. They are here now among us. When we are ready to become one of them, we will meet one. They will help us to reach our ultimate Vision."

He stopped talking. There was this silence, as if holy words had been spoken. I could have nodded or even said amen. But knowing what Fletcher expected of me, I didn't do that. Instead I questioned him.

"I don't see how you can believe all that. It seems pretty far-fetched to me."

Fletcher looked at me directly. "It's pretty far-fetched that a man was crucified then returned to life three days later. More far-fetched to claim he was actually the Son of God. It's also weird to believe that some Divine Being handed down two stone tablets to a bloke on a mountain."

I laughed to relieve the tension.

"Anyway," Will commented. "We have proof."

"Proof?"

"Yes," Fletcher said. "None of us here would have been convinced about the Light and Perfects had there been no proof. This is the twenty-first century. The age of science. We only believe what we know to be true."

"What's your proof?" I asked.

"Have you heard of near-death experiences?" Nick asked me.

"Yeah. People look down on their own bodies, right? See themselves on the hospital bed?"

Fletcher nodded. "If you compare accounts of near-death experiences from all over the world, they're surprisingly similar. People feel as if they're moving forward, and see a light. They're conscious of spirits welcoming them, and a sense of peace and love. When they return to this world, it's with a sense of loss."

"So that's your proof?" I had to admit this was interesting, but not conclusive. Then I noticed the three of them exchanging looks.

"I think he's ready," Nick said.

Will nodded eagerly. I was glad. I liked Will and was pleased at this evidence of his friendship. And I wanted to know whatever it was Fletcher was on the brink of telling me. I promised myself I would take it seriously.

Fletcher seemed to hesitate. Then he spoke. "Look, Joe. We don't impart this to everyone. A lot of people who are attracted to the White Ones are just sad and lonely souls, willing to believe anything in exchange for security. We think you're different. You're not afraid to speak your mind. You have a voice of your own. You have a brain. But not only that, we sense your past lives in you. We think you are meant to be here. This is your right place. We've watched you struggle a bit with us, fight your destiny. We've seen the Light in you sometimes and have felt glad. We think you are one of us and that we've found a brother. But we cannot make you join us. It's a vital part of our code that you come to us of your own volition. You must invite each stage. We can do no more than assist you."

Now I felt seriously weird. I didn't know what to think. It could be true – I could be one of them. I certainly felt different on the farm, more me, more significant. Maybe that feeling of being significant was what Fletcher meant. I had found a place or purpose. But on the other hand, I was still me, Joe Woods, with a mum and dad and a place at Bristol to read law in the autumn. Only none of that seemed very real at that moment. I needed to find out whether I was a White One now, whether Fletcher and Nick and Will knew me better than I knew myself. Most of all, I felt an overpowering curiosity to see their proof. What was it they knew, but weren't yet prepared to tell me?

Fletcher got up, and went into the bathroom. He came back immediately with a glass of water and placed it on the floor in the middle of us all. No one said a word. They were waiting for me. That's when I had this thought. This moment in front of me had more meaning than any moment I had experienced so far. Something extraordinary was about to happen. It was up to me to seize it.

"I'd like to know," I said. That was it. There was no turning back.

Fletcher took the glass of water and sipped from it, passed it to Nick, who sipped from it too, passed it to Will, who did the same, and then it came to me. I sipped from it, like them. The water trickled down my throat, softening and relaxing it. I handed the glass back to Fletcher.

"Give me your hand," he said. I stretched out my hand, palm outwards. I noticed it was trembling slightly. Fletcher took a penknife from his pocket. In an instant the blade was out and skimming the surface of my index finger, drawing blood. I felt no pain. Fletcher took my wrist and held my finger over the glass of water. A drop or two of blood landed on the surface and diffused through the water until it had dispersed completely. Fletcher lifted the glass again and picked it up, and handed it round once more. They each drank. Me, too. I drank my own blood.

Fletcher began again. "Colin Rendall, our leader, almost drowned with his friends over thirty years ago. It was when he was submerged in the water he was granted his Vision of the Light. But it was not with him as it was with others. He was admitted to the central chamber where he saw the Book. In the moment of timelessness he experienced, he was able to remember it all. All. And when he recovered he was able to write it all down, and more besides. That Book is both our proof and our Guide. It was time for a new prophet, and Rendall is that man. I have met him. Through him, I have seen the Book.

"But to argue for a moment," he continued. "Although I have proof, even I must concede that there is no such thing as absolute proof of anything. Even the most rigorously controlled scientific experiment is open to different interpretations. You believe in electricity but only because people you trust have explained it to you. People know about the theory of relativity because we trusted Einstein. No one person can know everything, and so we must find a teacher, someone we can place absolute faith in. We must trust the knowledge of other people, other people's proofs. Rendall knows. I know Rendall. I believe in his truth with the totality of my being. There is a chain of knowing. You, Joe, are part of that chain. You know me. You know. You can achieve Perfection."

At that moment, I was conscious of a warmth in my body. It seemed to start in my left leg, but in a few moments it had spread everywhere. OK, I know it sounds crazy. But it was like my body had filled with heat, with light, and I knew, I *knew* something stupendous had happened to me. There was a presence filling me. Then gradually it receded, but I was left with an afterglow, a deep happiness, a sense of purpose. So I knew what Fletcher said was true. I would be able to achieve Perfection.

PART TWO

THE ARRIVAL

7.

From Rendall's Laws Governing Purity:
Alternate Sense Deprivation

In order to free yourself from the temptations of this world, White Ones are encouraged to practise Alternate Sense Deprivation. In a five-day cycle one must abstain from each sense in turn; you shall not see, you shall not hear, you shall not taste, you shall not feel, you shall not smell. Those aspiring to higher levels of purity may, under supervision, attempt a combination of sense deprivations. Their gain is the greater.

————⋘◆⋙————

It's true – life is like a maze. Most of the time you wander around in it, sometimes thinking you're getting somewhere, but most of the time just coming up against dead ends. But if you were to see the maze from a helicopter, say, you'd see the pattern and be able to plot your route. And being a White One was like taking that helicopter ride. I could see the pattern, the pattern of my own life. Things were starting to make sense.

I'm not saying I was a White One – this was not exactly true. To be a genuine White One you had to undergo an initiation ceremony, and Fletcher had said that he would be my sponsor, which was quite an honour apparently – only Nick had been sponsored by Fletcher, no one else. Obviously I would have to prepare myself by studying and practising the Five Laws of Purity and ASD – alternate sense deprivation. I knew at any time I could opt out. The way I saw it, I had freedom. And I *wanted* to go further, because each step I took along the path, I felt better. Anything that felt this good had to be right.

I said that to Bea and she agreed vehemently. We had many long conversations throughout January. Bea was a few weeks ahead of me on the path to initiation but it felt like we were learning together. So her thoughts and experiences complemented the sessions I had with Nick and Fletcher. She sort of humanised the theory, she was the flesh and blood.

I could see now that what the White Ones believed was true. It stood to reason. All societies, past and present, believed something. Science is only an explanation of how things occur, not why. The *why* has to be open to interpretation. It seemed more and more obvious to me that the White Ones had to be right. Sun worshippers, Hindus, Christians, Jews, Ancient Greeks – everyone had a belief system and the White Ones' system was a distillation of all of them. It encapsulated the truth, the core of what we all know to be true. That there is a force beyond us. That it is good. That good conquers evil. That we have to strive to be good and only then can we conquer evil. How can *anyone* disagree with any of that? Don't try telling me the universe is just a random occurrence without form, shape or meaning. Like, how can that be true? That's harder to believe than accepting there is meaning. Most people don't want there to be meaning because it gives them the excuse to follow their own greed and selfishness. To accept there is a higher being is immediately to commit to following in his path. Most people don't want to do that.

I could go on. But the most engrossing things about training to be a White One were the Purity Laws and ASD. I had to give up cigarettes, alcohol, drugs, sex and all addictive behaviour. This wasn't too bad. I didn't smoke, although I'd experimented once or twice in the past. I could easily live without weed. I found, since I gave up drinking, my head was clearer and I felt good when I woke in the morning. Not being hungover, I didn't need coffee. As for sex, there wasn't the opportunity. I thought I would worry about that one later.

ASD was tough but rewarding. Doing without one sense sharpens your other four senses. It was very much like that when I spent a whole day at the farm, with Bea, doing without sight. We were both given blindfolds and Will and Auriel helped us when necessary. What Bea and I did was to sit back to back, blindfolds on, and we talked. It was the best conversation we ever had.

We were both on a high. Bea said non-White Ones would think we were missing out, but what they don't realise is the buzz you get from self-discipline. She said that paradoxically we have a higher quality of life than people who give in to every whim. And I said to her, what's so good about the Purity Laws and ASD is that they simplify everything. Each day, you know what you have to do. Bea agreed. She said there was nothing so good as *knowing* that you were doing the right thing.

Sitting like that, our backs touching, supporting each other, we began to share new stuff. Not seeing stopped us from doing so many things that we had unlimited time on our hands. Time to really listen.

I said to Bea, "Tell me exactly how you found the White Ones – tell me every detail."

She said, "It's hard to know where to begin."

I heard, and felt, her take a deep sigh.

"You know I'm an only child. My mother was a piano teacher. She wanted to be a concert pianist but she was unlucky, no one discovered her. Also she married young. My father was Italian – he was over here working as a waiter. It was love at first sight. Mum used to say it was one of those grand passions that blind you to everything that actually mattered about a person. She showed me pictures of him and I could see he was quite striking. But as you know, the marriage didn't work out. Basically he couldn't stay faithful to her. And she told me he would lose his temper when she confronted him, he would rant and rave about his rights. Not that I remember any of this. I was a baby at the time. They split up when I was three. But the whole thing took its toll on Mum and she had a breakdown. She was admitted to hospital and I went to live with my gran. She really loathed my dad, and she let me know that. Never trust an Eye-tie, that's what she used to say."

"That must have messed you up," I said.

"Not really. When you're a kid you just accept whatever situation you find yourself in. I was quite happy just living with my mum, and I wasn't the only girl in my class at school from a single-parent family. I studied the piano and things were fine, until I was thirteen, when Mum first got ill. It was breast cancer. They were able to take the lump out of her breast and then she had to have chemotherapy and radiotherapy. That was tough because by then Gran had died and it was just us on our own. Mum was the sort who never wanted to trouble anybody; she wanted to cope by herself. She accepted help from me, though. It made me feel good, in a way, being able to do something, but also I felt responsible for her. It wasn't as bad as it sounds, honest. Mum always believed she would get better and was determined to fight the cancer. Then she got the all clear."

I felt tense. I knew what was coming next.

"Things were OK for a while. But when she found a second lump my mum pretended it was her imagination. She couldn't admit that it was happening again, so she was lying to herself. By the time she went to the doctor it was too late. It had spread this time and they tried the chemo again, but it was no use. She was in a lot of pain in the end. Then they gave her morphine and that was the worst part. It was like she wasn't my mum any more. She said all sorts of bizarre things. And it was funny, I knew she was going to die, but on another level I couldn't accept it. I didn't believe it was going to happen.

"On the last day when Mum was thrashing about in bed, fighting it, the nurses insisted I go into another room. They thought seeing her was upsetting me. It was, but what upset me even more was that I wasn't there when she went. I felt so angry with them. I had to beg and plead to see her body, but when I did, it wasn't too bad. She looked so peaceful, as if she was in another place. I sat with her a while and hummed some Chopin. It was OK."

I could feel tears behind my blindfold. They moistened the

material. I reached behind me and felt for Bea's hand. She took it and held it. I didn't know what to say. I couldn't imagine coping in that situation. Me and my family, we're all going to die together in some car crash or something. That's what I've decided. I can't get my head round losing any of them.

Bea carried on. "After she'd gone, I was very low. I couldn't work, I missed days at school. The doctor tried giving me some anti-depressants but they made me numb and I didn't like them. To be honest, there was a point when I thought of killing myself because I couldn't see the point of carrying on. My mum was a good person, I loved her, so why did she have to die like that?

"I met Kate at college. She was finishing her art foundation course. Bit by bit I got friendly with her and she told me snippets about the way she lived. She never hassled me but just answered my questions. I felt drawn towards her, it was odd. That was the time things began to make sense. When Kate told me about Rendall's Book and its revelations, I could see that the cancer had struck Mum randomly. It wasn't our fault – cancer is antimatter and anti-life. It's one of the things we have in this world, but it's also our duty to combat it. Not just by research and nursing – though that's very important – but by increasing the balance of good in the world. How we live affects the rest of the world. But I also began to see how Mum had made decisions that had an adverse outcome on the disease. Like when she lied to herself – lying is never good. And also I knew the truth of the Light when I saw Mum at peace. That was all the proof I needed. Mum wasn't religious and yet at the end she was happy – I'm certain about that. So everything Kate had told me made sense. I visited the farm, and liked it. I came here more and more, and then I met you."

She squeezed my hand. I squeezed it back. I moved my fingers against hers. When she spoke again her voice was charged with emotion.

"I love being with the White Ones! Fletcher is right – we're a family. Apart from my music, this is all I'll ever need. And I wouldn't have met you if it hadn't been for the White Ones. One of my best moments was hearing that you'd decided to follow the path of Light. I just know we have a special bond!"

"Yes," I said quickly. "I can feel it too."

It was the truth.

So this was my life. I lived at home and read Rendall's Book, and kept fit by going to the gym – my dad bought me six months' membership as a Christmas present. I spent most evenings at the farm. Mum and Dad complained a bit but I explained that since both the Red King and Electric Avenue had dispensed with my services as it was the slack season, I had nothing else to do. I could tell they didn't like it but they were wary of upsetting me. Just as well. But it was getting increasingly hard to practise ASD at home. In the end it was the ASD that forced the issue.

Normally I worked my ASD round the times I was at the farm, so, for example, I'd deprive myself of taste – which meant fasting – at the weekend, when I was with the White Ones. I wouldn't risk it at home. The last thing I wanted was my mum worrying that I'd got anorexia or something because she saw that I wasn't eating. I was planning to explain to my parents about ASD, but I was waiting until the time was right. But recently I was worried that I'd been falling behind with my programme. That was why I risked doing a not-hearing day at home.

I inserted the earplugs in the morning after my mum had gone to work and put the answerphone on. Then I messed around on the computer – the White Ones have a website but the address is not in the public domain. I read some of Rendall's Book. Did you know, when he was coming back from his near-death experience the whole text was imprinted on his mind in one moment? He was able to recall every word later, every word. Fletcher says this is probably similar to the way Moses received the Ten Commandments. The stone tablet business was a myth so people would believe him. Most people find it hard to grasp phenomena which defy rational explanation. That's why so many religions employ stories to tell truths, like the parables. But I'm drifting here. What I'm saying is that the sense of time passing is something we only experience in this life. In the other world, there's no such thing as time.

I told myself that as my day inched forward. Not being able to hear much meant I didn't want to go out, and time was passing very slowly. I stopped myself looking at the clock and instead tried some White Light meditation. I reminded myself that time meant nothing, except it was strange that something that was nothing could weigh so heavily. The hands on the clock hardly budged.

In fact I was quite glad when Gemma got back from school and my parents came in. The earplugs didn't take away all of my hearing, but just muffled sounds, and Gemma's got such a loud voice it was easy to make out the gist of what she was saying and to react accordingly. Mum was busy in the kitchen. Neither of them had noticed that I wasn't hearing. It made me realise how little attention people usually pay to one another. Mum and Gemma just wittered without really listening to anyone else. I felt distant from them, one remove away.

So the day had gone well and it must have been about eight. We were watching TV – one of the soaps. That is, Gemma was watching it, an absent look on her face. Dad was upstairs working. Mum was flicking through the papers, looking up every so often. I didn't need to listen to know what was going on. Every so often she would be saying to Gemma, *What was that? Are they having an affair? Who's in trouble with the police?* And Gemma, irritated, had to recap the plot. My mum only ever drifted in and out of TV programmes; she was always doing two things at once.

I was looking at the screen thinking how pathetic the soap was, and how, in our bland, processed world we needed this charade of emotion and conflict because everything else was meaningless and devoid of interest. Most people are afraid to live fully so they surround themselves with second-hand lives – soaps, celebrity gossip in magazines, whatever. Two characters were arguing, their faces bulging aggressively. The camera was zooming in, zooming out, extracting every bit of emotion from the scene. You didn't need to be able to hear what they were saying to enjoy it.

Then I heard Gemma screaming, "Joe!!"

My head swerved round.

"Joe! Mum's *talking* to you!"

Quickly I removed one of the earplugs. I felt a bit guilty and hoped Fletcher would understand when I confessed at the next Evening Service. I hoped the Light would wash away my small act of cowardice. But I thought I'd better find out what it was my mother wanted.

"Honestly, Joe!" she said. "I've been trying to get through to you for the last five minutes. Anyone would think you were deaf."

I mumbled an apology and asked her what she wanted.

"It doesn't matter. It was nothing."

She always does that. Makes out something is a big deal, and then retracts. It's a guilt trip. The White Ones don't do that – they speak straight, no poses, no game-playing.

"Mum," I said, trying and failing to hide the impatience in my voice. "What did you want?"

She tutted a bit. "I only wanted to ask you if you thought the settee needed replacing or just re-covering. I told you it wasn't important. Your dad says new covers would do the trick but I can't see why we can't get a new one with interest-free credit. One day we're going to have to. It might as well be now."

"Shhh!" warned Gemma. Her expression was pained. Soaps were her religion.

"Get a new settee," I said, knowing that was what Mum wanted to hear.

It was relatively easy to replace the earplug. Then I closed my eyes and put my hands over my ears, partly to make up for the full-on hearing I'd just been experiencing.

Then I felt a sharp kick in my shin. It was Gemma.

"Joe, you moron! She's speaking to you!"

My mother was looking annoyed now. The soap was over and both of them were directing their attention to me.

"You haven't heard a word I've said." My mum looked daggers.

"TV was too loud," I parried.

Gemma turned it off then, and I removed an earplug again. I could see my mum thinking, wondering how best to tackle me.

"Joe," she began. "Is there something bothering you? You've been a bit preoccupied lately. I can understand if you're a bit fed up, still living at home."

I felt sorry for my mum. She has very limited vision. The only reason she could think of for my behaviour was that I wasn't at uni.

"I'm fine," I assured her.

She looked at me and raised her eyebrows slightly.

"You were talking before Christmas of travelling in the New Year. You haven't mentioned your plans for a bit."

"They're on the back burner," I said.

"This hasn't got anything to do with those people in Todmorden?"

"It's my own decision," I snapped at her.

I saw Mum and Gemma exchange a glance and I was seriously annoyed. I hate it when other people think they know what's best for you, when you feel their pressure moulding you into what they want you to be. Anger surged through me but I controlled it. Just.

"Well, I think you've been a total pain lately," Gemma commented.

I was annoyed, but I wasn't going to rip into her. She was just a kid. I took a deep breath.

"You don't understand," I said.

"Too right," she continued. "I don't think I want to understand. Like, in the old days, you used to tease me, and I know I used to go at you, but I didn't really mind. At least you noticed I was there. Now it's like I'm no one, and Mum's no one, and Dad's no one. We've all been talking about you. I just thought you ought to know."

"Gemma!" Mum said, threat in her voice.

So it was true. They'd all been talking about me behind my back. Great. For the first time in my life I'd found something that made me feel good – real friends, a sense of belonging, a mission – and my family were campaigning to take it all away from me. And they didn't even have the guts to tell me to my face. I'd had enough of their tinny, putrid cynicism.

"Cut it out!" I shouted at Gemma.

I must have shouted louder than I thought. There was thudding on the stairs and in came my father.

"What's going on here?" he commanded.

By this time Gemma had started crying. Big, whooping, theatrical sobs. Mum's face was ashen. I could see Dad twitching, itching to get to the bottom of things, to find a victim. It was funny, like I said before – since hanging out with the White Ones I could see so much more clearly. Dad's rage, Mum's distress, Gemma's histrionics, all like a soap playing out in front of my eyes. I was the camera. And at that point I realised the best way to deal with all of this was to detach myself, not to get drawn in.

"Joe – explain yourself," my dad bellowed.

"It's just the kids." Mum decided to step in. "Gemma had a go at Joe because he's been acting a bit distant lately. I think she felt left out."

Dad ignored her. His eyes were fixed on me. I knew he'd heard me shouting and he was spoiling for a fight. He had this idea that he ought to be the tough one, the superhero, the defender of family values, the one who kicks ass.

"Apologise to your sister – at once!"

"For what?"

"For a start, shouting at her like you meant to raise the dead."

That was unjust and stupid. I could see everyone's thoughts like clouds of poisonous mosquitoes obscuring my vision. I valued this new vision. I didn't want to be standing in the living room with my dad's red face and the beads of sweat on his upper lip, with my mum gripping the sides of the armchair, with Gemma gulping on the settee with its manky, worn cover. I didn't want to feel myself sucked into the backwash of emotion. I decided to remain silent. I just stood in front of my father, not saying anything. It separated me from them and I knew it would annoy him.

"Apologise!" he shouted.

"I don't need this," I said to him.

At all costs I wasn't going to lose my self-possession. I thought about Fletcher and Nick and the White Ones, how they would cope if they were beset like this. I knew that faced with impurity a White One kept himself pure, unsullied. The best thing to do would be to leave the room, but Dad was standing in the doorway. In my head I recited, *May it be my lot to achieve Perfection.*

Gemma stopped bawling and just looked at me. I thought she looked scared for some reason. But I was feeling OK now. I realised all I had to do was keep myself apart from all of this, not let myself get dragged down to their level. I knew my dad wanted to hit me but he wouldn't. I glanced at Mum. I saw tears in her eyes. That got to me. I knew I owed her an explanation. When my voice came out it sounded different, partly because I was wearing one earplug, partly because I heard myself speaking as a White One.

"I don't expect any of you to understand this, but I've found a way of life that suits me better than this one. It's not my intention to hurt you, but I have to move on."

"Move on?" asked my dad. "What's all this about moving on? You shouted at your sister and I'm demanding an apology."

I ignored him. "So it may be easier if I go and stay at Lower Fold for a while. I was thinking about it anyway."

"You're staying right here," my dad said.

I just shook my head. I knew now what I had to do. It was time to commit myself fully to the White Ones. I couldn't lead two lives, one here and one at the farm. There was a story in Rendall's Book about a man who wore two suits of clothes and looked ridiculous. It made the same point. I knew I had to choose, and if I chose my family I would have to give up the White Ones. I couldn't do that.

"Sorry," I said to Dad. "Sorry," to Mum, and then to Gemma.

Inside my heart was breaking. They didn't know it, but this was my farewell. I loved them more at that moment than ever before, and felt, in renouncing them, I was being brave, self-denying, pure. I felt free, light as air.

I went up to my room. I lay awake most of the night and packed my rucksack when I was sure they were all asleep.

When I'd done that, I wrote a letter.

Dear Mum, Dad and Gemma,

Please don't think that the argument last night caused this. Also please don't try to go after me. I'm safe and well and I'll be in contact from time to time.

You've always said to me that growing up was about finding out who you really were. That's why you never pushed me into making choices at school but let me find my own path. You also said that a person has to have values, a moral code to live by.

My friends at Lower Fold Farm have a moral code, but more than that, they have belief and purpose. They're not wasting their lives. They follow the path of Light. I want to travel with them and now I can see that means doing without the people I love most. I have learnt that love is not bound by space, time or physical proximity, so you can be assured I love you still.

I promise you, no one, absolutely no one, has talked me into this. I have not been brainwashed, whatever that is. I want to dedicate my life to a higher good and have found a way to do that. This is my choice. I want to say again, don't come and try to find me. I'm 18, an adult according to the law, and in my right mind.

I know it will be as hard for you to say goodbye as it is for me. I shall be praying for you. When you think of me, know that I am happy, bathed in Light.

Joe

I left the house at five-thirty a.m., and caught the first bus in the direction of Rochdale.

8

From Rendall's Book of Prayers: The Induction Service

The Service is to commence with one or two readings from the Book. The inductee, having fasted for the previous twenty-four hours, is led into the place of meeting by his sponsor. He is dressed in white undergarments and covered in white. After Prayers A and B the leader of the congregation then asks the inductee for an object which represents the past to him. It is placed in a crucible and burnt. The inductee is then led outside to a tub or container of water. He then divests himself of all of his clothing and stands in the water while the Dedication Prayer is read. He then immerses himself in the water, his head below the surface for a minimum of ten seconds. On his re-emergence all are to kiss their fingertips and touch the forehead of the newly born White One. His birth may be marked by a wedding ring, wreaths of white flowers, or gifts of commitment. All then say, "It is the Light, and the Light alone, that separates us and makes us Holy."

I can't believe it. I can't believe life can be this good.

That was the thought that kept going round and round my mind, those first few weeks, that spring, with the White Ones. Every morning when I woke I snapped awake, completely ready to get up and do whatever was planned for me – seeing to the greenhouse, cleaning, preparing the Gathering Place for the Dawn Service. Everywhere I went, people smiled at me, showing they liked me. The guys in the men's house were my brothers, the brothers I never had. Sleeping in the dormitory was like being alone because we were all one, and not being alone because of the different rhythms of each other's breathing, but we knew our minds were all set on the same goal.

But I'm racing ahead. When I got to the farm and told Fletcher I had left home he said he knew, or rather, he had been thinking of me all day, sensing a disturbance around me, knowing I had come to a rope bridge over a chasm. And he was right, that was what it had felt like, crossing a chasm on a rope bridge. He took both my hands and held them for a moment. I knew I had made the right decision. I had come home.

When Fletcher suggested I be initiated fairly soon, the breath was taken out of me. The White Ones recommend at least six months as an observer before commitment. Bea was scheduled to be initiated ahead of me. Now I would be a White One before her. I realised once I agreed to set a date for my initiation, there would be no going back. But then what the hell? I had just left home. It amounted to the same thing. I told Fletcher I was ready. Things were set up for a week's time.

Now when I look back, the ceremony resolves itself into a series of snapshots. I remember the headache I had from the fasting, a box of tension above my eyes, and also how my emotions were all on the surface – I could have cried at the slightest provocation. Fletcher said that was part of the purification process. Your emotions rise to the surface so they can be expelled. It made sense. I felt as if everything was about to be – here are some words from a poem Bea quoted to me – "changed utterly. A terrible beauty is born."

I didn't have any white boxers so I had to wear Y-fronts, which felt weird. But I was wrapped in a large white beach towel so that was OK. I handed Fletcher a photo of me, Mum, Dad and Gemma on the beach at Lido di Jesolo, taken a few summers ago. I watched him burn it in a white crucible. I reckoned it was only a photo, and what mattered was the symbolism – I was replacing one set of loyalties with another. I had spoken to my mum and it hadn't been easy. I had to promise to meet her in town soon, just to put her mind at rest. It did seem strange, watching this photo, which I used to come across from time to time in my desk, leaping into flames, curling, transforming to white ash in front of my eyes.

Next I remember the immersion. One impure thought escaped me, which was that I was worried the water would be cold. And if it was, would they know from my reaction that I thought it was? Here's the amazing thing. The water was cold and yet I welcomed it. Something above and beyond me took away the usual reactions of my body and I could do it, immerse myself fully in the water, tingling sensations of hot and cold all confused, holding my breath under the water and counting, one elephant two elephant three elephant as I did when I was young to make sure I was counting proper seconds – until fear and exhilaration rushed through me and I forgot whether I'd reached thirteen or fourteen. I found myself rushing up for air, freezing cold and then the cheers and applause from all the guys. Nick threw me my towel and I felt like

I'd run a marathon. The girls came in then and they all touched my forehead, which seemed to fill with light and gladness.

Fletcher gave me the ring and placed it on my finger – a thin, gold band – and it was Bea who placed the garland of white chrysanthemums around my neck. In a moment of silliness I felt like I'd just stepped off the plane in Hawaii or something. The flowers scratched my skin and for the first time I felt foolish. But then the drumming started and people came over and congratulated me. Fletcher gave me a white leather copy of Rendall's Book, Nick a white T-shirt. There were other gifts too, wrapped in white tissue paper. Bea told me she had something for me, but it was for later. Then people brought me food – I was ravenous now – and we all sat on the floor and ate, drank while the drumming continued. This was the best moment of my life so far.

Until that night with Bea. People had begun to disperse after the feast and I had wandered out to the back of the buildings and stood on the boundary of our land, looking up at the hill in front of me. Funny how from a distance it looked unclimbable, but standing here, I could see how to ascend it. There seemed to be a path on the left, overgrown but manageable. Like life. Like my life.

Back in October I'd thought I wouldn't be able to hack the coming year, but everything had turned out so differently. I had turned out so differently. I shuddered with the momentousness of it all. How can I explain this feeling? I was in awe of myself, what I had become. I had to recognise I was more than just me now. I carried the expectations of the White Ones – Fletcher had told me there was nothing I could not achieve – and had to come to terms with the fact that I was special. Me, Joe Woods, a White One.

I was about to feel it was all too much for me and I'd do anything for a drink when I heard what I thought were footsteps. Yes, they were footsteps. Bea's.

She placed her hand on my shoulder.

"I was looking for you everywhere."

I looked down at her and smiled. I always smiled when I saw Bea. She had that effect on me. It was dark now, and her face was only a suggestion of itself. There was a mystery about her. She had something in her hand. She gave it to me. It was a package, wrapped in a white silk scarf. Its softness was like liquid on my hands as I unfurled it. Inside, on a white thread, hung a tiny scalloped seashell. Even in the dark it had a pearly glimmer.

"I've varnished it," Bea said. "You can wear it round your neck. I like to think of it having been washed and purified by the waves."

I held it in my hand. It was delicate and beautiful; my eyes devoured each voluptuous curve.

"I made a special trip to Formby. I asked Auriel to take me in the car. When I found it, I knew it was right for you. Do you like it? Joe?"

I realised I hadn't said anything to her, not even thank you. But words seemed insufficient. A moment ago, all there had been was the enormity of what I had undertaken; now here, in this curved white shell, was perfection in miniature, cradled in the palm of my hand. A microcosm of all we were trying to achieve. I felt that Bea had understood me perfectly, understood my needs at that moment, understood who I was. I had never felt closer to anyone.

"I love this," I said to her, and realised I had wanted to say something else, that I loved her, but the words deflected themselves and at that time I didn't know why. I stroked her arm over the white cheesecloth shirt she wore. I could feel the firmness of her arm beneath it. Her arm did not flinch. I moved my hand up, to her upper arm, I felt the sudden, soft warmth of her neck. I placed my hand on her shoulder.

"Thanks," I said.

An owl hooted somewhere. Otherwise it was silent. My hand on Bea's shoulder, connecting with her beating heart and warm, living body. I took it away, kissed my fingers, and placed them on her forehead. She took her fingers and held them to her lips, and slowly moved them away and placed them on my forehead. She stayed like that for a while.

Twin souls. I'd read in one of the Commentaries on Rendall's Book, written by one of the earliest followers, that a soul can only be truly pure when there is an equal balance of male and female. There was some dispute about whether that means one has to balance the male and female within oneself, or find a female to balance you. Just then I knew that it meant the coming together of a man and woman. I could be the White One Fletcher wanted me to be, with Bea by my side. And Bea herself was being initiated in a couple of weeks.

I was filled with the desire to shout, laugh, pick Bea up in my arms, anything to express the exultation I felt. Already life was perfection. *May it be my lot to achieve Perfection.* I'd never expected it to happen so soon.

Things were busy on the farm. There was a lot of work to be done in the vegetable garden, and we were doing some redecorating and creosoting the sheds. I was active all day, always on the move, and sometimes the physical effort was back-breaking, but somehow the harder we worked, the greater the spiritual payoff. You'd feel utterly exhausted and then the exhaustion would transform itself into a high, as if you'd sloughed off your body like a snake his skin, and just your essence was left.

And when there wasn't physical work, there was study. Study was a vital component of being a White One. Our faith was demanding, physically and intellectually. It was important I was fully acquainted with Rendall's Book, and the Commentaries on it, the different interpretations, those which were allowable and those which were heresies, and after a few months I would be expected to write some Commentaries of my own. I had to study late at night. A group of us would gather in the dormitory, around a table, and discuss what we were reading. And then there were the Services, the cooking, the days of ASD: there was never a moment that wasn't accounted for.

In the beginning, there was quite a bit of trouble with my parents. The first time they came up to the farm Fletcher explained that I didn't want to see them. Even from inside the farm I could hear my dad shouting at the door. They came the next day too, and on that occasion Fletch went to get me and suggested I speak to them. He stayed with me while I explained to my parents again that this was my choice. That afternoon Mum and Dad were trying to win me over with reason and with bribes – a car, a holiday, stuff like that. I was gentle with them and explained those things had no value for me any more. Mum then backtracked and said she'd put up with me living on the farm if I saw her from time to time. I conceded that as I couldn't see what harm it would do. My dad banged on about the White Ones being a cult and brainwashing me and I had to explain to him again that every step I had taken I had *chosen* to take. I said that living on the farm was only like going to uni – if I hadn't taken a gap year they'd have lost me anyway. When they left, they were subdued. There was this arrangement that I'd ring home every week and if I didn't, they'd come to see me. Out of the corner of my eye I could see Fletch nodding so I knew it was all right.

About a week later Fletcher called me to his room unexpectedly. I saw him every week as he was my mentor and we used to discuss my progress. I guessed this was something different. It was bizarre, but I had this totally stupid feeling that I might have accidentally done something wrong. I could feel my pulse racing. I was already filled with shame for the sin I had not committed. But it wasn't that. Fletcher wanted to talk about the future.

A lot of what I thought he was going to say I had picked up from the other White Ones. Being initiated was only the beginning. Being a White One was like a journey, and initiation was the starting point. Soon I would be ready for advanced ASD – days where you did without two or more senses. There was this story that Fletcher himself had done without all five. He had spent a day alone in his room, blindfolded, his ears stuffed with rags, his body wrapped in a white shroud, cotton wool up his nose. None of us would have had the courage to go that far. But Fletcher was special. You could tell that, just by being with him. His presence exuded Light.

When Fletcher said we were going to talk about the future I

thought he meant advanced ASD, my Commentaries, my place at uni – I wasn't sure if I should still go or not and how I was to earn my keep at the farm. Also whether it was time for me to become an Attractor. Attractors are recruiters – White Ones who mix in the other world and find potential White Ones, as Kate and Nick did me. It was an honour to become an Attractor – it meant you were fully trusted. You had reached a level of purity where you were unsullied, incorruptible. I badly wanted to be an Attractor. I thought maybe that way I could still go to uni. There were White cells across the country and I hoped there was one near Bristol. I knew that it was up to Fletcher to think through what to do about me. Part of being a White One was showing utter faith in your mentor, and placing your life in his hands. If you could do this, it showed you were capable of surrendering entirely to the Light, when your time came.

But it wasn't my future Fletcher wanted to talk about, it was his.

"I got a fax from Rendall this morning, Joe. There's going to be a meeting of cell leaders in Orkney. In Carbister."

That was where Rendall lived. Carbister was his headquarters.

"Unusually for Rendall, he doesn't say why or when. Just that it will be imminent."

"What do you think it could be about?" I asked.

"We have business meetings from time to time. Or Advanced Purification..." His voice trailed away. "I have heard it said that Rendall's received a new language, the one they speak in the world of Light."

"That must be it," I agreed.

"Or if Rendall knows of a Perfect."

Fletcher sat on his bed, his chin in his hands, thinking. I was cross-legged on the floor. I knew I was privileged to be invited to share Fletcher's thoughts in this way and guessed I wouldn't have been if Nick had been around. But Nick had been confined to his room. His illness had recurred. The White Ones looked after him well – he was never alone – and people kept up prayer vigils at his bedside. I'd asked Fletch if I could take part in a vigil, and he said, in time, when I was ready. I guessed Nick's illness was tough for Fletch, as he used to be his second in command.

Anyway, so there I was, in white Levis, my white sweatshirt, rather grubby white trainers, feeling as I always do with Fletcher, privileged to be there.

"I wonder if all the cell leaders are going. If there was news of a Perfect, it would be..."

He didn't finish his sentence. Then he was silent for a bit. There was nothing I could usefully add. I smiled inwardly when I thought that Fletcher's relationship with Rendall was probably like mine with him. I guessed he was a bit scared of him, and hung on his every word. Then I wondered what Rendall was like, as a person. I would have given anything to meet him and lived in hope that one day it might happen. Rendall never left Orkney but he wasn't exactly a recluse. Chosen people visited him. I'd heard his voice once – Fletcher had a tape of him reading from the Book. He sounded quite old-fashioned, rather posh, and yet there was something about the timbre of his voice that made me tremble. Then I had this mad thought that maybe Fletcher wanted me to go with him to Orkney.

"There have been rumours about a Perfect," Fletcher continued. "I pray to the Light that He should come in my lifetime. Perhaps Rendall wants to prepare me. There's work on myself that I need to do. I have to be ready when the call comes."

His voice trailed away. I felt privileged to hear Fletcher thinking aloud like this. It made me realise how little I knew about him. Despite the fact that he was my mentor and – I had to admit it – my hero, we had never spoken about anything except me. I had taken that for granted. That was the way it was. That was the way Fletcher was. Entirely self-abnegating. His whole life was lived for a higher purpose. It was almost as if he had renounced his right to a personal life. I wondered if the responsibility of running the farm weighed heavily on him. It was a novelty for me to think of him in this way.

"How long have you been a White One, Fletch?" The words escaped before I had a chance to call them back.

"Eight years now."

I made some quick calculations. I reckoned Fletcher must be thirty, maybe older. It was hard to tell. He had a toned, wiry body, cropped fair hair, a firm jaw, a tight expression on his lips most of the time and eyes that blazed. I wondered if there had been a woman in his life, and if he found it easy living the life he did. My curiosity prompted me to question him further.

"Have you always lived on the farm?"

"No."

"But you have a local accent."

"I was brought up in Stoke," he replied absently. "Not exactly local."

"Are your family still there?"

"I wouldn't know. I have no contact with them. They want no contact with me. It's far better that way. The modern concept of the nuclear family being the best social unit is highly questionable. The family feeds on itself. It devours itself, and that's when it's working well. A dysfunctional nuclear family is hell on earth. Emotional antimatter."

I stored all that away. I knew I had a habit of quoting Fletcher or even occasionally borrowing his speech patterns. Bea caught me doing it once or twice and it made her laugh. Fletcher had a way of throwing emphasis on to key words, and lifting his hand as if he was on the verge of a great thought, then slowly lowering it again. He wore a white gold ring on his hand, symbol of his marriage to the Light.

"What was your family like? Were you happy at home?"

It was as if he hadn't heard me. He carried on talking as if my past few questions had no existence in time or space.

"I called you here to prepare you for the fact that I might have to go away at any time. Normally Nick would deputise, but he might not be well enough. I'd like you and Kate to look after things. I know there are other men more senior than you but probably not as pure."

Immediately I forgot about Fletcher clamming up. All that resounded in my head was his praise. My purity was greater than almost anyone else's! I only just managed to hide my deep pleasure at Fletcher's opinion of me. I was doing well, then. I was achieving purity. All that ASD had paid off and it was true. I had not lied, not once, never shirked a truth no matter how unpleasant, and I was even calm about not seeing my parents. I had achieved the emotional stasis that the Book describes as one staging post on the way to purity. White Ones feel emotions like the fabrics you wear on your body. They're on the surface only. Inside you have a still centre, a perfectly balanced soul unattached to anything, an effulgent globe, Rendall says, a source and a receiver of Light. That was me. I had that.

It was not arrogant of me to think that way. Modesty was not seen as a virtue at Lower Fold. We thought of it as hiding your Light. You owned your good points, admitted them to yourself and others. In the other world, most people either had one sort of low self-esteem which resulted in shyness and low achievement, or the other form of low self-esteem which compensated by coming across as bad attitude. Like the rap artists I used to listen to. But now their lyrics horrified me. Fletcher thought I was pure. And so I was. I had the knack of purity.

"I'll let you know," Fletcher said, "if I hear anything else from Rendall."

He got up and I knew our interview was over. I decided that in two days' time I'd have a total fast and wear the blindfold. I would get Will to bring me some Braille sections of the Book so I could study while I ASD'd. I would memorise verses with my fingers. I would prove that Fletcher was right to trust me.

I felt superhuman. I knew I could do anything.

9.

From Rendall's Parables: The Tale of the Stallion

A snow-white stallion lived in Arabia. He was fleet of foot and exquisite to behold. The desert was glad to bear his weight and the sun to warm his muscles. One day he galloped to a Bedouin encampment, where he was caressed by maidens who fed him delicacies. His senses dulled with physical cravings satisfied, he did not notice when a splinter entered his hoof. The splinter was poisoned and so it was that a fatal infection entered the stallion's bloodstream. He could no longer stand, his eyes darkened with pain and he collapsed to the ground. The pain of dissolution was followed by the agony of oblivion.

⸺◈⸺

I agreed to have a meeting with my mother a few days before Bea's initiation. I didn't really want to see her; the weekly phone calls were hard enough. I could feel her pulling at me. Her voice and the things she said stank of the old Joe, and I didn't want to be reminded of him. But Fletcher felt it was wise for me not to break all ties. Most White Ones kept in intermittent touch with their families.

So there I was, walking towards Rochdale Town Hall that Thursday afternoon. Mum was already there and I could feel her eyes greedily devouring me as I approached her. She kissed me; I kissed her back.

"Joe," she said. "You've changed."

"Of course," I said.

Her eyes scanned me again. She made me feel uncomfortable.

"Is it that you've lost weight? Your hair's certainly much longer. I think it suits you. Look, we can't just stand here. Shall we go somewhere and have a cup of tea?"

I nodded, and followed her over the road into a backstreet. She found one of those tea shops where little old ladies bustle about with trays of tea-things and saucers of sticky jam. Since I was having a taste-deprived day I only wanted water. Mum also avoided eating, and just ordered a pot of tea that came in a fussy little china pot with sprays of flowers all over it. She poured the tea and I noticed her hands were trembling.

"How are you?" she asked.

"Very well," I said. "And you?"

She said nothing, but gave me a stricken look. She seemed paler than I'd remembered her, and her face more lined. I could see she was unhappy.

"Mum," I said, "there really is no need to worry about me. I've never felt better. I'm studying, working, I'm doing what I want. I know it's hard for you, me leaving home, but all parents have to go through it."

"I know," she said, fiddling with her teaspoon, "but Dad and I are worried about the people you're staying with. We've been reading up about cults and we think – look! Why don't you come home this weekend? Just for a break. We can really talk about this, about your friends, what they do there, and Dad and I won't force the issue. I promise. I'll gag your dad if needs be."

Mum attempted a smile.

"No," I said. "I'm happy where I am. I know it's hard for you. I'm safe – listen. As a White One I've pledged never to do drugs, never to smoke, to drink – there's nothing for you to worry about!"

"A White One? What on earth is that?"

I deliberated for a few moments, and then decided to explain our philosophy to Mum. Maybe once she'd heard it, she'd understand why I had been so drawn to them. I told her about Rendall, about his Book, about the Light, about Purity, about our theories of the universe, and how they were no more extreme than any of the major world religions. I talked for ages, ignoring the pangs of hunger that assailed me every time I caught a whiff of scones and jam, or toasted teacakes. Listening to myself, I was impressed with how well I was explaining it all. I had learned a lot.

"So what do you do all day?" Mum asked.

I told her about our daily routine, although I didn't mention ASD. There was no point as I knew it would worry her. I mentioned I'd learned to cook and that I studied. I told her about Bea too.

"She sounds nice," Mum said.

I appreciated that and smiled. Mum smiled too. For one moment it seemed like the old times.

"Here," Mum said, scrabbling about in her handbag. "I've got something for you. A letter from Gemma."

She handed it to me. It wasn't in an envelope, just a folded piece of paper. I read it.

Dear Joe,

Look, I'm sorry for going ballistic at you. I was just upset that you were cutting me out. It's crap here without you. I want you to come home. It's a bit because I miss you and a bit because I'm scared for you. Your mates on the farm sound like a bunch of losers. Well, someone's got to say that. I don't care if you're angry. I hated it when you left home and you went all calm and funny. Mum is on anti-depressants and Dad doesn't sleep. So come home, you bastard.

Gem

"I don't know what she put in there," Mum said. "I had to promise her I wouldn't read it."

I was silent for a bit. Gemma was trying to make me feel guilty, but it was understandable; she was only a kid and had a very limited vision.

"Tell her I won't come home," I said to Mum.

For some reason that got to Mum. She suddenly started ranting.

"For goodness' sake, Joe, can't you see what's happened to you? You've been brainwashed. I don't know how, I don't understand it for one minute, and I've tried to be nice to you, tried to be reasonable, but if that won't work, then maybe some straight talking will. You've changed. You don't seem like my son any more. I know we can't come and forcibly take you away from the farm, but we've talked of it. We've been to see the local vicar, even though your dad and I haven't set foot inside a church for years. He'll talk to you, and he knows organisations that help people who've got involved in cults. Why don't you meet him? Joe – grow up and face the truth."

"The Truth," I said to her, "is the Light, and the Light is the Truth."

"Joe! Didn't you hear anything I said?"

"Mum, I did, but listen to me. I am happy. I'm doing what I want to do. If you can't accept that then I won't see you again."

"Any more tea?" asked the dumpy waitress.

"No," said my mother.

We were quiet for a bit. When I looked at her again, she was crying.

"Don't cry," I said. "I will carry on seeing you, but you must stay calm."

She said nothing.

"Next month maybe?" I suggested.

"You must ring next week," she said.

I nodded. She asked for the bill and as she paid, I noticed the waitress give us an odd look.

We left the tea shop.

"I love you, Joe," she said. "Remember that. We all do. And when you've finished with these White Ones, just come home."

"I hear what you're saying."

"Joe, I love you."

"Love you too," I mumbled.

She kissed me again, I kissed her back and turned and walked to the bus station.

Even though I coped very well that afternoon, it disturbed me. I was preoccupied for the rest of the day and the other guys noticed. Fletcher suggested I talk it through with them, as a number of them had similar difficulties with their families.

So Will, Kate and Auriel sat with me in the kitchen, and I debriefed.

"Yeah, my parents went nuts," Will said. "They even tried locking me in my room when I told them I was going. And they came to my cell – the one in Forres – and threatened to get the police."

"What happened eventually?" I asked him.

"They gave up. I didn't hear from them for ages and then they moved to Winchester. Sometimes I get a letter but I don't think about them much now."

"My parents visit me here – they know it's the best place for me," Auriel said. "But when I see them, it makes me glad I live here and not with them."

She got up then and went to the sink to wash her hands. I'd noticed Auriel was always washing her hands. Then afterwards she would dry them very carefully, then say something like, *this towel is dirty!* Then she'd start again. She tended to be over-enthusiastic about her purity, but Fletcher said that was hardly an error, and we were to let her travel her path as she saw fit.

Kate said, "It is difficult for your parents. There's a loss for them, and they're made to feel their own shortcomings. This often expresses itself in anger or grief. I went through all that too. But like you, Joe, I have an arrangement with my mother and I keep in contact. Everything is under control. These are early days yet, and you're doing well. Remember, just as the process of birth is painful to a mother, so is your process of rebirth."

Her words cheered me, and the scene with my mother began to fade. Kate had analysed it and put it to rest. It also helped me to think all my brothers and sisters had gone through what I had.

Fletcher entered then and came up to me. In a gesture of affection he ruffled my hair. I felt completely at peace again.

"Joe," he said, "how would you like to go and visit Nick?"

I jumped up, eager. I hadn't see Nick for some time – I knew he'd had a relapse. The duty of nursing him was not one of my responsibilities. But I had a bond with Nick, and liked him. I was only too ready to visit.

Together Fletch and I made our way upstairs. We went to a small room at the end of the landing. Fletcher knocked, then entered.

Nick was sitting up in bed. I had to admit I was a bit taken aback. He looked shrunken and the bones of his face stood out. I had to fight an impulse to run. I guess that was the antimatter emanating from whatever was causing Nick's illness. I mastered the impulse and went to sit down on a chair by his bed. I noticed Nick's hands were trembling like an old man's.

"I'm feeling better," Nick said to me. Without his glasses on his eyes looked small, timorous.

"Good," I said.

"I asked if I could see you," he said to me. "I wanted to know how you were getting on."

Fletcher was silent so I knew it was OK for me to talk. I updated Nick on my life at the farm, hoping the distraction would cheer him up. He smiled when I mentioned my clumsy attempts at bricklaying and the vegetable stew I made that no one would eat. I also told him about my mum, and he said, "It's hard."

That struck me as profoundly true, coming from Nick, looking so ill.

While I was talking, I scanned the room. It was bare for a sick room. There was a jug of water by Nick's bedside, and someone had put a spray of flowers in a vase. I wondered again exactly what was wrong with him but I thought it would be rude to ask. So I tried an oblique approach.

"How are you feeling?" I asked.

"Better today," he said. "There's been a very exciting development." I saw Fletch nodding out of the corner of my eye.

"What? Is your medicine working?"

Fletch answered that. "Carbister is taking an active interest in Nick's case and they're taking over his treatment profile."

Nick looked as if he wanted to talk, so Fletch let him.

"Yes – it's essential to starve whatever is still in my system, which is, of course, essentially antimatter. I have been ASD'ing but alone it's not enough. I need something more rigorous. I want to try this, Joe, because otherwise it'll have to be conventional medicine. Fletcher has promised me that."

"One last attempt," Fletcher said.

"What are you going to do?"

"I'm waiting for Carbister to send through the details," Fletch answered me. "But meanwhile, Nick has something to ask you."

I felt so sorry for him I would have said yes to anything.

"Joe – I've not been much use to the White Ones lately. My

Attracting days are over. I've spoken to Fletcher and he feels – we feel – you should step into my shoes. We want you to be an Attractor."

My heart leapt with joy. It was the one thing I'd been secretly hoping for. I knew how to be an Attractor. You see, it wasn't like other evangelical religions, where you stand around on street corners handing out leaflets. You just *mingled*. Then at a particular moment someone would come to you. Or you would see someone and know he was a potential White One, just like Nick and Kate found me.

Fletcher said, "The world is a maze and people get lost. Like a shepherd looking for his flock, you must find the missing souls."

I knew how to do this. I was sure I had an instinct for it – I was a good judge of character. It was important I kept my purity – I mustn't be sullied by the world. And I wasn't to preach – that wasn't the point. And just like Perfects, immortals who live among us but retain their Perfection, I would stay as a White One in the outside world.

"We thought," Nick said, "you could start by going with Will to the shop. There you'll come into contact with different people. It will be a starting point."

"Yes," I said. "I'd really like that."

Nick smiled at me, then turned to Fletcher and said he was tired. It was our cue to go. I waved goodbye at the door and left, my heart singing with happiness.

I continued on that high for days. I was a trusted and honoured White One, and had just been given one of the highest accolades. The Light shone in me and through me.

Everyone said so. And then it was the day of Bea's initiation.

I remember just before the ceremony looking at myself in the long, speckled mirror in the men's washroom. I only caught my reflection in it by chance. It surprised me because for a split second I didn't recognise myself. But it was me all right. Same old Joe, except my hair was considerably longer and I'd dropped about a stone. I looked older too. I tried to decide if I preferred myself thinner and older and I decided that I did. It kind of made me look more interesting. More intelligent. It expressed what I was becoming. It was as if my body was taking its cue from my spirit. I stared myself out, looking for the intensity in my eyes that the other White Ones said I had. Then I rotated my shoulder blades, flexed some muscles. The physical work I had been doing was making me stronger; it was much more effective than anything I ever did at the gym. And more meaningful too.

Then I told myself my body was only a vehicle and that I had better move away from the mirror and instead think about the significance of the occasion. And I did. I believed Bea was fully ready to commit, and knew it would bring us closer still. We were good for each other. I didn't need anybody to tell me that and, besides, no one, not even Fletcher, had commented on our spending so much time together.

That hour or so, before Bea's initiation, was my happiest, purest hour.

So it's hard to even begin to account for what went wrong. But I must try. White Ones don't lie, even to themselves.

We all congregated in the common area which led into the Gathering Place where Bea's immersion was to happen. It was good

– it made me remember my own act of commitment not many weeks ago. We all greeted and hugged and there was a happy, yet awe-filled atmosphere. Then the girls left us and went to join Bea in the Gathering Place.

The guys sat cross-legged on the floor and hummed, pressing our fingertips together so that our individual energy was contained and circulated in one continuous stream. As we hummed we thought about the significance of the occasion and how each initiation increased the Light in the world. We were to focus on the Light. I did, but I had to admit I was thinking of Bea too. She was special to me, and there was no one I wanted to be initiated as much as her. So as I meditated I visualised not only the Light, but the shell she had bought me, the shell which even now was hanging around my neck, in fragile, pristine whiteness.

Then it happened. I thought – bizarrely – of that old painting. You know the one – what's it called? *The Birth of Venus*. Some Italian guy painted it. There's Venus, the Goddess of Love, standing on a shell on the sea, naked – like Bea would be emerging from the water now – with one arm covering her breasts, and her hair sweeping free, and curling round her stomach to conceal the place my eyes were always drawn to. And so I thought of Bea next door, coming out of the water, her hair dripping over her full breasts, which I had never seen. I imagined the curve of her stomach and thighs and thought about embracing her now, naked, her arms and legs wet, pressed against mine – what did she look like naked? I didn't know. I wanted to know. My meditation was shattered and I became aware that I was getting a hard-on.

Shit. This wasn't supposed to happen. I was the pure one, the strong one. I didn't know what to do. I had to stop thinking of Bea, that was for sure. I tried to refocus on the Light, but there was nothing. Just Darkness. Just the chaotic whirl of antimatter. I tried to think of my mother, saw her face and gradually I regained control of my body. But my heart was racing and there was a flush on my face. I hoped the other guys wouldn't notice; luckily they were all deep in contemplation.

I tried breathing deeply in order to calm myself. What bothered me was that the deviation from purity had come from me. I had let myself down. This was bad. When the foe was outside yourself – your family, food that tasted good, whatever – it was easy to withstand it. But I had produced my own antimatter.

I wanted to pretend it hadn't happened. I wondered what the other blokes did about this stuff. Before, I had thought that all the ASD affected you so that you didn't react physically in the way you did in the other world, where all round you there were pictures of semi-naked bimbos flouncing their way through pop videos, and women lying prone on posters in the streets and girls who used their sexuality to get you – I thought it was their fault. Like, what's a guy to do? But maybe there was something about *me*. The thoughts came from *me*. Maybe I wasn't so pure after all.

Then the other worrying thing was, ought I to tell Fletcher? Answer – I had to. He was my mentor. Then it struck me I would be compromising Bea and risking her reputation, which I wasn't prepared to do. Besides, I didn't tell him everything. Like, maybe, I was digging and accidentally sliced a worm in two. Well, I wouldn't tell him that. Or that my back ached so I rested for a couple of minutes. He would be bored stiff if I told him everything. So maybe I could just omit this. For all I knew, Fletcher had hard-ons. It was just something you weren't supposed to talk about. Maybe being a successful White One was about what you chose to do when your body let you down. As in, nothing. No sex. It was one of our vows.

There was movement from next door and the guys were invited in. I lingered at the back. I still didn't feel ready to face Bea. I felt my sinful thoughts still clinging to me. Eventually I entered the room and saw Bea wrapped in a big white towel. I joined in the cheering and clapping. We all pushed forward to greet her in the usual way, and when I did I found I couldn't look at her properly.

"Joe?" she questioned.

She had noticed. Then I made my eyes meet hers and there was such pain for me as I saw her. She was so beautiful and I wanted her so badly. Her wet hair framed her face and she looked like the Virgin Mary now. I felt worse and filthier than ever. And more determined to have her. And more determined than ever to fight that impulse and not to have her. Ever.

When the others gave her their gifts, I shoved mine forward. It was a music manuscript book which I had painted carefully with white nail varnish. With it was a white fountain pen. I gave it to her and then went. I saw Fletcher and explained to him that I felt I needed to have some solitude. Meditation, prayer and reflection were an important part of our way of life, and it was quite usual to want to have time out.

I made my way to the Reading Room at the front of the house. Someone had turned off the light, as we were all at Bea's initiation. I switched it on again, closed the door behind me and sat at an upright chair by the wooden table. There were several copies of the Book on the table, as well as some service sheets. I began to stroke the leather cover of the Book, felt its rough skin and the smoothness of the gold-leaf-embossed letters spelling Rendall's name. My fingertips had never seemed more sensitive.

May it be my lot to achieve Perfection.

I opened the Book at random. I hoped my eyes would light on a passage that would help me in my confusion. But the first page I turned to just gave instructions on how to purify food that had come from the wrong source, such as a supermarket or fast food outlet. It held no relevance for me. Maybe I was floundering in such a deep Darkness that even the Book could not reach me. But reading about food made me realise I was very hungry. I had fasted for the last twenty-four hours and was weak and light-headed. There was food in the kitchen but to go there would be to break my enforced solitude.

Then I decided that prolonging my fast was just what I needed. The flesh had to be subdued. Only then would I regain my sanity and be able to face the others and Bea. And to help that, I could calm myself with some ASD. I glanced quickly round the room and as I hoped, there were some blindfolds in a heap on one of the shelves. I helped myself to one and, fumbling, put it on. It took some doing but finally it was in place. I felt my way back to the chair and sat down. The blindfold cut into my cheekbones and it felt good. I stared with my inner eye into the darkness and discovered the darkness was not dark but multicoloured. Perhaps the Light was returning to me. I regulated my breathing and tried to visualise the rise and fall of my diaphragm.

I don't know how much time had passed when I started. Someone had entered the reading room. But it was OK. They wouldn't be surprised to see me here. *Now* I was doing nothing wrong. I expected the person to respect my right to privacy and leave quickly. I heard the click of the door closing but then there were footsteps and I felt a displacement in the air. The person was with me, in the room. My heart raced. It was instinctive to want to remove the blindfold but I knew I mustn't. So I remained still.

"Joe?" Bea said. "Why aren't you at my feast?"

She sounded puzzled and hurt. I didn't know what to say. With her Bea brought the aroma of food, freshly baked bread, the crispness of salad. My stomach contracted with hunger.

"Joe? Say something. This isn't like you."

I felt myself heat with embarrassment. I couldn't begin to explain to her. But if I lied, then I would be breaking my vow to utter the truth at all times. If I told her the truth, I could never speak to her again. I felt my way carefully.

"I needed to be alone," I said.

"Why? Is it anything to do with me?"

Oh, God. This was getting worse. I didn't want her to think she had done anything, or that I'd gone off her. But to tell her the truth, I would have to say that it was to do with her. Again I side-stepped without exactly lying.

"It's to do mainly with me."

I heard her pull up a chair and she sat beside me. Then she stroked my arm. Because I was blind her action was startling. The sweep of her fingers on the skin of my arm felt dangerous and ran through my body like the tremor of an earthquake.

"Joe, tell me. You can. I'm a White One now, remember. Share it."

Now she squeezed my hand. I could still smell food.

"Look, I have some bread," she announced. "Eat this. You'll feel better."

She brought her hand to my lips, parted them, and inserted a morsel of bread. I couldn't help it. I ate it. She put the rest in my hand and bit by bit I finished it all.

"That's better," she said. "Now tell me what's wrong."

I was glad I was wearing the blindfold. It's easier to say difficult things to people when you can't see them.

"It was just... while you were being initiated. I began to think about our relationship. Whether – you know – if it was getting out of hand. If maybe I was in danger of breaking a vow. Because of my feelings for you."

That was as near the truth as I could manage. Bea didn't speak for a while. I could hear her soft breathing.

"So you thought you'd be better apart from me for a while?"

"Yeah. That's right. So I came here," I said.

She didn't respond to that either. I couldn't know what she was thinking as I couldn't see her. I didn't even know what I wanted her to think.

"Joe," she said, after a while. "We haven't done anything wrong."

Her voice sounded fragile, as if she was fighting back disappointment.

"I know. But I'm scared we might, if we spend too much time together."

There was another gap in our conversation. It was wrong of me, but I was pleased that she was upset. If she didn't care about me, she wouldn't have minded that I wanted to back-pedal our relationship. Except I didn't want to back-pedal our relationship – I wanted more from Bea. I wasn't being entirely honest. And not to be honest was to break a vow too. My head throbbed in confusion.

"But people see us spend a lot of time together," Bea said plaintively. "No one objects. Kate would have spoken to me if we were in danger. Has Fletcher said anything to you?"

"No."

"Well, there we are. We can carry on as we were before."

"No," I said, surprising myself by my sudden determination. "We can't. My feelings for you are getting stronger. I want us to have a proper relationship."

My hand found her hand and my fingers prised her fingers apart. We interlocked.

"I know what you mean," she whispered. "I've been feeling that way too. But I can't see what's wrong in us being boyfriend and girlfriend. We're not breaking the vow of physical purity. I need you, Joe. It's hard, being a White One. When it's the two of us, it isn't hard."

I was taken aback by what she said because I felt exactly the same way. And if that was true, if our relationship actually helped us keep pure, then it *had* to be a good thing.

I could even imagine myself explaining that to Fletcher.

"And since both of us are initiated now," she continued, "it brings us into a closer relationship anyway. You need both male and female. It says so in the Book."

"And it says that love and purity are connected," I added.

We were still holding hands so I increased the pressure. Then she moved closer to me. The next thing I knew, she pressed her lips to my forehead above my blindfold and kissed me, her soft lips pressing themselves eagerly on the skin and bone of my forehead. My other hand found its way behind her head just to keep her close to me for a moment or two. Then I lifted my face and our lips met.

It was the best kiss I'd ever had in my life. All of me was in that kiss. I revelled in the sensation of our lips meeting, the way they opened, the way our tongues caressed each other as if they were alive. I could taste Bea, I was feeling my way inside her – in my darkness, all my senses were on fire. But it wasn't just that it *felt* so good – it was being so close to her that counted, being inside her like that, seeing nothing, feeling nothing, nothing but Bea.

I don't know how long we kissed for. Too long, and not long enough. I don't know which was stronger, my joy or my guilt. When eventually I pulled away, it was more because of the fear of discovery than any desire for us to stop.

"That wasn't wrong," Bea said, reading my mind again.

I wished she was right and feared she was not. With my fingers I caressed her face.

"Joe – I bet we're not the only secret couple here. Have you seen the way Will looks at Auriel?"

That struck me as slightly blasphemous. But Bea was probably right. Now she began to untie my blindfold.

"Please don't worry," she said. "Being a White One is as

important to me as it is to you. We'll never do anything wrong. Come and join the others now."

I blinked as my eyes accustomed themselves to the light. I looked at Bea. She was beautiful, her hair still damp, with some dry tendrils curling at the sides. Her cheeks were flushed and she looked at me with such tenderness that I wanted to kiss her again. Only I didn't dare.

"It'll be fine," she said.

I only wished I could believe her.

She took me by the hand and led me out of the room.

10

From Selected Commentaries on Rendall:
"They were male and female together."

They were male and female together. These words, taken from Rendall's Vision of the Light, have been interpreted in various ways by different commentators. Laban North says they confirm that the greeting angels were both male and female, denoting that both male and female can follow the path of Light and achieve Perfection. Paul Telford suggests that the angels were hermaphrodite, therefore suggesting homosexual White Ones are acceptable. Laban North has disagreed and says that "male and female together" implies that male and female White Ones may marry to produce pure White offspring.

———— ((()) ————

Did Fletcher guess?

I didn't know. I didn't want to tell him about what had happened with Bea, unless it became relevant. I didn't feel I had to; it was clear that our vow of purity related to the act of sex itself. Our kiss was not exactly wrong, not exactly right. And the Book was ambiguous. I took the coward's way out, which was to wait and see.

Meanwhile, it was time for me to re-enter the world as an Attractor. I was to work with Will in the shop in Hebden Bridge.

Maybe someone would come in and feel my magnetism. It would also give me an opportunity to readjust myself to the Outside. I was keen to get started. I didn't think this desire to get away from the farm was a bad thing. It was more like my will was in tune with Fletcher's will for me. Maybe my instincts were beginning to attune themselves to my spiritual welfare. In that case, it was possible my feelings for Bea were healthy too. Yet there was always the possibility that since Bea also lived on the farm, Fletcher thought I was best away from it. And thus my thoughts went round in circles; they spun themselves round me like the mesh of a spider's web with a gossamer touch and sticky insistence.

I'd seen the shop once or twice but I'd never been inside. It was just like any other charity shop, the window brightly lit and full of a jumble of goods, old clothes, piles of books, small items of furniture. The inside was surprisingly small, or maybe it was just the effect of the clutter. There were rails of clothes, stools, chairs, a wall of shelves with stuff on it, books, a pile of records, and a counter at the rear. Behind that was a door which I later discovered led to a small storeroom, a sink and toilet. It was all fairly basic but I didn't mind. Life on the farm had got me used to roughing it.

"Do you take much money?" I asked Will.

"You'd be surprised," he replied. "You get plenty of bargain hunters coming to Hebden Bridge. But making money isn't the point. Too much money corrupts, anyway. It's a moral poison."

"The glister of gold is a thief in the night," I repeated.

That was a line from one of Rendall's poems. We often did this, quoted at each other. It might sound feeble, but it's only what I used to do with my old mates if we were discussing a match or something. You'd describe something you saw that everybody else knew about anyway. You just said that stuff to bond. As Will and I did then.

"Money deafens the ears to the needs of the poor," Will added.

"It's true," I said. "When you possess, you fear to lose."

But the odd thing was, standing in the shop, which seemed so normal and everyday, these words sounded hollow. We seemed to be parroting them. But never mind.

Will showed me how to work the cash register and found a couple of chairs for us nearby.

"So where do you get this stuff from?" I asked him.

"People bring it in. Or there are house clearances," he said. "The other guys fill the Transit occasionally. Fletcher comes down in the evenings sometimes and goes through the consignments, to see if there's anything valuable. He keeps what he finds separate."

"What do you say to people when they ask what charity we are?"

"Didn't you see the sign outside? We're The Sisters of Light."

"Sisters?" I queried.

"Yeah, well, the story goes it was the girls who had the idea for fundraising like this. And then Fletcher thought it would be better for the men to help out too. But there was no point in changing the name."

"It sounds like we're a holy convent or something," I joked.

Will laughed. His laughter seemed to tangle self-consciously with all the junk. I wondered, not for the first time, what sort of customers we might have. I couldn't see that this would be a hotspot for potential recruits. I always got the impression that it was old folk that came into charity shops, and White Ones were generally – actually, they were all – young. But Fletcher knew best. And anyway, I was here as a sort of halfway house. Later, Fletcher said, I would be sent further afield, into Manchester maybe. Nothing much would happen today.

But when the bell rang and someone pushed the door open, my pulse raced.

Two people. Blokes, both big. One in a puffa jacket and denims hung low, under a jutting stomach. The other in a football shirt, long hair like rats' tails and a tatty briefcase. They couldn't possibly be recruits. Instead I felt myself repelled by them. They looked the sort of geezers who might mean trouble. I glanced at Will. He didn't seem worried – in fact he evidently knew them.

"Have you got anything for us?" the long-haired one asked.

"Yep," Will said. "It's in the back."

He left me alone in the shop for a moment while he went into the back room. He emerged just a moment later with a cardboard box full of old clothes. While he was handing it over to the puffa jacket, the bottom gave way, and the clothes cascaded to the floor. The bottom must have been damp, or the clothes too heavy for the box. Will got a black bin liner from under the counter and I helped him fill it with the clothes. There weren't just clothes. There were several Jiffy bags sealed with thick masking tape. The long-haired bloke also helped us with the bag. The puffa jacket took it when we'd finished.

"Cheers," he said, and they left.

"Who were they?" I asked Will.

"Market traders. They have a stall out in Dewsbury. I pass them the stuff Fletcher tells me to – things he wants to sell on, or get rid of, whatever. He sees to the business side of it. I don't understand the accounts."

"What was in the Jiffy bags?"

"Those? I guess small valuables, watches, jewellery, stuff like that. I dunno, really. Fletch passes them to me. But it doesn't do to ask too many questions."

I laughed. "I can tell you were in the army," I said. "It's the way you accept authority."

Will laughed now. "Heck, you might be right. But if it wasn't for the army, I wouldn't have become a White One."

I knew what was coming next. Will was going to tell me the story of how he became a White One again. We all did this from time to time. It stands to reason. Becoming a White One was the most important thing that had ever happened to us. We all felt compelled to repeat our stories and had learned to love each other's stories too.

"My dad was in the air force. That meant we moved around a lot and lived on army bases. We stayed for a time at Findhorn – in northeast Scotland. It was a bit bleak. I wanted to be in the forces like my dad, have a uniform, be in a parade, or fly one of those bombers. He used to take me round the base. School was a bit tough because we moved so much. I had to fight my way to being accepted – well, nothing unusual about that. I ended up not really trusting anyone, like, I was permanently on my guard. Defensive. My parents were all right but they didn't talk much. They had their own separate lives. That's what I thought you did. You each had your own life. Mum lived in the kitchen mostly or sewed in the back room – she didn't reckon much to the other women on the base. When Dad wasn't on duty he watched TV in the lounge. I had my own room."

"Sounds lonely," I prompted.

"Yeah. Next to the base there was this commune of weirdos, people who talked to trees and grew enormous vegetables. They'd cycle around and lived in caravans. Dad used to take the rise out of them. I watched them, like kids do. I went there, once, and this woman said she could see my aura and it was all white. At the time I thought she was batty."

I was silent.

"My mum insisted I worked hard at school because she had ideas for me. She wanted me to get a civvy job. But I was no good at school, I couldn't concentrate, I just messed around. It all seemed pointless. I thought I could just join the army when I was sixteen and they'd sort me out. And I could travel, see the world, learn a trade. So I ignored her and I did, I joined the army. It was tough and yeah – you were right – I was always obeying orders. But then, when we were off-duty, we'd go out, get rat-arsed."

I started at the word. It was a little strong for a White One. But I guessed away from the farm standards might be more lax. Will was unaware of my reaction. He continued.

"It was one of those nights. We were all out drinking and one by one my mates went home. One or two had work in the morning, another one was ill and someone else took him home. I forget the details, but they all deserted me. I was in this club and however much I drank, it was like I wasn't getting drunk. I was stone-cold sober.

"So when I saw Pete looking at me, I was edgy. It wasn't a gay club or anything, but you couldn't be sure. I reckoned if he came over and offered to buy me a drink I'd just flatten him. But he just started talking, and everything he said, I agreed with. About the club being a dive, the girls just on the pull, the fact that even booze didn't make the sadness go away. By rights, I should have walked. Like, a bloke doesn't come up to another bloke in a club like that. But there was a click, know what I mean?"

I did. It was what I had felt with Nick and Kate. We call it Galvanisation.

"We went for a coffee after that and, as it was too late for me to get home, he gave me a bed at the place in Forres. I met the other guys and thought they were weird but better than anyone else I'd ever met..."

I knew all the rest, from my own experience. But it felt good to have one's own convictions confirmed by somebody else's experience. Will had started his life as a White One in Scotland, but you would never have guessed because he didn't have a Scottish accent. Even then, he'd never met Rendall or been to Orkney. The place in Forres was closed down as they couldn't make it viable. Will was sent to us, just a little time before I joined. He was probably my best mate on the farm.

We fell silent. I played around with the idea of opening up the subject of Bea with him. I was certain Will wouldn't give me a hard time about it, and talking to someone might help tease out the tangles I was getting in. When you talk things through they always seem more logical. So I rehearsed what I might say.

Something like, *Will, I need to talk about my relationship with*

Bea. It's not just friendship. I fancy her – not even that. I think I love her. I want to have a proper relationship with her, and I know about our vow of chastity and all that, but I don't see why two White Ones can't have a relationship – even a physical relationship – because what we feel is more than just sex. And if we did the stuff normal couples do, then maybe I wouldn't have these dreams I've been having – mad, crazy dreams, disgusting dreams, I'm doing stuff in them I wouldn't have ever imagined doing in my old life even, so I've been trying to stop the dreams by jerking myself off, which makes me feel even more guilty, because White Ones rise above that kind of stuff – don't they? Do you?

No. There was no way I could have said any of that to Will, or to anyone. I'd have to puzzle it out all by myself, or give up Bea. But every time I saw her I just melted – I would look at her and feel suddenly weak, because I wanted her so much. And I knew she felt the same because she told me. And it was so ironic that we should meet now, when we couldn't have each other. Or could we? Was there a way round it? I scoured Rendall's Book and all the literature and found some promising Commentaries. I would have written some myself except I reckoned Fletcher would be able to guess what was going on in my mind. My biggest fear was that Fletcher would separate me from Bea. Except, surely he could see that we were good for each other. We studied the Book together, cooked together, worked in the allotments.

Like, if he'd said, I know how you feel about Bea, and we've decided you two guys can get married, I'd have jumped at the chance. I know that sounds crazy, me being only nineteen, but being a White One had made me so much more mature. I knew about commitment in a way that few people did. I knew what it was like to make sacrifices. I'd had one bad relationship in the old world and now I had a good one, and I knew the difference. It made me sick to think about the things I did with Tash but – Christ! – I wanted to do them with Bea. And that was making me doubt my purity. And sanity.

I give thanks to the Light for true Vision. I give thanks to the Light for warming my flesh and giving me life. I yearn for the Light and crave the day we are united. May it be my lot to achieve Perfection.

Will saw me mouthing those words and made no comment. Later, he said, "There's some blackcurrant tea in the back. Do you fancy some?"

I nodded. Reality was reasserting itself. I walked over to the pile of vinyl records and sorted through them. They were mostly easy listening or old rock and roll groups that even my parents hadn't mentioned. I quite missed listening to the sounds I used to like. But that wasn't really a problem. Bea played and sang for me and the others. It didn't bother me that I missed some aspects of my old life. There would be no sacrifice involved if I didn't.

I sipped at the blackcurrant tea and found it too sweet. Will must have loaded it with sugar. I wondered whether that wasn't an infringement of our principles, and decided next time he made a brew to specify that I wanted mine plain. I glanced towards the door. Business was slow, or rather non-existent.

"Do you prefer it here to the farm?" I asked Will.

"I've got used to it," he said. "I prefer being outdoors but sometimes I lock up and go for a walk around. There's a canal round the back."

I was about to ask him if I would be allowed to do that, when there was a ping and the door opened again.

"Oh, no!" muttered Will.

I could see why he said that. The bloke who walked in was obviously a nutter. You could smell him before you saw him. He was in his fifties – maybe sixties – but he wore a filthy baseball cap turned back to front. He staggered a bit as if he was drunk. But what you noticed first of all was the placard he wore on his chest, saying *Doom Is Nigh*. I heard Will sigh exaggeratedly.

"Prepare yourselves," this bloke said. "It's the end of the world."

"Oh, yeah?" Will was obviously used to him. "So when would that be exactly?"

"Next Tuesday," said the bloke. "Quarter to three in the afternoon. Thirty-three devils and thirty-three angels will arrive on horseback at Stoodley Pike."

"Must arrange to get front-row tickets," Will said. "And by the way, last time you came in you said the world was ending last Wednesday."

The bloke ignored him. "Thirty-three devils and thirty-three angels. The sky will fall and the beast from the scarlet sea will rise again and kill the infidels. You wouldn't have some spare change for a cup of tea? And the mountains will move and Darkness will fall upon the face of the earth. And God will pass judgement upon the waters. And the firmament will explode in fireworks. Just 50p will do."

Will chuckled and went to open the till. The bloke shut up then and cleared his throat noisily. Will handed him a couple of quid. As the bloke moved over to take it there was a miasma of dank, sweaty clothes and urine.

"Thank you kindly. You will find yourself among the saved. You'll be bathing in milk and honey. And dancing with maidens. Do the hokey cokey and you'll turn around."

He shuffled out of the shop.

"You get all sorts here," Will said.

I wished we had some air freshener.

The day dragged on. We chatted a bit, and had a study lunch break where we read the Book and I helped Will with a Commentary he was working on. Only five more people came in, three old ladies and a young woman with a toddler in a pushchair. I felt no pull to any of them. Later we rearranged some of the second-hand paperbacks we had on to a shelf. I began to feel homesick for the farm. Fletcher called for us about four and I was glad to lock up.

It was a beautiful evening. The sun seemed reluctant to go down and back at Lower Fold I realised I was living in a kind of heaven. Gentle, fading sunlight bathed the buildings, and the people out in the fields and allotments were my brothers and sisters. Among them was Bea. When I went into the kitchen for some water she was there, stirring something on the cooker. Her face brightened when she saw me; she stopped what she was doing, and just smiled at me. I stood in front of her, dumb, not wanting to break the spell. Our eyes locked on to each other's, our mutual gaze bringing us closer than any physical union could do. Again I felt perfect contentment.

As the evening wore on, that feeling didn't go away. At the Service I felt surrounded by love and light. I said the words of the prayers with conviction. As I washed away my sins I felt the water charged with a healing warmth. I noticed Fletcher look on me approvingly. I knew then I was a chosen one, more fortunate than I deserved to be.

So I don't get why it was that the nutter from the shop wouldn't leave my mind; why I felt I loathed him, and dreaded seeing him again, why his stench invaded my nostrils, and I wished he could be taken from the face of the earth.

May it be my lot to achieve Perfection.

11.

Letter to all Cell Leaders: From Colin Rendall

Brothers,

A recent Vision has implanted in me the conviction that a Perfect walks among us now. As contact with this Perfect will help us achieve our own Perfection, it is imperative that we locate him. He is young and fair of skin and, I believe, it is likely he is already one of our number. He will not know of his own Perfection, for is it not logical, brothers, that the nature of Perfection is humility and the absence of all ego? It is therefore the duty of all cell leaders to bring here to Carbister that member of your cell who might be the missing Perfect. Seek him whose personal purity is above all others. Once the candidates are here, the Light will guide us to his true identity. You are requested to reacquaint yourselves with those rituals necessary upon encountering a Perfect. These can be found in the Reserved Manual.

May it be your lot to achieve Perfection.

———◈———

I'd been working in the shop for a few weeks when Fletcher said he wanted to see me. There was something serious in his demeanour and my first thought was that he wanted to talk about me and Bea.

I knew it was coming and I'd been planning a defence in my head – sort of like we haven't done anything, we won't do anything, we couldn't help it... He told me not to go in to Hebden Bridge with Will but wash the kitchen floor.

I hoped Bea would be there – she was often in the kitchen. I'd noticed that among the White Ones men and women still kept to their traditional roles. Once Bea had asked why that was and she was told nurturing and compassion were female qualities and tasks relating to those virtues devolved naturally on women. In contrast, activity and order were male attributes, so each White cell was led by a man, and men did the bulk of the physical and outreach work. It resulted in harmony, she was told.

In the old world, I used to say I was into women's rights because it stood to reason that you can't generalise and different people were good at different things. So why couldn't women be lorry drivers and men stay at home to look after babies, if that's what they wanted to do? But now I could see that society would become chaotic if individuals all chose to do precisely what they wanted, and that many individuals had unhealthy struggles with their true natures. And the modern idea of "finding yourself" was wrong too. What you needed was to find your role, the job you had to do. The job of a White One was to bring forward the Time of the Light.

But Bea wasn't in the kitchen and I was on my own. Breakfast had been cleared away, and I was a bit disappointed, because I was pretty hungry. Yesterday I had been fasting and nasal-blocking and the kickback today was that I was obsessing about food. It usually happens like that. Double ASD is so powerful that the antimatter tries to force a way in – so if you fast, you get hungry the next day too. So, to help us, there was never much food around on the farm unless it was a feast for a special occasion. Most of the time I was pretty hungry but also so exhausted at the end of the day that I didn't care. To be a White One you had to deny yourself stuff, but other people gave you so much more – all that love and sense of belonging. It was good for me – I was getting tough. I was learning to submit and endure.

I sat at the scrubbed kitchen table, just listening to the noises around me, the banging of the building works, some stray bird chirping repetitively outside and was about to start the cleaning when Auriel came in.

"Joe! Thank God it's you. Have you got a razor? An electric razor?"

"Just my shaving stuff but it's in the men's bathrooms. What do you want a razor for?"

"This," she said, and in a wild gesture lifted her mass of hair off her shoulders.

"For your hair?"

"It's filthy," she said. "Crawling with things, disgusting things. And it's impeding my purity. You see, Joe, it makes me vain, having all this hair. I think about it too much. I think how I should wear it. I think whether Will likes it. It's a net, trapping antimatter. Sometimes I love my hair and I think it's beautiful and this diverts me from the path of the Light. But the truth is that my hair is a spider's web and I'm the fly. It's vile. I've made the decision. I don't want it any more. Help me get rid of it. Give me a razor."

I was a bit alarmed. Auriel's hair was her best feature and it seemed a shame for her to lose it. Also the way she was talking sounded desperate to me, and White Ones took actions calmly, through conviction, not in the heat of the moment. I wasn't entirely sure what to do. I tried to stall her.

"Look, Auriel. It might be a good idea but why don't you think about it first. Speak to Kate. She'll know what's best."

"No, I can't. I want to be perfect. And clean and pure."

Before I could work out what she was doing she moved over to the cutlery drawer and found a pair of kitchen scissors.

"These will do," she said, lifting a clump of hair, and cutting it.

"Auriel, don't!" I shouted.

She carried on. "I need to do this, Joe. Then I can think clearly. It stops me thinking. All the time, my thoughts run in circles like my hair. And I must not be vain. Vanity is my shortcoming." As she spoke, her curls drifted to the floor. I wasn't sure what to do. Ought I to get someone? Yet as she cut her hair she seemed to calm down. That made me think the best thing to do would be just to stay with her, keep an eye on her. Bit by bit her voice became more normal and she spoke of other things. I thought it best to join in, bizarre as the situation was, with Auriel's hair spread all over the kitchen floor, and me watching her.

"What was that letter Fletcher received this morning?" she asked.

"What letter?"

"That's what I thought you might be able to tell me. The way he acted, I think it was something important. He went into the Meeting Room with it and prostrated himself in front of the Book."

"He's said nothing to me," I told her.

She carried on cutting. She'd almost finished. Her hair was now spiky, like a punk. Her eyes looked larger than ever. Yet now she seemed serene. Maybe cutting her hair was a good idea, how was I to know? She took the broom from the cupboard to sweep up the mess.

"Do you get on well with Will?" she asked.

"Yeah. Fine."

"You're lucky, working in the shop. Do you think Will likes girls with no hair? There – I'm being vain again – I'm a lost cause! You don't know how hard I find it not to be vain. It must be deeply-rooted antimatter. Bea is so lucky. She looks gorgeous but she never seems aware of it. She is gorgeous, isn't she?"

I didn't want to give anything away.

"As much as any White One."

"But you're special friends, aren't you?"

"It's true we discovered the Light at around the same time and that's made us close."

"You spend a lot of time together," Auriel prompted.

"Sure," I said. I felt nervous. I didn't know why Auriel was questioning me like this.

"Look. I don't want you to think I'm jumping to any conclusions and probably what I'm going to tell you, you don't even need to know, but I like you both and I don't want you to get into trouble. A couple of years ago there were two White Ones, Luke and Anna. They liked each other. Well, it was more than that. People knew but thought it didn't matter. Then one day neither of them was there in the morning. Luke had been sent to another cell somewhere in South Wales. No one knew what happened to Anna.

But there was a rumour – oh, God, I know I shouldn't be spreading rumours. I'll confess tonight, but I'll say there was a positive intent to the rumour. She had a breakdown. And then they threw her out. And she was lost."

"What do you mean? That someone stopped them seeing each other? Someone broke them up?"

"I don't know. We weren't allowed to speak about it. It wasn't Fletcher, at that time Jacob was in charge – he's in Orkney now. Fletcher was his second-in-command. Jacob used to scare me. Do you ever wonder about all the people here, Joe? A lot of them are a bit frightening. Not you, not Bea, not Will – you're my best friends. But Layla sobs at night – I hated it the night she told us about all that abuse. And Nick is dying, I think, and they won't let him have any medicine. Kate cuts herself at night – on her thigh – I've seen her do it. She can't stand the pressure of all the Perfection, you see. And what about Fletcher? I don't know anything about him. I know how he found the Light – that time when he was homeless and walked the streets – we all know that story, but what about before that? I haven't found anyone on the farm who knows anything about him. But he must have a past – so why won't he talk about it?

"When I think like this I reckon I must be the worst White One of all. I have all these wrong thoughts and I can't help it. I question things and I hate myself for being so awful and think I shouldn't be here. But then where would I go? Just to some mental hospital. Did you know my parents pay the White Ones for my keep? But I'm glad – I'm free here – and here they're all as mad as me. I have these times when I see everything very clearly, you know. I need someone to help me, don't I? I shouldn't be talking like this. I'll see Kate later. Kate's all right. I don't mind that she cuts herself. We all have to suffer because we want to achieve Perfection. That's why the antimatter is more out to get us than anyone else. It's like a war, isn't it, Joe? We're in the front line."

I didn't know if I should be listening to her. I thought I'd better go and get Kate. But at that moment we were interrupted by Jenny, a new girl who Kate had Attracted. Auriel started.

"Yes – I forgot – we were going to study together. I'm sorry, Jenny. Be with you in a moment." She turned to me. "Don't repeat any of this. I'm not well today. I envy you. You're special, Joe. Bea is lucky." And she went.

I sat there for quite some time, thinking. Auriel was in a pretty bad way and I hadn't noticed. I would have to discount all the rubbishy things she had said as they were dangerous. I thought I might hint to Fletcher that Auriel needed special care. I wiped my forehead and discovered it was damp, even though I hadn't been exerting myself. I felt sorry for Auriel. I liked her and I feared she was cracking up. I would pray for her, pray for all of us.

It was after lunch when Fletcher came for me. He knew about Auriel and said she was spending the rest of the day with Kate. It seemed there was no need to debrief to him. Instead he said that since it was such a good day, we could walk somewhere and talk at the same time. That wasn't unusual. Leaving the farm was the best way of having a private conversation as no one could surprise you – you'd see them coming. Fletcher was in his bleached jeans and a white vest top, revealing his sinewy arms. He made me feel a bit inferior. I'd borrowed an old T-shirt of Will's as mine were grubby and I hadn't had time to wash them. My baggy white combats made me feel skinnier than ever. We set off out of the farm and walked down the road. There was an occasional car so we faced the oncoming traffic. I noticed an old bloke staring at us from the front garden of a house on the opposite side of the road. I knew the locals thought we were a bit strange, but we knew we were lucky, privileged to be together.

Fletcher and I fell into step together at an easy pace. "How have you found working in the shop?" he asked me.

"Fine, but there's not a great deal to do. And I've Attracted no one." I was a little ashamed of that fact.

"I know. The shop is only a halfway house. I don't believe it's your final destination. Has your purity stood firm?"

"Pretty much. One morning I did stop to read the poster about the film on at the Picture House."

Fletcher was silent for a bit. "Nothing else?"

"No, I don't think so." This was the truth. The shop had simply reinforced my belief that the old world was sordid and confused and rather pointless. I didn't feel like rejoining it. I had done nothing that did not befit a White One. The daydream I had didn't count. It was the one where the door opened and Gemma walked in, or my mum, or Dad. I made up this story they'd driven to Hebden Bridge for a walk around, saw the shop and fancied something in the window and then they came in and saw me and...

"Have you ever thought, Joe, why those who have attained Perfection choose to return and walk among us?"

I liked these kinds of theological puzzles. "When you think

about it, it's weird. Because to be at one with the Light is all you could ever desire. So maybe it's to spread the word here. Like, part of what being Perfect means, is to wish to create more Perfection."

"A good answer. To emulate a Perfect, then, no White One should think only of his or her own Perfection as if that were the ultimate end. What we do affects others, and should affect others. That's why our dealings with other White Ones must always be calculated to work towards their Perfection. We must think about each other's good."

"Completely!" I agreed vehemently. That was the side of being a White One that I liked. I followed Fletcher as he turned down a rutted footpath towards the moors. I kind of hoped we could climb up to the top where the television mast was, and get over to the other side. Just to explore.

"And you can say that in all your communication with your brothers and sisters, you have been of profit to them?"

"I think so," I said.

Fletcher didn't respond to that. I felt sure there was a criticism hovering somewhere. I knew it was up to me to guess what it was and own it – White Ones never criticised each other. They only facilitated self-reflection.

"Will and I get on well together. We study and pray. I can't think..."

"Have you always been pure with your sisters?"

I looked down, pretending that I needed to watch my step. I focused on my dirty trainers and concentrated on trying to avoid clumps of grass. Then I realised by not answering Fletcher's question directly I had in fact answered it indirectly. I had implied I had not always been pure – and that he had guessed about Bea and me. Christ – it wasn't difficult! Now I dreaded what was coming. I remembered what Auriel had said and desperately began praying that it would all turn out all right. Like the coward that I was, I retreated to a safe island.

"I haven't broken my vow of physical purity," I said. I could hear my pleading tone and hated myself for it. Still Fletcher did not respond. "I've done nothing wrong," I added, sounding more pathetic than ever. Where had my courage gone?

And then I couldn't stand it any longer, couldn't stand the horrible pressure of the fact I was keeping a secret from Fletcher, and more than anything I wanted to spit it all out, confess everything, start from the beginning, fill the vacuum around us. And as weird as this might sound, for that moment I wanted Fletcher to reprimand me, to rip out my feelings for Bea from my chest, to make me clean again. Just then Bea wasn't real but Fletcher was. With a horrible sense of inevitability I knew this was the end of the road for me and Bea. I hoped she would understand. Perhaps it just had to be this way. As long as Fletcher did nothing to hurt her. It was my lowest moment. I took a deep breath, let it out, and began.

"I've got involved with Bea," I said. "I know she's involved with me too. Maybe I've encouraged it. I've allowed myself to think about her in the wrong way, the way I would have thought about her in the old world. Fletcher, I don't know what to do."

He still didn't speak, but I glanced at him and his face was tight, his lips compressed. I feared the worst and wanted the worst to happen so it was over with. He made for a hillock, and sat there.

There was a small amount of room by his side and he invited me to join him. I looked down at the tufted grass and saw it wasn't damp. Gingerly I eased myself down. I was aware of the very close proximity we were in, hip to haunch. It had this effect on me – like I wanted him to hug me, reassure me, tell me he still liked me. I wanted his arm round my shoulders. I couldn't stand the gulf of silence between us.

"I'd suspected this," he said. Sitting so close to him, I could feel a tremor travel through his body. Then he asked me, "Do you love her?"

It wasn't a question I had anticipated so my answer was spontaneous. "Yes," I replied.

"I thought so."

"Is it permitted?" I asked.

Fletcher was breathing heavily from the exertion of the walk.

"It is permitted," he said.

What? What was permitted? That I could carry on loving Bea? Or even more? That we could have a real relationship? What did Fletcher mean? I wanted him to be more specific, to spell it out.

"What is permitted?"

"If you need her," Fletcher said, "then you must have her."

Wild joy filled me. My love for Bea surged back, and I loved Fletcher too, and Will and Auriel and Nick and Kate and everyone I could think of. I knew it – I knew I was right to live among the White Ones. The dark, worm-like doubts I had been having secretly squirmed and died. I could live Perfectly, love Bea and be among the company I cared for most. I was right to put my fate in Fletcher's hands. Surrender was good.

Fletcher spoke again. "You should tell me everything, Joe."

"I will," I assented eagerly.

"That's good," he said. "Because I'd been considering sending Bea with you when you next Attract. I will, if you keep no secrets from me about your relationship with her. You need to confide in me, for your own sake. Anyway, you can go nowhere alone. I don't want to risk your personal safety at this stage. And now Nick and Kate can no longer work together we need a new male/female pair."

I could hardly believe this. Bea and I together – Attracting! We would have time alone together and do good work. I'd been right to confess to Fletcher – he wanted nothing but my welfare and Bea's welfare.

"Stand up," he said to me.

I did so. Fletcher got up too and stood in front of me. He placed his fingers on his lips then moved them to my forehead.

"May you be a vessel of enlightenment to all who you meet. May the Light shine upon you. If you should be who I think you are, may the Light forgive me for my ignorance. May you light me in my Darkness."

His fingers were hot on my forehead and as he spoke they pressed more and more heavily. My skin throbbed under them.

"May we both be enlightened," he said. Then he stepped back and regarded me – really looked hard at me – and I flinched under his gaze. His mouth curled with the suggestion of a smile, an intimate, knowing smile. For a moment I was afraid of him and wanted to get moving again and get back to the farm. There was something intense in his expression that prevented me from returning his gaze. A nerve jumped in my face. Then I quickly looked up at him and saw – no – it wasn't sweat on his brow. Those were tears. Fletcher was crying. There were tears escaping from him.

"May it be my lot to achieve Perfection," he said, his voice breaking.

I was scared, exhilarated, and feeling quite weak. Fletcher wiped the tears from his eyes and did not refer to them.

"Come on," he said. "We must be heading back."

I fell into step beside him.

12

From Rendall's Laws Governing Purity: Degrees of Passion

Passion is permitted to White Ones; indeed, passion is our aim. But there are degrees of passion. The lowest is the passion between man and woman, an animal passion which consumes itself. Next is the passion between man and man, a devotion which, if used correctly, may assist purity. Higher still is the passion a man may experience alone, in meditation, in contemplation of the Light. Highest of all is that which we all desire, the passion of utter purity, the passion we experience on merging with the Light at our final Elevation. The moment of Elevation cannot be spoken of in a way that would make it intelligible to those still living. This bliss waits for you, like a lover hungry for the touch and scent of the beloved. Know this: you are not yet born. This, too: fear nothing. And this: the end of days is to be desired.

⸺⬥⸺

The first person who I looked for when I got back to the farm was Bea. I found her taking Auriel back from the bathroom – Auriel was blindfolded now and needed assistance. Presumably Kate thought some ASD would help her. But to me, for a moment, she looked liked a prisoner: shaven head, blindfolded, led by the hand.

The delusion passed. I noticed Bea was wearing gloves – for her it was only a touch-deprived day. She wore the rough linen ones the girls had made for all of us to wear. Once Bea had taken Auriel back to the Reading Room, I indicated I needed to speak to her urgently. She followed me out to the allotments where luckily no one was around.

"It's OK," I told her.

"What's OK?"

"Us. I've been speaking to Fletcher. I've got some news. Look, I told him everything, I explained how I felt about you. And he was absolutely all right about it. I forget his exact words. But the gist was, he doesn't see our relationship as a distraction from our journey to enlightenment. There isn't a problem. I feel great about this. I wanted you to know. And there's something else."

I could hear myself babbling, not giving Bea a chance to respond.

"So you told him. I thought we'd agreed—"

I cut in. "But it was for the best. Because he acknowledged us, our relationship, and said we could go out Attracting – together! Together, Bea. We can have everything. It's what we wanted."

Slowly Bea began to smile. I took both her hands, cursed the gloves that meant I couldn't feel her, and kissed her softly on the lips.

"Are you happy?" I asked her.

She nodded silently. The afternoon sunlight made her hair look golden. Fletcher had said I could have her. That made me feel kind of powerful, macho, stronger than I knew myself to be. It was good.

During the next few weeks I only went down to Hebden Bridge

twice a week. For the rest of time I helped the guys build an outhouse which was going to be a meditation chapel. It was hard work and my hands developed calluses from all the digging. Most nights when I went to bed my back ached like an old man's. Services, study sessions and celebrations provided a welcome break. The familiar words of Rendall's Book, our prayers and readings were so comforting they sometimes sent me to sleep. Fletcher was keen I should step up my ASD. I hardly had a moment of leisure – no space to think, even – and the times I spent with Bea were short and snatched. But I was happy, I think. Apart from my dreams, but Fletcher said dreams were like a sewerage system for antimatter. Bad stuff seeped out in the night. Stuff about my parents, Gemma, scenes from the past. Once I woke up and I had been crying. Fletcher said that was proof absolute that bad old matter was draining away, like pus. Whatever. I was so tired some days I would have accepted anything. I just hoped for a change, any change.

And it came. What I think kick-started it was the letter from my parents. Fletcher called me to his room one morning. He was sitting on his bed, the letter in his hand. But I'm rushing ahead here. I didn't know at that point the letter was from my parents. He beckoned me over and I sat by him. He put the letter down a little way from us and put his arm round my shoulder.

"You've got a decision to make, Joe."

"OK," I said. I waited to hear what the decision was and what Fletcher thought I should do about it.

"I've got here a letter from your parents." Now I glanced quickly at the letter and saw Fletcher had put it back in the envelope. I noticed it was addressed to me. Fletcher had opened it. He had that right. "They say that Bristol University have asked you to confirm you'll be taking up your place there next month. They want to come and talk to you about it."

A tremor went through me which Fletcher felt too. He tightened the pressure of his arm, then removed it.

"What shall we do?" he asked me.

I couldn't believe I had forgotten about Bristol. But I had. This reminder of what I had planned was a bolt from the blue. My first thought was that I couldn't go because I hadn't done any academic work for so long. I was totally unprepared. But then I realised that always at the back of my mind I'd imagined myself going to Bristol, as a White One, Attracting, maybe, coming back to Lower Fold in the holidays. Only I couldn't cope if I was away from Bea, away from Fletcher and Will and everyone. I hadn't realised how much they would all come to mean to me. The thought of Bristol scared me. I would be on my own. I'd forgotten what that was like. And what if I went, and I was tempted? Better not risk it. I wanted to stay where I was. And while I was thinking all of this there was a whispering voice in my head, saying, what's happening to you, Joe? What's happening?

"I'm not going to Bristol, Fletch."

"That's OK."

"You see, my Perfection has to be my primary concern. Just now I feel I'm making progress. Two days ago – you know, when I did my triple ASD – things really began to come together. You remember that vision I had, the light streaming in and illuminating caverns, and how the caverns looked like the tissue of my brain – I'd never experienced anything like that before. My journey lies here. Bristol is part of the old me. I've moved on."

"I'm glad," Fletcher said. "I think you'd better write to your parents and I'll post the letter."

I did, there and then, and thought when I rang them at the weekend I'd explain why I'd chosen not to go in more detail. I hadn't seen them for a month or so. The last time was ugly – there was shouting and tears. Mine, theirs, I forgot whose. I tried not to think about it. It was better not to. Then I filled out the slip the uni had sent me. I noticed I was shaking while I did that. I guessed the shaking must have been muscle cramps, the result of all the hard labour.

"Take the rest of the day off," Fletcher said. "I want you to build your strength up."

I loved Fletcher then. He understood my needs so well. He was a better parent than my parents. I went from his room back to the dormitory, made for my bed, and lay there, my mind spinning until the exhaustion in my arms and legs spread through my whole body, and I slept.

I woke up suddenly, late afternoon. Jerked awake. I don't know why that was. And a thought slammed into my head. What if the White Ones were wrong? What if everything was made up? What if it was all nonsense? I felt myself go cold. My stomach clenched tight.

Joe, Joe, use your reason. This works, the way of the Light is right. Here there's love and harmony, people supporting you all the time. There's meaning in what we all do. So much has been written by so many – they can't all be wrong. You have everything you need here. United we are invincible. Treat your doubts like arrows that miss their target and fall away. May it be my lot to achieve Perfection. May it be my lot to achieve Perfection. My it be my lot to...

It was because I'd rested. The trick was to keep busy, to keep moving forward. I'd better help with the bricklaying. But Fletcher had said I could have the rest of the day off, that I needed to build up my strength. I felt my pulse return to normal. I began to appreciate just lying there, doing nothing. Then I tensed again as I heard the door to the dormitory open.

"Joe?"

It was Bea's voice. I answered her immediately. She came running over.

"Joe! Are you all right? Auriel said she thought you might be ill."

I sat up on my bed.

"No. Fletcher's given me the day off. I was sleeping. Come here." She got on the bed with me, I put my arm around her, and we both marvelled at our good luck in having some time and a place to ourselves. I told Bea about Bristol. She was quiet for a bit.

"I'm glad you're not going away, Joe," she said. "But maybe one day you will go to uni. It's a shame to waste any ability you've got."

"I know," I said. "I thought that. And there will be a time. Just not now."

"We're lucky," Bea said, after a while, but I thought her voice sounded flat.

"Are you OK?"

"A bit low today. Kate said I should go and play my guitar for a bit, but I thought I'd look for you first."

"I'm glad you did."

I nuzzled her face. She turned towards me, and we kissed. It was only the second time we'd kissed, but already she felt completely familiar to me. As our mouths moved together nothing seemed to matter any more, not Bristol, not the White Ones, only us. Nothing else was real. In a moment we were lying on the bed, wholly entangled, our bodies moving against each other, almost despite our will. All my aches had vanished. All I could hear was our breathing. In my hunger for Bea, everything else was blotted out. I stroked her face, her back, and my hands found their way inside her sweatshirt. Her breasts were warm to touch and soft like silk. In my eagerness to hold them firm in my hands, I tried not to hurt her. She kissed me harder than ever. I didn't care about anything, not even if we were discovered. Then I felt her hands over my trousers, finding my hard-on. She read my mind and then began to unbuckle my zip. I was breathless with excitement. I could hardly believe this was happening, at last. Our kisses got more desperate, deeper and deeper.

And then we heard voices outside the dorm. We froze.

"Hey, Bea." I sounded husky, not like me. "We're not supposed to do this."

"I know."

She extricated herself from under me. She looked more beautiful than ever, flushed and dishevelled.

"It can't be that wrong, can it?" she whispered.

"No. Fletcher said it was OK." But I could read her mind. We'd been told we could have a relationship, but not break our vow of chastity. It was a thin line. And she knew, as I knew, that just then, our bodies had betrayed us. If it wasn't for those voices, if we had been free from discovery, we'd have gone all the way. Guilt welded us together. I'd never felt closer to her.

"Joe – listen – I think I'd better go," she said.

"Look, don't worry. Whatever happens, I'll stick by you," I told her.

"I know you will. And I'll stick by you."

I wanted to kiss her again, but knew it would be wrong. I watched her get up and leave the dormitory. The movement of her body departing made me want her more than ever.

At the Evening Service when it was time for transgression cleansing, I washed my hands and said some stuff about feeling too smug about my progress, having slept in the afternoon and having lied. Only I didn't say what the lie was. The lie was a lie of omission. I should have spoken aloud what happened with Bea, but I didn't. Nor did she. We glanced at each other, then looked away.

So it came as no surprise to me when Fletcher indicated he wanted to speak to me. I followed him to his room. For some reason I was feeling slightly mutinous. I admired Fletcher – yeah, I suppose I even hero-worshipped him. I'd never known anyone like him. But recently I'd found his attention suffocating. He'd been watching me more closely than ever. That whispering voice said, get off my back. I didn't know why I was thinking in that way. I decided to deal with it later.

Fletcher shut the door to his room behind him. He didn't sit down. He eyeballed me, his face a mask.

"Joe. You need to be more careful of your purity than ever. As you progress, there are more temptations. antimatter is attracted by Perfection. You know this. So be honest, be absolutely honest. What did you hold back tonight?"

I couldn't hold his gaze.

"I have negative thoughts," I said.

"I thought so. Pray that they vanish."

"I will."

"And Joe?"

"Yeah?"

"What about Bea? I saw her go into the dormitory. She was with you a long time."

"Yeah. We were talking, and stuff."

"What stuff?"

I shrugged.

"Tell me. You promised to tell me. What happened?"

I swallowed hard. I didn't like the tone of his voice. It was pleading, desperate.

"We kissed."

"Just kissed?"

"We didn't sleep together!"

"So you're telling me you just kissed."

"And other stuff – you know."

"I don't know, Joe. Explain."

"Stuff you do with girls. Leave it, Fletcher."

"I need to know."

I noticed his fists were clenched. I was afraid now.

"I... I just felt her a bit. She felt me. Over our clothes."

"Over your clothes. But no more. Did she touch you, Joe?"

"We stopped when we heard voices."

"But otherwise you would have carried on."

I shrugged. The interrogation was over. I wished I could go but Fletcher was barring the exit. I looked up at him and watched his expression move from a hard stare to an apologetic grin.

"I have to do this," he said. "And maybe it's time to tell you why."

He walked over to the sash window and stood by it, looking out over the farm.

"I have to go to Orkney. There's been a message from Rendall. A Perfect is among us, but the Perfect himself does not know who he is. Rendall is convinced that the Perfect is a White One. We've been asked to use our intuition to sense if the Perfect is in our midst." He paused, turned, looked at me, his eyes alight.

"Joe – I think it might be you."

"Me?"

Now Fletcher approached me, kissed his fingers and pressed them to my forehead. "There have been signs," he said. "Signs I'm not allowed to divulge. Also, Rendall and his men have been reading runes. There's to be a Gathering in late September. We must be there, you and me."

I was incredulous and exhilarated, all at once. Of course I wasn't a Perfect. I was Joe, but maybe Fletcher was right, maybe all these whispering thoughts were antimatter out to get me, maybe there was a revelation coming, a revelation that would blow me apart, and everything would finally make absolute sense, every question would be answered. I could get away from the farm, travel to Orkney. Meet Rendall. See Carbister.

"Before then, Joe, I want you to go out on your first Attracting mission. I want to test you in the world. A Perfect can move safely anywhere. You are an immortal."

I knew I wasn't an immortal, but then, I believed my soul was immortal, and so in a way, Fletch was right. And I wanted to go Attracting. Except there was one condition, one condition I thought I'd better make clear now.

"I'm not going anywhere without Bea."

Fletcher paused. "I said that was all right. You can take her with you."

"And to Orkney." I was getting bold now. I was fired up by this idea I might be a Perfect. It was stupid, I knew I wasn't, but it was easy to act as if I was as Fletcher thought so.

"No. Not Orkney."

"Then I'm not going."

I'd defied Fletcher. I awaited the explosion. But there was none. I heard his heavy breathing.

"You are going," he said.

"With Bea," I added.

Then to my surprise he said, "With Bea."

I grinned at him, and then he hugged me. I would never have imagined I'd be alone in another guy's room, hugging him. But we broke apart after a moment. Fletcher seemed charged now, rapping out instructions, full of excitement.

"It seems a risk to send you Attracting but Rendall will want to know that you can survive unsullied in the outside world. Go to

Manchester, a place where there's lots of people. Where the clubs are."

"The Gay Village?" I suggested.

"No! No – a different place. Not Deansgate."

"Down by the university?"

"Yeah – that's good. Go on a weekday night – you'll be safer. Then you can stay late. Take a morning train home. The Light will protect you. I'll keep a vigil in the Service Room with some other White Ones. I'll get you a phone, and one for Bea too, so you can keep in touch. There'll be an allowance – you'll need some money – and you must build your strength up. You look thin. The time approaches. It comes quickly. We must be ready. I praise the Light that lights up the Truth, that reveals Perfection to the unworthy."

I bowed my head. Fletch had begun a prayer.

I couldn't pray. My mind was reeling. Me, a Perfect? Surely Perfects would know they were, or maybe not? I was stunned, but who's to say that Fletcher wasn't right? I ought to look after my purity. I'd better not be alone with Bea again. Except when we go Attracting.

To be honest, I couldn't wait.

The Sentinel Wednesday, May 6th, 1985

A young man was killed last night after being stabbed in a drunken brawl outside the Potter's Arms. Witnesses say the trouble began when several revellers started an argument inside the pub, and then were ejected by the bar staff. The fighting escalated once the men were on the pavement. The victim, Keiran McDermott, 19, of Turnham Street, Stoke, leaves a mother and two sisters.

A man is helping police with their enquiries. The victim's friend, John Elliot, 21, who witnessed the attack, said, "I know who the bastard is. He thinks he's hard, but tell him from me, if the police don't get him, I will. Keiran was a great mate, one of the best. His mum is devastated."

Another witness, Trevor Harrison, 58, said, "They were all tanked up. I knew there was going to be trouble. Kids today can't control themselves." Other bystanders said the quarrel seemed to be personal in nature.

See our leader, p 23 – Violence in the City – what the council should do to stop it once and for all.

13.

From Rendall's Laws Governing Purity: antimatter

We cannot recognise antimatter with our senses but know it by its effects. We know the man who plants the bomb, the absence in his eyes. We know the force that floods the rivers and drowns the fields. We know the cell that grows cancerous. We know the dark seeds of doubt which feed leech-like on our heart's blood.

━━━━◉━━━━

I tried to joke about it to Bea. I told her Fletcher had finally flipped, he thinks that I'm a Perfect! But she didn't seem to find it funny. She questioned me closely and asked me how I felt about it. Her seriousness calmed me down.

"Well, if I am, there's nothing I can do about it," I told her.

We were facing each other across the table in the kitchen.

"I can't really believe I'm a Perfect. I can say in absolute truth that I have no consciousness of being anyone but me. Only I feel I have to go along with this. It doesn't seem that I have a choice."

"I suppose," Bea said, "it's like those little boys who are discovered to be reincarnations of the Dalai Lama. They wouldn't know, either. Only I find it hard to believe too. It makes me feel a little scared of you."

I didn't like that. "Don't be. Nothing's changed. Except we can go out Attracting and then to Orkney. And the chances are we'll go and meet Rendall, and he'll shake his head, and send us back, and everything will be as it was before, and we'll have had a holiday."

Bea smiled at me. "I guess. But I wish things were as they were before."

I knew what she meant. Sometimes when I looked back it seemed the best times as a White One were behind us. I loved the lead-up to being initiated, those early days full of new discoveries. Now there were responsibilities, work, and darker moments. All part of the journey. And then this. Because if Fletcher was wrong about me, then what else was he wrong about? And if he was right, then what?

"We must just try to carry on as we were before," Bea said, with decision. "We must take one day at a time."

"Yeah, Fletcher said to carry on as normal."

"Well, there we are!"

But the truth was, in the intervening days before we went Attracting, I thought of little else. At times I was so excited to have a destiny, and almost thought I had intimations of it. When I was small, there were times I had felt my parents were not my real parents. Was that an inkling of what was to come? Then I would look around me at the farm, the stone floors, the wooden chairs, and the reality of everything told me that I was real too, not an immortal, and that Rendall would realise this, and Fletcher would be let down gently.

As the days went on, I partly got used to it, the seesawing, believing and not believing. The only thing that kept me going was the thought of Attracting with Bea. She was looking forward to it, too. I saw it as my chance to show myself how much I'd changed, how immune I had become to the temptations of the world, how I could see through the shallow fripperies of so-called Western civilisation. Or so I said to Fletcher. I saw myself as a knight surrounded by an armour of Light that would carry me, immune, through the mean streets. This was the image I focused on in my visualisations.

But the reality was a smelly, almost-empty train that stopped and started all the way to Victoria. I told Bea that it was easy not to be seduced by the old world because it was so sordid and disappointing. What we had was so much better. She nodded vehemently in agreement.

We finally reached Victoria, and a memory ignited.

"This is where it all started!"

"Victoria Station?" Bea asked.

"Yeah – I went on the tram with Nick and Kate to Victoria. This is where they got off."

She squeezed my hand. We were holding hands, had been for all of the journey. I suppose we were nervous. We hadn't been to Manchester for ages and it dwarfed us. At that moment I had never felt less like a Perfect. I was just a kid again. I sensed Bea felt the same.

The station was cavernous and grand, and you had this sense of the old Manchester that was linked with steel umbilical cords to all its satellite towns: Bury, Rochdale, Preston, Blackpool – I knew the names of all these places were carved in stone outside. But now the station was a pit, the ticket booths were closed and anyone who had any sense was elsewhere. Late at night was not the best time to be in a railway station. We had to move on and find places where people might be Attracted to us. We had to cross Manchester in the direction of the university, wait, and see what happened. There was something about the early hours of the morning that made people ask big questions.

Bea and I left the station. I was coughing a bit – I'd had this cold I couldn't shake off. Luckily it was a warm, autumn night. We weren't in a rush. We wandered up to the Printworks and gazed up at the bright lights of the cinemas and restaurants. The laughter of people out partying, the throb of traffic, the blasts of loud music, the smells of exotic food, they were all too much for me. I couldn't relate to it any more, and yet just a year ago this was my stamping ground: me and my mates would go out and get plastered, eye up girls, queue up outside clubs. Altogether, I felt like I did when I was getting over glandular fever, remote, disassociated, my mind and body weak.

Bea disentangled her fingers from my hand and put her arm round my waist. I felt better immediately. Partly because it was her, partly because, for a moment, we felt like a normal couple going out together, boyfriend and girlfriend, camouflaged. We walked down Cross Street, opposite Marks and Spencer, and suddenly I felt a rush of happiness. I was away from the farm, free! Just for a moment I didn't care about anything.

"We're in Manchester, Bea!"

"Yeah – I'm happy too."

I kissed her then, and the kiss felt like a tiny moment of rebellion. It may even have been the spark that ignited the slow-burning fuse. But not yet. Bea was feeling chatty now, going over the things we had to remember.

"Kate said not to feel bad if nothing happens. We're not evangelicals, and the right person might not turn up. All we have to do is be there. And she said you just *know*. It's weird, Joe, how all the White Ones are young, isn't it? Have you noticed that? I think that was why Fletcher was happy with us starting at the university. Have you asked yourself why we're all young?"

"Rendall's in his fifties."

"Sure, but Fletcher's the oldest one at Lower Fold. I hope we do meet someone tonight. I love the way that being a White One has challenges. Like this. It's a journey, isn't it? A journey towards enlightenment. It's so clever the way it all works."

I glanced over the road at the Royal Exchange Theatre. I went with school a couple of years ago to see *Waiting for Godot*. Two blokes under a tree. I didn't know what the hell it was about. But it was good, though. It was good not knowing what it was about. I was only half listening to Bea. It was enough to have her alone with me.

"It makes you wonder who thought it all out. The structure of it all. Because if the Light is just Light, it wouldn't have the practical intelligence to construct a system that hooks so neatly into human psychology. But if Rendall devised all the stages on our journey, then how? And why? Do you ever think about these things? Joe? Joe!"

"What?"

I was looking in at the Cross Street Chapel. Those guys had a faith too. It seemed so ordinary compared to ours, a chapel on the ground floor of an office block.

"Joe – you're not listening! And I was going to say something important."

"Say it." I smiled at her, and stopped walking.

"It was nothing. I suppose I was just thinking aloud. Being away from the farm, it's funny. You see things from a different perspective. Just ignore me."

"It's weird being in Manchester again," I said to her. "It's doing my head in."

"I know what you mean," she said.

We walked on. We got to Albert Square. There was the Town Hall, floodlit, massive. Once me and Tash had been shopping on a Saturday and when we got to Albert Square there were all these temporary stages and people were performing – it was some sort of music festival. There were these black guys doing a reggae number and everyone was joining in, clapping and that. Old ladies were waving their arms in the air. I laughed but found myself tapping my feet. Tash was going on about how good it was to see such cultural diversity – she used to talk like a dictionary.

I said to Bea, "You don't get any black White Ones either."

"Black White ones? What are you on about, Joe?"

Opposite the town hall Caffe Uno was still open but I didn't reckon we had enough money to eat there. A shame, as I was hungry. I hadn't been to a restaurant for ages. I knew that food as entertainment was morally corrupt because I had often said so.

"Did you eat tonight?" I asked Bea.

"Yes," she said, "but I'm still hungry."

We cut through to the Central Library where I revised for my A2s. So did a few of my mates. We spent more time sitting on the steps and stressing than actually working. It was weird the way I wanted good results more than anything, but half the time I couldn't be arsed to work. And I got the grades but I wasn't going to uni now. So it had all been pointless.

Pointless because my destiny lay elsewhere. I was a White One, possibly a Perfect, entrusted with an understanding of the world, given a part to play in its destiny, with a family, a structure, a purpose. A tram blazing with lights trundled past. On our right the Midland Hotel oozed wealth and grandeur. Once I went to a Bar Mitzvah there. There was this Jewish kid in our class, Adam Goldblatt. His parents were rolling in it. They'd even invited some Manchester City players to the reception. I got their autographs. Earlier, at the synagogue, I'd reddened with embarrassment as I watched Adam singing some Hebrew with his voice that was breaking, and wondered what the hell it was all about. Then we had this huge dinner and we all got pissed. Adam threw up in the toilets and his mum was in floods of tears. It was a good night. I wondered what was going on inside the Midland Hotel now.

"Joe – you're very quiet."

"Sorry."

Guilt washed over me. Here we were, on our first Attracting mission, and all I'd been doing was reminiscing. We'd reached the top of Oxford Road, and the university was about a mile away. Just then I didn't feel as if I had the strength to make it.

"I need something to eat or drink," I told Bea.

We began to look for somewhere. Mainly it was just bars and restaurants that were open. We felt like going somewhere quieter, and cheaper. But the small coffee shops and cafés which were open during the day were closed now. There was only McDonald's.

"We'd better go there," Bea said.

So we did. We queued up at the counter and my mouth began to water at the thought of the burgers and fries. All we could have was fruit juice.

"Or maybe a milk shake," Bea said.

It wasn't a stimulant, that was true.

The guy at the counter eyed me suspiciously. I bristled at that. Hadn't he been trained to deal with the public? Then I caught a partial reflection of myself in a mirror, in my dirty white denim jacket, my white tracksuit bottoms and white T-shirt. My face was pale and my eyes had dark rings under them. I suppose he thought I was a druggie waiting to shoot up in the toilets.

"Large fries," I demanded, "and a chocolate milk shake. And a Diet Coke."

We would have to confess all of this when we got back, but it would be worth it. Anyway, I'd heard that White Ones on Attracting missions often had to make compromises.

I carried the tray of food to a corner table and Bea and I squeezed behind it and fell on the food. The fries were like manna. It was hard to slow myself down so that Bea could have a fair share too. I had half a mind to go back and get some more, which would have cleaned out our funds completely. Then we took turns slurping at the milk shake. It was sickly and wonderful. Neither of us said a word. The ice in the Coke bobbed against my lips, temporarily numbing them. When everything had gone, I breathed deeply. I felt much, much better.

Bea said, "They've been starving us."

"Yeah, there's not much food. It's difficult to feed us all."

"When I fast," Bea said reflectively, "it sort of removes a barrier. I feel more spiritual."

"Yeah – me too."

"So have you ever thought that the spiritual feeling is a result of the fasting and not of the Light?"

"What are you saying?"

"I don't know."

McDonald's hadn't changed at all. The décor was bright, upbeat and garish. The people in it were a blend of post-cinema diners, some students and a few lonely people with nothing better to do. Someone was washing the floor at the other end of the restaurant. I knew McDonald's was the ogre of Western civilisation, but when I was little I wouldn't eat anywhere else. It drove my mum mad. I wouldn't touch her burgers, only McDonald's. Gemma always had a Happy Meal and hoarded the toys she collected.

"I keep thinking about my old life," I told Bea. "Because I'm here in Manchester."

"Me too," she said. "My mother used to take me to the Opera House whenever there was a touring opera company. Or a ballet."

"Do you miss that?"

"Of course I do." Bea looked blank, unfocused.

"And do you sometimes think, we're all a bit mad, hiding ourselves away on the farm?"

"Maybe we have to do that for now."

"What do you mean, *for now?*"

She was silent.

"Are you saying," I continued, "that there'll be a time in our lives when we're no longer White Ones? Or do you mean that some White Ones could live in the rest of the world, keeping the beliefs, but having normal jobs and families and that?"

"I hope so," she said.

"So do I."

And that was when it hit me. I had only ever seen being a White One as temporary. Like a serial relationship. I needed it back in November. I was grateful, I'd put a lot back into the community, I believed, more or less, in most of the stuff, and loved some of the stories in the Book. But the ASD was an ordeal, it was humiliating, and then at other times, I looked at everyone, and just thought they were stupid. But every time you had a negative thought you were supposed to say, *it's the antimatter*.

Bea said, "Would they let us – you know – leave?"

"Yeah. Why not? Everything we've done we've chosen to do. No one brainwashed us. So we could just leave."

"I'm scared to leave," she said.

"We're not going to leave," I reassured her. Maybe I was reassuring myself too. "It's still working for us. It's because we're away from the farm, we're looking at it differently."

Bea fiddled with the straw of the milk shake. I thought about what I'd just said, and saw the individual White Ones pass in front of my eyes. There was Will, who, when all was said and done, wasn't very bright. Kate, who, despite her composure, mutilated herself. Auriel, who was profoundly disturbed. And Nick. Nick was sane but desperately ill, and there'd been no news of him for days, only rumours. Finally there was Fletcher himself. I shuddered as I thought of him. God knows why. Then my mind's eye flicked to last night's Evening Service when we were all together in the twilight, hands joined, singing, and it was all incredibly beautiful.

I thought, so what if they're not perfect?

And then I thought, but they're supposed to be perfect. And me, I'm supposed to be a Perfect, but I'm not. I found myself wishing I was the guy in the baseball cap behind the counter stoking fries into a bag. I reached out for Bea's hand.

"I don't feel good tonight," I told her.

"Maybe this is normal for the first time you leave the farm," she said, with a forced brightness. "What we ought to do, is wait and see. We'll Attract tonight, and leave it a couple of weeks, and talk again."

"Yes. That's good. We'll have a clearer picture then."

Or maybe we shouldn't even go back to the farm at all. Maybe Bea and I should just walk and walk until we get back to my old house, and ring my parents' bell and just say, hi. And the nightmare would be over.

Maybe.

I concealed that hope, that intention, like a secret weapon. Later on tonight I would let Bea know what we could do. But not now. I wasn't ready yet. And I'd been looking forward to being able to Attract for months. I was determined to find out what it was like.

One way or the other, it would resolve the issue. If we Attracted, then there was meaning. We were being guided by an Unseen Hand. If we didn't, if it all went pear-shaped, then we could... then we could...

"Let's go, Bea," I said.

14

To: coolbabevicky@hotmail.com

It's me, Gem. Thanks for inviting me to your party and I might come. I'll see what things are like at home.

Actually, they're crap. My mum's seeing this counsellor person and I reckon it's making her worse. Mum is like, he's been brainwashed, I don't even know if he's well or ill. Do they have any doctors there? Is it my fault?

I told her it wasn't her fault but I fucking HATE!!!!****!!!!! that bloody stupid fucking cult. They've stolen my brother. And you'd think I'd get used to it but I haven't. Like Mum says, you don't know how he is or what he's feeling.

And I think they're cowards, Mum and Dad. If it was me I'd go up there with the police or the SAS or something and get him. But they say he's 19 now and it's his choice. Some choice.

And then I meet people, and they're like, d'you have any brothers and sisters? I dunno what to say. Sometimes I say, I had a brother. Coz in a way he is dead.

Sorry to babble on like this but sometimes it like all builds up and I feel like kicking and screaming or something. But it's not fair on M & D if I let it all out.

So thanks for reading this - you can delete it now.

Luv, Gemxxxxxxxxxxxxxxxxxxxx

Once we got back out into the street, we felt a lot better. Having that meal had been the right thing to do. I found myself cheering up.

"Hey, Bea. It's weird. Like, we were in McDonald's and we had all those bad thoughts. Like the place itself was infecting us. Do you reckon McDonald's is a channel for antimatter?"

"It makes sense. When you think of the animals killed for burgers, and all that suffering, it has to have a reaction somewhere down the line."

"Yeah. You're right."

I was back in the rhythm again, feeling in tune with myself, having a purpose. Perfect. And so we carried on walking south, under some scaffolding and past the *Big Issue* seller by the Cornerhouse. We talked about social diseases like avarice and quoted the Book at each other. I noticed some people looking at us oddly, but that was no surprise.

We came to the Royal Northern College of Music. Bea paused.

"I had lessons there once," she said.

"You told me."

"Yes. And I was in the youth orchestra for a while, before Mum was ill. That's where we had our concerts. They were good times. I miss the concerts. Maybe by joining the White Ones I was searching for the same thing, that sense of belonging."

"No, Bea. You were searching for the White Ones and found the youth orchestra by mistake."

It was bothering me, the way she was talking. We'd finished with all that negative stuff. I wanted everything to be simple again. I needed to find someone to Attract. I was getting tired. We reached the Whitworth Art Gallery. Bea was quiet now. Groups of students passed us on their way into town. It gave me the illusion we were heading in the wrong direction, a small boat setting sail against the tide.

By the time we reached the Student Union, we decided to rest. We sat on the steps. I was thirsty and thought longingly of the Coke I'd had at McDonald's. That was bad, and so I spoke some prayers silently in my head. I begged that the right person should be drawn to us, that we should be of service. I asked the Light to use me as a channel. People shot us curious glances but no one approached us. The Union was shut and I realised, too late, that we should have stayed in town where there would have been more chance of striking up a conversation. We waited for five minutes, ten. Fewer and fewer people were around. Ten minutes, fifteen. Maybe even longer than that. Nothing happened. I was shivering with the cold and snuggled up to Bea.

"This seems pointless," she said.

"Have faith," I told her.

It was easier to tell someone else to have faith than to have it yourself. The truth was, I was beginning to feel more and more uncomfortable. It wasn't supposed to be like this. We were to have met someone, dazzled them by our vision of what life could be. But to an outsider, we looked as if we were the ones who needed help.

"I think we ought to go back into town," I said. I heard Bea sigh.

We got up then. As we did so I realised someone had been watching us. He was a bloke who looked a little older than me, but not much. It crossed my mind that he could be the one, the one we had been destined to meet. My heart pounded as he came towards us.

"Have you got a light?" he asked.

"Sorry," I said. "I don't smoke."

"Cheers," he replied, and wandered off.

That was the moment it happened. The whole absurdity struck me. I thought this guy was my destiny and all he wanted was to light a cigarette. What sort of idiot was I? What the hell had been going on with me? I asked myself what I was doing here, on the steps of the uni, trying to convert people to a half-baked belief system I had stopped believing in? Until then, I hadn't realised that I had stopped believing in it. Maybe I had thought there was too much to lose if I admitted it. Now there was nothing to lose.

I had this experience once before. When I was fourteen, I went out with a girl – Tracey – for a couple of weeks or so. It was mainly just so I could show everyone I could pull. Then one night we went to see a film and I thought, what am I doing with her? I didn't even like her. She giggled all the time and kept poking me in the arm. Then it was just a matter of working out how to finish with her. At the time I thought it was weird how I could go off her in one moment, kind of.

Remembering Tracey helped steady me. The first thing now was to let Bea into what I was thinking. As much as I wanted to loosen the bonds between me and the White Ones, my relationship with Bea was the one real thing, the thing worth saving.

"Come on," I said. "Let's head back."

Bea linked arms with me and we fell into step together.

"Are you disappointed?" she asked me.

"No. Maybe this was meant to happen. Like, finding no one who was interested."

"I don't know. I'm getting fed up with thinking that everything has a purpose all the time."

I knew it. Bea was thinking in the same way as me. Yet such was the hold of the White Ones that even then I was tentative in expressing my thoughts, or getting her to express hers. It seemed dangerous. Blasphemous, even. So I was careful.

"What do you mean – fed up?"

"Oh, I don't know. Like, don't you wish you could just take time out? Watch TV, maybe, or leaf through a magazine and look at the latest fashions? Just for a break. To get away from the intensity of everything."

"I've been thinking, I wonder what goes on in people's heads when they're supposed to be praying. I watch them at Services. They don't concentrate on every word. They just make out as if they do. To be honest, that's what I do. I try to make it all mean something, but most of the time I'm thinking, are the others watching me, and am I praying convincingly?"

Bea's voice, when she replied, was urgent. "Yes! *I* can't concentrate on the prayers all of the time, even on a good day. I reckon two-thirds of what we do is pretence but we have to, to encourage everyone else, and just in case..."

"Just in case what?" I asked her.

"Just in case it *is* true."

"So you think it might not be true," I insisted.

"No! I believe in the Light and the importance of Perfection. Well, I want to believe. There's so much wrong with the world. But I miss the world, and I want some of it back."

"This is what we'll do, Bea. When we get back to the farm, I'll talk to Fletcher. I'll say I feel we need a break."

"He won't agree."

That chilled me. I wanted to take issue with her. "No. He's always been reasonable. Like, I thought he would freak at us and our relationship, but he didn't. He might be upset, but he's never stopped me doing anything I wanted. All we're going to be dealing with here is that he's going to be disappointed – big time. It'll be tough but we're going to have to break free. He won't stop me doing what I most want to."

"But you've never tried to leave before."

We'd reached the city again, and I'd hardly been aware of our walk – our conversation had been so vitally important. Bea and I had talked ourselves into wanting out. I could never have imagined our Attracting mission would have ended in this way. Normality had never seemed more tempting. I thought, if I went home now, I could sleep in my own room. In a comfortable bed. In the morning, I could fry up some bacon and eggs. I could introduce Bea to my parents. They would love her. I could begin to assess what had happened to me.

Maybe, if I was going to leave, now would be the best time.

"Bea, what if we were to go home – to my home?"

"Could we?"

"Why not?"

I looked at her to gain strength and I think she was doing the same to me too. I couldn't believe it was all unravelling so quickly. At least Bea was for real.

"OK," Bea said. "But look. I need the loo."

I guessed she was feeling the same terror that I was. Luckily we were approaching McDonald's again. It was still open so she said she'd go in there. I said I'd wait outside. I wondered whether to ring my parents, except they might be asleep. I had the mobile Fletcher had given me. Did I have the courage to ring them?

I got out the phone and unlocked it. The screen lit up. Only some yobbos were arsing about on the other side of the road and I wanted to be able to hear properly. I thought about going into McDonald's but this was going to be an important conversation. I needed to be alone. I needed quiet. So I walked round McDonald's to a bus shelter, stood by it and dialled home.

There were no warning signs. They were on me in a moment. One grabbed my phone, the other punched me so that I doubled up in agony. I was on the floor, someone was going through my pockets. Then the kicking started, boots connecting with my legs, my crotch, my face. Pain crashed around me. I saw nothing. It lasted for ever but was over in a moment. There was a whimpering heap on the pavement and that heap was me.

Slowly my mind cleared. I thought I had better go into McDonald's and get Bea. So I tried to get up but my body didn't belong to me any more. Which struck me as strange. I noticed some people across the road who glanced at me and walked on. I suppose they thought I was a drunk. I tried to call out to them but my voice was tiny, like in those nightmares when you try to shout and you have no voice. Pain radiated from my middle, reverberated around my head, but if I didn't move, I would be OK.

I told Bea that when she found me. "I'm OK," I whispered hoarsely, "but I can't move."

Her face was blank with horror. I wished she would smile because that would have made me feel better. She kept saying my name, then stood up and shouted for help. Soon there were a few people around me, gawping.

Bea explained later why she did what she did. She was scared. And she couldn't imagine explaining what we were doing out late, dressed in white, with just a few pamphlets, to the police. It made sense, she thought, to ring Fletcher. In the short-term, he would be the best person. So she rang his mobile.

It seemed to me he was there in a just a few minutes, which I thought was strange, as he had been on the farm in Todmorden. But I didn't care because I was glad to see him. He knew what to do. Gently, gently, he got me to sit up against the wall. He put his jacket round me. He wiped my mouth with his handkerchief and I realised the dark stain was my blood, the lumps that came away were my teeth. I heard Bea sobbing hysterically. I wanted her to stop because I just wanted peace. Fletcher helped me to my feet and got Bea to support me on my other side. I found I was just about able to walk. People were still staring at us and some offered help. But Fletcher said it was OK, he was seeing to me, and the car wasn't far away. A voice from a spectator offered to ring for an ambulance; Fletcher said he would do that.

And the van was just down the street. He laid me in the back and my head rested on Bea's lap. She stroked my face and her fingers were smeared with my blood. Fletcher drove as slowly as he could and it was only the bumps in the road on the approach to the farm that jolted me awake. I heard myself moaning. Bea was going, shhh, shhh.

Fletcher, Will and some of the other guys took me to the dormitory. Fletcher got me something to drink with a weird taste.

Oblivion.

15.

From Rendall's Book of Prayers: Prayer for Recovery

We implore the Light to surround the body of our brother/sister and bring, in its rays, healing. Our love, focused like arrows, pierces the antimatter, destroying it for all eternity. As the Light is Perfect, so let the body of our brother/sister be Perfect, whole and firm. As our love is unending, may the healing continue. May it be our lot to achieve Perfection. May it be his/her lot to achieve Perfection.

———◦((◦))◦———

It's hard to remember the order in which things happened.

I woke up, or maybe I was woken up. Fletcher was there. Maybe Will. I thought I saw my mother but that was a dream. Then I thought someone took me out into the cold and I didn't want to go. When I woke up, I saw a mushroom-cloud explosion and a three-bar electric fire. I was in Fletcher's bed. Will poured me some water. Or was it Fletcher? All I wanted to do was sleep.

Then I had another dream in which everybody was in the room and filling my head with Light. I felt the pain diminish and liked it when they all laid their fingers on my forehead, avoiding the gash. I don't think it was the mugging that made me feel so woozy, maybe it was the medicine.

When I was properly conscious again, it was dark. I can't say whether it was the middle of the next night or earlier than that.

Different bits of me were hurting – my ribs, my head, my right arm – and my legs felt so weak, like lead. I could hardly move them. Fletcher was with me. I was glad I wasn't alone. I asked for Bea, and he said, later.

He asked me to tell him exactly what had happened. I explained about Bea going into McDonald's and the mugging. He shook his head.

"I should never have sent you out Attracting," he said.

"It could have happened to anyone," I told him, as he looked so upset.

"No! You see, if you are a Perfect – if you are, then antimatter is more likely to seek you out. It always happens that way. Think of Gandhi, think of John Lennon. Evil is drawn to destroy good. That's always been the way. Bea never should have left you."

"But she had to—"

"She should never have left you," he repeated. "And up till then, what sort of night did you have? Did you find anyone?"

"No – it was strange. It was..."

My voice petered out. I couldn't say what had really happened. But Fletcher sensed something.

"Was there anything that happened that created a channel for antimatter? Did you and Bea do anything you shouldn't?"

His face was like thunder and I was scared.

"No! Nothing like that, nothing at all."

"But something happened," he persisted.

"We were just talking," I said.

"Talking? Talking about what?"

"I'm tired, Fletch."

"Tell me what you were talking about."

I didn't have the strength to resist him. "Just things about the White Ones. Questions, kind of."

I expected his fury. I tensed myself. I thought he might hit me or something. But I couldn't have been more wrong.

"Oh, Joe," he said, and his voice was full of compassion. "This is all my fault. I should have realised. Without us to support you, doubts are bound to creep in. It's the way antimatter works. Doubts are fifth columns that topple the edifice of belief. They usually start with a woman. Like Eve in the Garden of Eden, giving Adam the apple. Like Samson and Delilah. Like Lady Macbeth. But thank the Light you are safe. Had you been lost, cosmic disaster would have followed. The Beast would have risen."

I was so glad he wasn't angry and I wanted to believe in all the things he was saying. It was the easiest thing to do, to let myself fall back into the ways of the White Ones. They would look after me. And maybe the attack *was* a punishment for my thoughts. Who could say? Last night seemed a blur now, and the thoughts I had then seemed like traitors. I had been so near to throwing it all away. Praise be to the Light!

Fletcher said he was needed elsewhere, but he would give me something to help the pain and make me sleep. I took it gratefully.

Then I had a nightmare. I thought I saw the Beast, the one Fletch had been talking about. Its glistening green scales flaked light; it dribbled yellow vomit; its underbelly had no skin but exposed bone and sinew. My wounds throbbed even in my dream. I moaned but no one was there in the abyss. Then I walked up from my living room to my bedroom where a table was laid and we all ate, my mum, Dad, Gemma and Fletcher. Big Macs, chips and milk shakes. But I couldn't reach my food. The Beast was sitting on my chest, and I couldn't breathe. I tried screaming, but it came out like a whimper. My whimpering woke me up.

It was still dark and I was alone. I tried calling but no one came. So I got out of bed, feeling surprisingly dizzy and tried to open the door. It was locked. I thought I must be mistaken and tried it again. That didn't make sense. Why would they lock me in? Half thinking this was all part of my nightmare, I went back to bed. Sleep overtook me, and then it was the morning. Late morning. Sunshine poured in through the window above the bed.

I lay there, weak, still in pain, remembering parts of my nightmare, the Beast, my family, being locked in. I looked round the room now and saw nothing had been moved since last night, no one had been in to see me. I had this sense that all was not well. Automatically I muttered the Morning Prayer. It calmed me, and I decided to get out of bed and go to the bathroom. I got to the door and tried it. It was locked.

I was worried now. I banged on it repeatedly. No response. I banged louder. I tried shouting, too. Where was everyone? Why had Fletcher left me? And Bea? I called for her as she was the person I most wanted to see. I don't know how long I was banging for. I was frantic, like a kid who'd been abandoned.

Then suddenly someone put a key in the lock. I stood back, expecting Fletcher. But it was Auriel, looking wild as ever. She had a jug of water with her and a hunk of bread. I let her in and she shut the door firmly.

"These are for you," she said. "I asked Fletcher, I said, could I look after you? He said, yes, just this morning, while we have to make arrangements. You must drink this water and eat this bread. And we must pray to the Light."

She put the water and bread on the bedside table and fell to her knees. I did, too, but I couldn't concentrate on the prayers. When she'd finished we both got up and sat on my bed.

"He has been Elevated," she said. "He is with the Light and the Light is with him."

"Elevated? Who?" We used the word "Elevated" to say that someone had died. Because it was better being dead, in a way. You were on a higher plane.

"I saw him afterwards. He was at peace. He was full of Light."

"Who? Fletcher?"

"Fletcher was with him. Fletcher removed the shroud. It stunk."

"Auriel! What are you talking about?"

"May it be his lot to achieve Perfection. But he has achieved Perfection, so I suppose we don't have to say that any more. What do we say, Joe, when someone has died – I mean – been Elevated? I forget. May he rest in peace. Is that right?"

"Auriel! Who has died?"

"Nick."

She stared straight ahead, her eyes glassy. I was shocked. I knew Nick was very ill but I never, ever thought he would die. I just saw him as a chronic invalid or something. I couldn't take it in. I realised death was just as shocking when you were a White One as when you weren't.

"What happened?" I asked.

Auriel clutched my hand and squeezed it so hard that it hurt.

"Don't let them know I'm telling you all this. They wanted to make him better. They wrote to Carbister. They had a reply. Nick was to undergo full ASD for twelve hours, to erase the antimatter. They gave instructions. He had to be wrapped in a shroud – a white one – tightly, tightly. But first he had to be bound. I helped do it. He looked like a mummy swathed in bandages. But he didn't mind. His eyes were shut. We chanted about the Light. We covered his eyes and nose and mouth with the bandages – I thought he would still be able to breathe through them – the Light would help him breathe. He was so thin, Joe. They said, if he mimicked death, then the antimatter would have nothing to feed on and it would leave him and move somewhere else. We were fooling the antimatter. Cheating it. That's the only kind of cheating you're supposed to do as a White One. Shall I recite the Laws Governing Purity? I know them off by heart. One: You shall not—"

"Stop that, Auriel. Tell me about Nick."

"Nick? Oh, yes. We wrapped him tightly, he couldn't see, and I strapped his arms to his body. When we were done we laid a white blanket over him, with a wreath of white chrysanthemums on top. From the Garden Centre; Gordon Riggs. Kate ordered it specially. And we left him. But we didn't go far. We held a prayer vigil in the next room. We said the Recovery Prayer ninety-nine times. Fletcher read from the Book. When we heard thumps from Nick's room, Fletcher said that was the antimatter leaving his body. We prayed louder, to cover the sounds.

"Joe – listen – you've got to get out of here! They're all mad. Because, later on, when the vigil was over, we went in there, and Nick had fallen off the bed. He'd been struggling to get out, and there was this stink (he'd soiled the bandages. It was the antimatter – no, it wasn't. He'd messed himself. And Fletcher quickly removed the bandages, but Nick wasn't moving. He was limp, white, but his eyes were open, staring, like he'd seen something so horrible there weren't words to describe it. And Fletcher tried breathing into his mouth and Kate shrieked (but it was no good. They couldn't bring him back. And Joe, he died like that, all wrapped up, all alone, and nobody came... I'm not going to die like that. I'll find another way... Fletcher's making arrangements about Nick's body, so he can't be with you... The body. I helped unwrap it. It stunk... I prayed to the Light. May the Light help me in my Darkness... Fletcher said you must eat and drink. Fletcher loves you, Joe, more than he loved Nick. But he doesn't love Bea... Would you like me to sing you a song?"

I said no, that I needed the bathroom. I went there, and was violently sick. When I got back to Fletcher's room, Auriel had gone.

I needed to think. If what Auriel had said was true, then... Then... I found I couldn't bear to think about what she said about Nick. Everyone knew Auriel was mad, anyway. Maybe she made it all up. But what about Bea? Was she there? And they wouldn't do that to me, would they? Wrap me in a shroud? Everything felt wrong and I couldn't decide whether it was me, or the antimatter, or the White Ones. I felt as if I was getting a temperature – my forehead was burning but my arms and legs pricked with cold. It reminded me of when the glandular fever began and I hoped it wasn't starting again. Panic seemed to make me burn up more.

I sipped at the water Auriel had left, then Fletcher came in.

"Joe," he said. "I have some news."

"About Nick?"

"Nick's been Elevated," he said. "Praise be to the Light."

"Praise be to the Light."

"He is now well and his antimatter is no more. We were victorious."

Fletcher looked so happy it made me think it was a good thing that Nick had died. Which, in a way, it was. Because he had been so ill.

"He was in no pain at the end," Fletcher said. "We were all with him, praying. The last words on his lips were about the Light. I sensed the angels coming for him. Peace was everywhere. You should have been there, Joe. I had half a mind to come and get you."

"But Auriel said—"

"Do not listen to Auriel. Our sister is not well. Kate found her trying to cut her wrists in the bathroom. The girls are taking care of her. Auriel sees things through a veil of antimatter. It is the nature of her delusion. But Joe – are *you* feeling well?"

"A bit feverish, I think."

Fletcher felt my head and frowned. "You'd better rest. There is a journey ahead for you and you will need every bit of your strength."

"What journey?"

"Rest now."

It was hard for me not to do what Fletcher said. I got back into bed and tried to think about these two versions of events, but my mind wouldn't stay focused. I really was getting ill. The blankets were irritating me, making me unbearably hot. Then I was cold, and there weren't enough blankets. I fell into a sleep that was more like a stupor. I woke to a pain in my chest. I thought, I'd better not breathe. Because every time I breathed, it hurt.

I don't know how long that stage went on for – a day, two, three? I can't say whether it was glandular fever or just another virus, brought on by the trauma of being attacked. Or maybe I wanted to be ill because, while I was ill, I didn't have to think – and I didn't want to think. There were times when I knew where I was, and other times when I was in a room with the walls closing in on me and squeezing all the air out, or fighting my way out of a shroud. But wherever I was, Fletcher was there, wiping my forehead, taking me to the bathroom, giving me water and other stuff to drink.

I remember Fletcher bringing me some soup and feeding it to me slowly, but it tasted of nothing. I ate it to please him. And then there were people again, imploring the Light to come and heal me. But I didn't want the Light because it was too hot and I was burning up.

Then one day I woke up and felt very, very weak, like a baby. Gingerly I raised my hand to feel my glands and I thought they were enlarged. It hurt me to swallow. It hurt to breathe, but not as badly as before. My legs were heavy. My face was still sore. But for the first time I felt like me, Joe, even though I was in Fletcher's bed. And Fletcher was there beside me.

"The Light has spared you," he said. "It is a sign."

He kissed his fingertips and placed them on my forehead.

"What's been wrong with me?" I asked.

"A struggle between the forces of Darkness and Light – it hardly matters what other name you call it by. Your spiritual crisis was enacted in your body. But you've recovered, Joe, and for that we are all truly thankful."

"Was it glandular fever?"

"It doesn't matter now. All that matters is that you must regain your strength for our journey."

I couldn't ever imagine regaining my strength, I felt so weak. It was good to lie in bed and be taken care of. Fletcher looked after everything.

"I'll bring you the phone later, Joe, so you can ring your parents and tell them you're fine. I want you to try to start eating again, and drinking as much fluid as possible. Then we can start to study in preparation, and all will be as it should. I won't leave you, you can be sure of that."

I didn't want him to leave me. While he was there my life was easy. While he was there I felt as if Nick and Manchester and the illness and Auriel were all a bad dream – it was all antimatter, and my experiences in the past few days only proved everything I had ever believed as a White One.

Outside the room I could hear the sounds of people building or repairing something, and voices, cheerful voices. My bed was a safe, warm haven, and I didn't have to do anything. Fletcher smiled at me, and straightened the sheets.

"There is great news, Joe. The call has come from Carbister. Rendall has requested to meet you. If, as I believe, you are the Perfect he knows is among us, it will be the dawn of a new age. As soon as you're well, we're going up there, you and me. We'll take the Transit and get the ferry. It's an incredible place, Joe."

I'd never seen Fletcher look so happy.

"But I don't think I am a Perfect," I said.

"If you did, then you wouldn't be one. It says so in the Book."

I didn't know what to think any more. Maybe I was a Perfect. Who was I to say? I remembered that moment in Fletcher's room – here – when I was filled with the Light. I remembered the moments of exultation I'd had. Was that a sense, an intimation, of what I really was? Joe Woods could just be dead clay, the mask of a Perfect. As Fletcher said, my journey might only just be beginning. And I didn't mind the idea of going to Orkney. With one proviso.

"Fletch – where's Bea?"

"Let's not speak of her."

"But I want to know. You promised she could come with us to Orkney. You did."

I was aware I sounded like a child, but I wanted Bea.

Fletcher shook his head sorrowfully. "She's let you down, Joe."

"If you mean she went to the loo at McDonald's, that wasn't letting me down. She had to go. And those doubts I had, they came as much from me as from her." I struggled up in bed. "I have to see her, Fletch. I want to make sure she's all right. I won't go to Orkney unless she can come. I mean it." I could feel myself getting feverish again.

"She's left you, Joe," Fletcher said.

"What do you mean, left me? She wouldn't. We were in this together."

"Relax. Lie down in bed again. That's good. I know this won't be easy for you, Joe, but better you should find out from me than from the others. Bea's gone. When we got back from Manchester Kate stayed with her, and the next morning we prayed with her. But she was possessed by the Darkness – it was too late. She used bad language and profaned her purity. She stole from other White Ones. And when she was unattended, she ran away. We went to look for her as we know Bea has no family, no one to run to. And we found her. She was in a pub in Rochdale with a young man. His arm was round her. They were drinking and laughing. She kissed him, Joe. We tried to stop it but the man threatened Will with violence, so he retreated. Accept this – the Bea you loved, Joe, only existed here on the farm when she was filled with the Light. The Light has left her. She's common, no good. She didn't care about you. She led you astray. Grieve for her, Joe. Pray for her. But do not hope."

"No," I said. "I don't believe you."

"Ask Will," he said. "Ask Kate. Ask anyone. We should never have let Bea come among us. Not all who are attracted to the Light are worthy of its radiance."

"You're wrong!"

"You're getting feverish again, Joe. It was a risk I had to take. The love of a woman is a vastly inferior thing – it says so in the Book. You will forget her. The Light will come with healing in its wings. She is not worthy of you, Joe. You're better off without her."

The way Fletcher was talking now really brought home to me what had happened. *She isn't worthy of you. You're better off without her.* It was the way my mum talked when Tash dumped me. It's what people said when they thought you were a loser. The reality hit me then. Bea had left me. On one level I couldn't accept it, but then, girls dumped me, that seemed to be the pattern. Even Bea.

I can't began to describe the rush of emotions I had. I felt humiliated, bereft, bereaved. And angry, betrayed and puzzled. I couldn't take in that just a moment ago, in my mind, we were still one. Now she'd ripped us apart. My rage fought with disbelief. I was sorry for myself, but also, weirdly, sorry for her. I hated her but I still loved her. I tried to harden myself and make myself determined never to let something like this happen again. But most of all, I wanted to see her just one more time, her lovely face, that look she always had for me. I began to cry. Sobs shook me. Fletch was by me in an instant, his arm around my shoulders.

"I know," he said. "It's tough." There was no reproach in his voice, nothing but compassion. He let me cry it out.

"I felt like you once myself," Fletcher said. "I lost someone I loved. The consequences were far-reaching. But I don't complain as it brought me here, and brought me to you, where my duty and allegiance lie. Bea was a necessary stage in your journey. I think we'll start out for Orkney as soon as possible. There's nothing to delay us. Will can be trusted in my stead. And when we return, it will be in glory."

I said nothing. I didn't care any more. Without Bea, Fletcher could do what he liked with me. Without Bea, there was little point in anything. I may as well go to Orkney as stay here — better go to Orkney, as every inch of this farm would remind me of her, places where we talked, places where we kissed, where we prayed. I needed to get away. It would be my convalescence. When I spoke to my parents, I wouldn't mention Bea. I would tell them I was going to Orkney, for a course, or something. I needed the space.

Fletcher could tell from my silence that I wasn't going to put up a fight.

"I'll put a call through to Carbister now," he said. "I'll tell them to expect us the day after tomorrow. You'll be well enough for the journey – I'll make you up a bed in the back of the Transit. Think about the future, Joe, your future. Leave the past behind. The past is dead."

He said *dead*, and I thought of Nick, I thought of Bea's love for me, and wondered why the path of the Light seemed to lead to death, but my head couldn't handle it. I lay back in bed, completely and utterly exhausted.

PART THREE

THE REVELATION

16.
Bea's Story

They took Joe away from me. Fletcher carried him in his arms upstairs to his room. I begged to go too but they said no.

Kate took me instead to her room and made me tell everything that had happened. At first I wasn't going to tell her about the conversation we had, for Joe's sake. But she was pushing and prodding and probing and I was so tired – it must have been five o'clock in the morning, or six, or seven – there wasn't a clock in the room. Then in the end I thought she needed to know the truth, because we all needed to – our faith is worthless unless we're free to come and go, unless it works for our good. So I told her everything, how Joe and I began to question everything, how we were going to visit his parents, and that we still wanted to. When Joe was better, I told her, we were going to go. And I begged her, take me to see Joe, I want to know how he is.

But she wouldn't. She said, not until after the Morning Service. So we had the Morning Service and it didn't work for me any more; it didn't, and I was frightened. I thought why was Fletcher so quick to rescue us? Had he been following us? Or just following Joe? All the time I pretended to the others that I was praying. I thought it was safer to pretend.

Then Kate took me into the Reading Room, the room where Joe and I first kissed, after my initiation. She locked the door and then she said I had to give him up. That we poisoned each other. That I had to abjure all contact with men. I had a weakness, it was a weakness of the flesh. I told her she didn't understand – I loved Joe, and it was normal to love someone and want to be close to them – she was the mad one. I got angry, hysterical. That made her shout for the other girls and they all came, and she said, "Bea isn't well. We must pray together." Kate put the blindfold on me and I struggled, but they held me down. They tied me to a chair and encircled me, and began the prayers for exorcising antimatter.

I was scared, really scared. It was the way they were surrounding me. It was also the way they all believed what they were saying. I thought they would be capable of anything because they were all so caught up in it. I tried to work out what to do. I couldn't run. But, if I sat still and listened, I thought I might start believing in it all again. I had to keep my mind intact. I had to fight.

So I started talking to them. I said, I want out. I'm fed up with your bloody religion. Let me go. Just let me go. I swore at them – I must have sounded mad. But I wouldn't cave in. They prayed louder and louder until they were shouting. So I stopped in the end and tried to think of something else I could do. Eventually they came to an end and Kate said again, "Our sister is not well. She needs confinement." They dragged me to a room somewhere, and locked me in.

I took off my blindfold and saw I was in a store cupboard, with mops, brooms and buckets. I took a mop and tried to break the door down with the handle. I felt like a wild animal – it must have been my survival instinct filling me with rage. I wanted Joe and I was so angry they were keeping him from me.

I was hungry. They wouldn't even let me go to the toilet. More and more I could see they were all demented. But I wasn't really thinking then, I was just desperate to get out. In the end I ran out of energy and fell into a kind of half-sleep, sitting up, my back against the door.

Then the next thing I knew was that someone was opening the door. Auriel. She said, "Quickly, Bea, go! They're all upstairs with Nick. Go now – here's some money." She stuffed some notes in my hand. I asked her where Joe was and she said that he was safe, that she would look after him. She said, "Go! You can help him more if you go."

That decided me. I left there and then.

I had to walk down to the main road to get a bus. No one would give me a lift – I must have looked a mess. I didn't know where to go. I checked to see how much money Auriel had given me – there was eighty pounds. I didn't know there was so much money on the farm. I thought about going to Joe's parents but I realised I didn't know where they lived – I knew he lived in Whitefield, but not his address, not his home phone number. Anyway, would they want me? Looking like this? Would they blame me for what happened to him?

Then I thought of my old piano teacher, Mrs Blake. She was a friend of my mum's. She would know what to do. Eventually I managed to hail a taxi, and had to show the money upfront to prove I could pay. The driver didn't like the look of me. I sat back on the leather seats, feeling so disorientated, and thought, am I doing the right thing? Should I have left the farm? Should I have left Joe?

But it was too late. The cab arrived at Mrs Blake's house. I paid the driver, ran up the garden path, and rang her door bell. And rang and rang.

The person who eventually answered the door wasn't Mrs Blake, but an old lady, still in a dressing gown, who turned out to be Mrs Blake's mother. She apologised for being hard of hearing. I asked for Mrs Blake, but she was out, teaching. I felt sick hearing that, nausea swept through me and it reached my head in a kind of fug.

I knew I was going to faint just before I did.

17.

Early the next morning we left for Orkney. I was able to walk by myself to the Transit, although my legs were shaky, like an old man's. The day was overcast and the sky was a white blanket of cloud. Fletcher had made it cosy for me in the back of the van – there were a couple of mattresses, some cushions and sleeping bags. He'd packed the small amount of belongings we had in an old, battered brown suitcase. He said I could either lie down in the back or travel with him in the front. I chose the passenger seat – I wanted to watch the farm recede and see the road in front of us.

Once we'd left Hebden Bridge it occurred to me I hadn't been away from the area for months. It was refreshing to see new things, new places. Fletcher didn't say much, but later played a tape we'd all made of prayers, chants and songs. It was good to listen to. It insulated us against the world, Fletcher said. He didn't notice when the recording of *They have all gone into the world of Light* began. But I did. I could hear Bea's voice. It hurt me so badly to hear it, so pure, so clear, knowing what I know now. Fletcher hinted there were more things about her, things it would pain me to hear. How could I have been taken in like that? In the end, it was too much for me, listening to her. I told Fletcher I was tired and wanted a sleep. We stopped at a lay-by and I got into the back of the van. The wind was cold and damp and there was a flurry of rain.

I lay on the mattress and put the sleeping bag over me. The trouble is, I thought, you can't learn to unlove someone. You can't turn off a switch and forget about them. So I kept trying to think of what could have gone on in Bea's head to make her forget about me, or maybe that there was another explanation for what happened. I made up stories about how we would meet again. Sometimes she explained everything and we got back together. Other times she wanted me back and I told her no way, not after leaving me like that. Eventually the van rocked me to sleep.

We drove and drove. In the early evening Fletcher pulled into a twenty-four-hour lorry park because he said he needed to sleep. He bought us both some food from the café and I fell on it hungrily. Then Fletch bedded down on one of the mattresses at the back and was asleep in almost an instant. I noticed he'd forgotten to pray. I couldn't sleep, and spent time thinking. I thought about what lay ahead of us, and how I knew I wasn't really a Perfect, but that I wanted to get away and Orkney suited me well enough. I remembered Fletcher had promised I could ring my parents, but he never brought the phone. I thought about Bea – it was like probing an open wound. And I recalled, bit by bit, the things we'd said to each other that night in Manchester, and how I'd wanted out. All that seemed very distant now. I watched Fletcher sleep. There were frown lines between his eyes and occasionally he twitched, like a corpse receiving an electric shock. Later he muttered something, and I thought I heard my name. But it could have been my imagination. Eventually I slept too.

We started on the road before dawn. Fletcher said the ferry left around midday and we still had a fair way to go. We drove through the wild and remote Scottish countryside, through swathes of bleak, windswept hills, mountains – it was all a blur to me. Arriving at Scrabster was a relief. There were other cars, families, and ferry workers going about their jobs. The air of normality was reassuring.

Fletcher dealt with the tickets and I saw we were queuing to drive on to the car deck. As stupid as this sounds, I was excited. I've always liked travelling, especially on planes and boats. It was also good to be out, back in the world. I was feeling better, cheering up. And then a thought about Bea would hit me and the world would lose all its colour.

Once the van was safely stowed we went on deck to watch us pull away from the coast. Quite a few people were on deck, wrapped up warmly against the biting wind. The coast of Scotland receded, its hills fading to soft curves, then just a thick line on the horizon. In front of us was the open sea. There was a tang of salt in the air and a cold wind that penetrated our clothing. The wind blew the clouds around above us. The oily, woody smell of the boat reminded me of other holidays. I told Fletcher I was hungry, and he said he'd get something from the café below. I took a seat on a bench and stared out to sea, lulled by the gentle motion of the boat.

Once again, things were making sense. My journey to Perfection was taking this shape, a voyage across the sea. I was sure and certain that this was precisely where I was meant to be. Then, just as the sun disappeared behind a heavy cloud, my confidence vanished. I realised if the other people on the boat knew why I was there, they would be astonished. They would think that Fletch and I were mad. Just like I did when nearly a year ago I went to Lower

Fold for the first time and saw them all in the Evening Service. A bunch of nutters, I thought. Harmless, but nutters.

But then I got intrigued with them and somehow they knew how to draw me in. At first it had been like a game, but soon every step I took was in earnest. I couldn't even remember when it was I began to think like them and use their language. And so it was I had left Mum and Dad and Gemma, given up my place at uni, lived the life of a labourer, fallen in love, got let down, all for... For what exactly? To achieve Perfection. What Perfection?

Some gulls wheeled above me. The wind messed around with my hair. What if I'd made a terrible, terrible mistake? What if the White Ones were living a lie, or they had all deluded themselves as I had deluded myself? No – I wouldn't go there. Not yet. I was still weak, physically and emotionally. I needed to look after myself, take it easy. Treat this trip as a break, a chance to recuperate. And then I would think what to do with my life. Later. When I'd had a rest. I noticed the sea was getting choppy, so I focused on a stack of rock that was coming into view.

Fletcher arrived then with some cheese and tomato sandwiches and some Cokes. We ate our lunch in silence. Then Fletcher spoke.

"You know, Joe, the other candidates have failed."

"What candidates? What do you mean, failed?"

"Other cells have sent potential Perfects to Carbister to meet Rendall. They have all failed the test. A lot is riding on you, Joe."

"Don't talk like that."

"I'm sorry. I understand how you might be feeling. But promise me one thing, Joe. Should it be you who is Perfect, grant me the chance to serve you."

He was talking like a bad movie. I wished he'd stop it.

"Yeah, whatever," I said.

Then he took my hand and held it for a few moments. And I thought, fuck this! What if the other people see him do that? What the heck will they think about us? I wriggled my hand out of his but he didn't seem to notice. The rock stack was straight ahead now. I could see birds nesting in the crevices. And dots of bird shit everywhere. I tried to remember how rock stacks were formed but it had all gone from my head. I thought, had I been brainwashed? No – I'd brainwashed myself. Or had I? The doubts were coming back even though I'd decided not to have them. I didn't like this. I was beginning to feel a little seasick too. I mentioned that to Fletch, and he said it was better to stay on deck and look out to sea. I told myself to ignore the cold.

After what seemed like an eternity, the coast of Orkney came into view. Soon I could see a higgledy-piggledy collection of houses and boats, the houses looking like they were scrambling up the hill to get away from the water. It wasn't like English harbours where the houses face the sea, looking out at it with a sense of ownership. Stromness was different, chaotic, a jumble. I watched us dock and then went with Fletcher to reclaim the van.

"Do you know how to get there?" I asked him.

He nodded, and I got the impression he didn't want to talk, which was fine by me. We got out of Stromness fairly quickly – it was only a small place – and I tried to keep an eye on where we were going. Most of the signs seemed to lead to Kirkwall, and there were loads of those tourist signs pointing to various monuments. I remembered one – the Ring of Brodgar – it kind of struck me. I guessed it would be something like Stonehenge. But mainly my impression was of gently rounding grey hills and a sky which was so pale it seemed to run out of colour at the horizon's edge. Farms and cottages were dotted about here and there but there weren't towns or villages as such. It wasn't that different from the English countryside, except there were no trees. None whatsoever. But instead I noticed jagged fingers of stone pointing to the sky, just one in a field from time to time. I guessed these were standing stones. Relics of a past religion. People must have lived here for thousands of years – why? It was so remote, so empty and ghost-like. Orkney seemed like the end of the world to me.

We didn't go in to Kirkwall. We turned off and headed north up the A966. There was hardly any other traffic. The light was fading. I was getting twitchy. The remoteness of the place was affecting me. Even Lower Fold seemed like the middle of civilisation. The further north we went, the more pointless it seemed. We weren't getting anywhere.

"Are we nearly there yet?" I asked Fletcher, and smiled to myself as I thought of Gemma, who had said that on every car journey I could ever remember sharing with her. "We'll get there when we get there," was my mum's gnomic reply. An acute sense of loss stabbed me. I missed them badly. If I ever returned to them, would they forgive me? I had no right to expect they would. And yet I couldn't ever imagine them cutting me off.

"Not far now," Fletcher said.

I also became aware that we were coming towards the sea again. On Orkney the sense of being on an island was very strong. The sky and the sea spilled into each other. The road climbed a bit, then descended, and there was the sea again, closer than ever, silently watching us. Then I saw a large, white, L-shaped bungalow surrounded by Portakabins, smaller cottages and various vehicles. There was a sign saying Carbister. For some inexplicable reason, I was jolted by fear. Perhaps I'd been on the road too long. Fletcher pulled up in front of the drive – metal panels protruded and prevented us from getting any closer. He pressed a button on the wall, quoted a line from the Book, and identified us. The metal panels receded into the ground, and we drove in.

While we were getting our stuff out of the back of the van, a guy came to meet us. He looked my dad's age, but unlike my dad he had his hair in a ponytail. He was English but wearing one of those white dresses over white trousers that I'd seen Asian guys in. He'd tied a white rope round his stomach. He embraced Fletcher, and then embraced me. I wondered if this was Rendall.

"This is Jacob," Fletcher told me.

A moment of anti-climax.

Jacob took a long look at me, nodded and smiled. I heard seagulls guffaw overhead. He led us towards one of the Portakabins, talking as he went.

"Welcome to Carbister. You've got here in time for the Evening Service. You'll find it different here, Joe. Carbister is, if you like, the centre of operations, the hub of everything. It's our Rome, it's our Jerusalem, as it was before the Destruction of the Temple. We're close to where the Light first revealed itself."

"May the Light be praised," said Fletcher.

"May the Light be praised," responded Jacob.

They seemed to want to compete in piety.

Already the sun was setting – you could see the sea from where we were. There was certainly something impressive about Carbister – its location, the sheer fact that our faith had built a stronghold out here, the spread of the buildings. It excited me to think Rendall was near. Hardly anyone at Lower Fold had met him. It was crazy, but I felt as I did when me and my mates went to the Manchester Evening News Arena to see Oasis for the first time. Awestruck, electrified. I gave in to the feeling happily.

We got to the steps of the Portakabin.

"You have fifteen minutes or so to unpack," Jacob said. "The Evening Service is earlier up here, naturally. Rendall has requested an audience with you, Joe, after the Service."

I could feel my chest tightening with excitement. Fletch unlocked the Portakabin and entered. I followed.

At one end there was a cubicle with a door that stopped nine inches or so before the floor. A toilet, presumably. Next to it was a steel washbasin. On each side of the Portakabin was a bed. There was a white table to our left. On the right was an old-fashioned coatstand looking embarrassingly out of place. There looked to be about four feet or so between the beds. This was where Fletcher and I would be sleeping. Just me and him. I didn't really like that but I guessed I had no choice.

"How do you feel, Joe?" he asked me, his voice gentle, fatherly, almost.

"OK," I said.

He smiled at me affectionately. I turned, quickly, and lifted the rucksack on my bed to find my stuff. "You'll like it here," Fletcher continued. "This is how it ought to be. When I first found the

White Ones this was where they brought me. I would have stayed, but there was a job for me to do. Which I have done. But who was to know that mine was to be the greatest honour of all?" Then he fell on his knees and began to intone a prayer.

I didn't know what to do, then. By rights I have should have joined him, but his prayer seemed highly personal. So I just took things out of the rucksack and reflected how little I knew about Fletcher, and yet how well I knew him. It was a paradox. I was completely familiar with the sound of his voice, his interpretation of our literature, his mannerisms, but I knew nothing of his past. I knew also that he cared for me, but I couldn't begin to work out why. There was nothing special about me, yet Fletcher genuinely believed I might be a Perfect. It would probably help him to discover I was just a normal human being. Maybe Fletcher needed a dose of sanity too.

18.

Bea's Story

I woke up in the hospital. I had to tell the nurses who I was and why I'd ended up on Mrs Blake's front door. They said I was undernourished and dehydrated and they were going to do blood tests. They were careful not to be too nosy about me which I was glad about, because I knew they'd never begin to understand what I'd been through. They kept me in for observation for twenty-four hours.

Mrs Blake came to visit me. I told her a little about the White Ones and she looked very serious. She said I'd done the right thing to run away and also that when I came out of hospital I could stay with her for a while. I was glad, but also I felt as if I was being an imposition. I said that, and she said, of course not – your mother would have been glad you came to me. Which made me cry. It was good to cry. I cried because I wanted my mother, because I'd been so stupid, because I felt guilty for running away, and I cried for Joe. I told Mrs Blake – she said to call her Beverley – about Joe. She looked serious about that too. She said we would think of how to help him. That calmed me down.

When I got out of hospital they wanted me to get some counselling but I didn't want it yet. I just wanted Joe. Only I wouldn't go back to Lower Fold and I didn't want anyone else to go up there on my behalf. Doing that would make me feel as if I was betraying them, or as if I was about to destroy everything they'd built up, like an antimatter missile. And they loved me, they thought they knew what was best for me. I knew I shouldn't act from revenge. Away from them, I found my feelings soften. Because you can't just start not loving people – you can't just flick a switch.

But Beverley said we ought to try to contact Joe's parents and tell them about the mugging. I agreed, but had to explain I didn't have their address or phone number. She made me dredge up everything Joe had ever told me. When I mentioned his sister was called Gemma, Beverley looked pleased. She said that on Monday we could ring round the local schools until we found a Gemma Woods, and then it would be easy to check details and trace Joe.

I was happy with that. She said I needed the weekend to rest and recuperate. I did. I slept for fourteen hours at a stretch. Beverley cooked me delicious meals, with meat, but it was hard for me to manage much. Her mother, May, kept bringing me cups of tea, even when I didn't want them. I felt grateful but very guilty. I hated myself for being so foolish, and only the thought that Joe had been taken in too kept my self-respect intact. But at other times I saw myself through the eyes of my fellow White Ones, and knew I was a traitor, knew I was weak and unworthy.

On Sunday afternoon Beverley played some Mahler. The beauty of it made me cry, and later on I went to the piano but my fingers were clumsy and wooden. The notes sounded all wrong.

By midday Monday morning Beverley had a result. She'd tracked down Gemma and was on her way to visit the school to explain face to face what the situation was, and why she needed Gemma's address. All my energy came back in a rush. More than anything I wanted to meet and speak to Mr and Mrs Woods – it was a way of getting close to Joe.

So that evening we drove to Joe's house, and when his mum opened the door to us, she just said, "Bea!" as if she'd known me for ages, and she hugged me.

I started crying again.

19

We went to a building they called the Croft for the Evening Service. It was freezing and the cold penetrated to my bones. I hugged myself to try to keep warm. Fletcher pushed open the door and we entered.

It wasn't like our Gathering Place. Inside it was more like a church. At one end of the room was a table with a white cloth over it and loads of candlesticks with candles waiting to be lit. Behind, on the wall, someone had painted a large, golden sun, with rays coming out like in a kids' book. Above the sun were shapes that I recognised as runes. There were rows of chairs facing the sun and the table, and there looked to be about a dozen blokes assembled. They were all silent. Fletcher and I took our seats in the middle. I noticed Jacob in the front row. The walls of the Croft were painted white over bare brick. On my left were some shelves containing literature. On my right was a board with names painted on it in gilt lettering. *Matthew Chalmers, Trevor Norrington-Smith* – they were at the top – *Keiran McDermott* was another I remembered, and there were two that looked bright and new at the bottom – *Anil Khatri, Simon McConnell*. Fletcher saw I was reading the board.

"Nick's name will be inscribed there, too," he said.

So it was a memorial board, for White Ones who had been Elevated. For a moment I felt awe and respect, but then memories of Auriel's account of Nick's death took over. If she had been telling me the truth – but Auriel was hardly the most reliable witness. I shut my thoughts off.

At that moment, two guys dressed like Jacob entered from a

side door by the table, carrying a silver basin and silver jug. They took it to the table and poured the water from the jug into the basin. Presumably this was for recounting our sins. There was total silence. I could hear Fletcher breathing beside me. I swallowed nervously.

The side door opened again, and one man emerged. His bearing was erect, his hair was grey and reached to his shoulders. When he turned to face the gathering I knew immediately this was Rendall. He had a presence that seemed to draw us all in, and all together. He *was* special, I knew it for certain. My eyes drunk him in greedily. I wasn't interested in the externals – his purple vestment like an archbishop's, the purple skullcap he was wearing – but in his face. Despite some wrinkles and a somewhat weathered look, he was handsome. There was confidence in his manner of looking at us. He reminded me of a poet who once visited us at school, a bloke who looked like an eccentric but seemed a lot more certain of who he was than we were. And examining Rendall now, I could see it was his eyes that did it. Their expression was intense, magnetic, even. You felt that if he was to look at you, your life would change. Or that he would know everything about you in an instant. They were deep set but they seemed to glitter.

I said it was his eyes that set him apart, but that wasn't all. When he began to read, his voice was compelling. It was low, a bit posh, like an old-fashioned newsreader, but set at a pitch that vibrated through you, rich, resonant. As he read, he seemed to weigh each word, allowing it due space and consideration. As he spoke aloud the words of his Book, I wondered how I could have ever doubted them. Once more I felt connected to the Light.

That was a relief. To be honest, in the past couple of months at the farm I had rarely focused on Services in the way I used to. I was either too tired or obsessed by something else. Now I felt reborn. I let Rendall's voice enfold me until the words seemed irrelevant. I was safe.

I decided to stay in my seat when it was time to cleanse us of our sins. I thought it would be drawing attention to myself if I made a public confession, and although there would be a time when I would have to admit my treasonable thoughts with Bea, I didn't want to do so yet. Instead I watched other White Ones come out. I noted with interest that they were all male and, on average, slightly older than at Lower Fold. That gave a different flavour to the Service. I felt I was where the power was. Then I could hear Bea's voice teasing me, saying "Sexist!" – I cut it off.

The Service was coming to an end. I looked straight ahead at the back of the man in front of me. When we'd sung the concluding hymn he turned to shake my hand, and Fletcher's. He seemed about Fletcher's age, a stocky guy with a thickset neck. I could tell by the way he spoke to Fletcher that they knew each other. The introductions were made.

"Laban, this is Joe. Joe – Laban."

I noticed the way Laban's shrewd glance moved from Fletcher to me and me to Fletcher. Then it settled on me. I could sense him weighing me up. He made me feel uncomfortable.

"May it be your lot," he said to me.

Perhaps it was the way he didn't finish off the greeting that made me not like him. I don't know. Or maybe it was the smile he gave me which looked almost manufactured. I just didn't take to him.

"So this is your Potential?" he asked Fletcher, referring to me.

Fletch nodded curtly. I could swear I saw Laban raise his eyebrows ever so slightly. But maybe he didn't.

"All will be revealed," Laban said.

Jacob approached us then.

"Rendall requests your presence," he said.

"I am honoured," Fletcher replied, flushing.

"No – just Joe," Jacob said.

"OK. Right," Fletch mumbled, and I felt sorry for him. It was an embarrassing mistake to make. Jacob led me out of the Croft and into what seemed like the main building, a sprawling bungalow. Neither of us spoke. I remember the excitement I felt. I was living entirely in the moment. I was tense with expectation.

Jacob rapped on a closed door, and I heard Rendall's voice saying, "Enter!"

Jacob opened the door and stood by it.

"Thank you," I said, and walked into Rendall's room.

Jacob shut the door and departed.

I say Rendall's room. It was more like a study. It had one whole wall of books, a number of which I recognised, Commentaries, editions of the Book. There was a roaring fire, and two old-fashioned easy chairs by it. I noticed a desk full of papers, and a mahogany cabinet. I saw a red velvet chaise longue, too, with embroidered cushions, and everywhere a strange, cloying, fragrant smell. I traced it to a pipe which had gone out. Someone – Rendall? – had obviously been smoking scented tobacco. I also remember an old-style record turntable with a stack of long-playing vinyl records next to it.

At the time I wasn't aware of taking all this in, only afterwards. Because the truth was, I was mesmerised by being so close to Rendall, Colin Rendall, our Father and Guiding Light.

"Sit down, Joseph," he said to me.

I didn't bother to correct him. Joe was my real name, as on my birth certificate. No one had ever called me Joseph.

"Joseph," he said. "The youngest of Jacob's sons. The most loved. The redeemer of his Brothers."

His looked me in the eyes and smiled. I smiled back nervously and nodded. I thought it was best that he kept the conversation going, rather than me.

"There are those who would argue that Joseph was a precursor of the Christ figure in his purity – he denied Potiphar's wife, and his incarceration, if you like, was a kind of death and resurrection. You see, Joseph, there are recurrent themes in all religions, basic truths which reassert themselves. There must be death before life. Three days Christ was in the tomb, and then he rose. Ancient civilisations used to throw their gods in the water. They drowned so that they should live. Those were pearls that were his eyes – T. S. Eliot!"

The breadth of his knowledge impressed me. He was coming over like a headmaster, or how I imagined a university professor to be. He was quality.

"And so, Joseph, Terry Fletcher believes you are a Perfect."

So Fletcher's first name was Terry! I never knew that. The revelation distracted me.

"How do you feel about that? About the prospect of Perfection?"

"I can't say I... I have no knowledge... It's not up to me." I sounded like an imbecile. But Rendall didn't seem to mind.

"The flower has no sense of its being a flower; the bird aloft even in the very act of flying knows nothing of its bird-ness. Thus it is with Perfects. It is for us to divine your true state."

"How will you do that, sir?"

Damn! The sir just slipped out. I hated myself for that. I was messing up big time.

"Later, Joseph, later. But first I want to get to know you. I want you to tell me about yourself. Excuse me." He got up and went to the mahogany cabinet, which he opened to reveal a whisky decanter. He poured a generous glass for himself.

"I can see your surprise, Joseph. But there is a stage of purity when it is acceptable to take back into your life those substances which you have had to abjure at an earlier stage of your journey. Now the whisky means nothing to me. I am as a eunuch with a damsel." He took a mouthful of whisky, savoured it and swallowed. "You have been among the White Ones for...?"

"For nine months," I said.

"Ha! The period of gestation. Nothing is accidental. When I established Carbister, I commanded that there should always be thirty-three. A company of thirty-three. I myself was twenty-one when I had my Vision. Even now, the refulgence irradiates my vision. Unlike other men of my age, I have never needed glasses. My eyes, you see, achieved Perfection. In witnessing what they did, they were beatified."

I looked at his eyes. Only they didn't seem to have that magnetism I'd seen earlier in the Service. Maybe it was the whisky, but his eyes looked watery, there was a yellow discolouration at the corners. As he spoke, I noticed flecks of spit at the side of his mouth.

"And after the Vision, my life was changed. I went back to Cambridge but conventional study had lost its appeal. But there were those, few at first, who recognised the immensity of what I had been through. I committed my Vision to paper, and shared it with my followers. Soon there were six of us who could testify to the power of the Light. Those were the days of ongoing revelation. We began alternate sense deprivation and the confession of transgressions. When we went down from Cambridge we set up the first cell near Mablethorpe, in Lincolnshire. I had inherited money, Joseph, on the occasion of the Elevation of my parents. But my desire was to return to Orkney, the birthplace of the Light. It is no coincidence, Joseph, that this island has Stone-Age settlements – here is where things begin, and where they will end. The stone circles represent the eternal cycles of birth and death, birth and death, and the standing stones the male principle. We have no women here, Joseph. At least, only as visitors."

I thought, Rendall had begun by asking me about myself, but in fact he'd been talking about himself. I was flattered he'd told me this much, and relieved I didn't have to give up all the details of my life to him. But still, I felt let down.

"If you prove to be the Perfect Fletcher believes you are – and Fletcher is a good man, a sound man – you will stay here with me. We cannot let you go back to Lower Fold."

I hadn't been expecting that. I'd just assumed we'd go back home. I didn't know how I felt about staying in Carbister. I shifted uneasily in my chair. Rendall didn't seem to notice.

"Because, you see, Joseph, I am no longer young. Like Moses, who was not allowed to lead the Children of Israel into the Promised Land, it will not be my lot to see the Kingdom of Light established here on earth. I have to find a successor. Who better than a Perfect? You will live here by my side and receive my teachings. In the fullness of time, when I am Elevated and rejoin the angels, you will rule in my stead. If, as I said, you are who we hope."

"And if I'm not?"

"Then you are not." He sipped contemplatively at his whisky. "Let us pray."

Without leaving his seat he began his Evening Prayer. I joined in with him, my voice and Rendall's voice together. I wish Bea could have heard me. Bea. It was the first time I had thought about her since entering Rendall's room. It still cut through me to think what she had done. What Fletcher told me she had done. But it was only Bea with whom I could have shared my impressions of Rendall. I would have said, he's amazing, brilliant, but he drinks whisky! And he's like... he's like... a real person.

And that was what worried me about him. He was a person. Until I'd met him, I thought of him like Christ or something. And he certainly did have a presence, for sure. But basically he was just a man, getting on a bit. And seeing him sitting in front of me it was actually *harder* to believe everything he said. Because he was *real*, and because of the way he'd been talking to me – it was pompous, he was a bit of a poseur. He was glib, he used his gift of language to make everything suit him. I could see why people followed him, but I... I tried to stop my thoughts. The prayer came to an end.

"Tomorrow night, Joseph, your trial will begin."

"My trial?"

"You see, since you have no intimation of your own Perfecthood, we must ask the Light to reveal you to us. We cannot do this by a written or spoken examination, or by feats of physical endurance. We must find—"

"What do you mean, a trial?"

"Like Jesus Christ, like the Gods of old, you must show us your ability to drown and return, to walk through the fire, to survive the Darkness."

I was panicking now – my whole body was shaking.

"What do you mean?"

"Do not be unduly perturbed. Fletcher informs me your ASD experiences have been positive, and at all times someone will be with you. Twenty-five hours of full sensory deprivation is considerably shorter than the three days between crucifixion and resurrection. Twenty-five hours is, in fact, the length of the Jewish Day of Atonement. And at the end of the day, when you re-emerge, we shall know you."

"What if I can't do it?"

Rendall must have heard the hysteria in my voice.

"Someone will be with you at all times," he said.

Full SD. No way. Auriel told me what happened to Nick. He died. The SD killed him. Fucking hell. I wanted out. But I couldn't run – I mean, there was nowhere to run to.

"I don't feel too good," I said. The truth was, I was wetting myself.

"Your modesty becomes you," Rendall commented. He rang a brass bell by his side. Jacob knocked and entered.

"Joseph and I have completed our business," he said. "You may return him." Rendall rose, kissed his fingertips, and pressed them to my forehead. And as he did that, I thought, he's a sham, the religion is nuts, and I've got to run. But where? I had nothing, no money, no maps. Fletcher was my only hope. When he heard what they were planning to do, he'd stop them. Full SD. No way.

20.

Bea's Story

I tried to find Joe's face in his parents' faces. Maybe he had his dad's chin and nose, and his mother's eyes. Or maybe I just wanted them to look like him. But Gemma – she looked like Joe. She was very quiet, nothing like Joe had described her, all mouthy and aggressive. She seemed to tiptoe round me and kept asking me if I wanted a drink.

Beverley was the one who explained the sequence of events, and I was grateful to her. I just nodded and said, yes, at various points. As she spoke, I could see Joe's mum's eyes dart about anxiously, I saw the looks she gave Joe's dad, and the way Joe's dad made fists of his hand until his knuckles were white. As Beverley repeated what I'd told her of the White Ones, Joe's dad muttered, "I knew it, I knew it was a cult, we should have gone and taken him away by force."

I interrupted. "He wouldn't have gone. Not then. Don't blame yourself."

Joe's mum looked at me gratefully. "He told me a lot about you, Bea. I'm glad you came here." Her voice was kind. I was so relieved to discover she didn't blame me either.

"We were ready to come here last Wednesday night," I said, and told her about our time in Manchester. Joe's parents listened hard. I explained how he was mugged and we were taken back by Fletcher to the farm. I told them only very briefly how I got away because I knew it was Joe they were interested in.

"So you don't know how he is?" Joe's mum asked.

"I think he was being looked after. Fletcher would never let any harm come to him. He's very fond of Joe." And as I said that, partly to reassure Joe's parents, it occurred to me that Fletcher really was very fond of Joe, and I began to ask myself, how fond? I'd certainly thought he was jealous of me sometimes.

"This time," Joe's dad said, "we're going to get him. I don't care what he says or what this Fletcher says. I'm taking the police if necessary."

"No," I interrupted. "You won't have to. I know Joe will want to go with you. We were heading here on Wednesday night. He was missing you very badly."

"Was he missing me?" Gemma said.

"A lot."

There was a pause in the conversation. I looked at Joe's family and I'd never seen people look so scared and bereft, so shrivelled. I realised then the price we White Ones paid for our selfishness. With me, it was different, having no family. Still, I thought, no religion should ask you to do what we all did – leave the people who loved us. That was the moment that turned me. After that, I never looked back. I knew that Joe and I had a made a dreadful error. I would do everything I could to rescue him and help his parents. Joe's dad looked at his watch.

"Is it too late to go up there now?"

"We— they go to bed early," I explained.

"So I'll wake them up," he said. Just then, when his face was fierce with determination, I saw a reflection of Joe. Joe, digging hard soil in the allotments, or unravelling a difficult passage in the Book.

He left. Beverley and I decided to wait. Gemma then became quite chatty, and offered to show me Joe's room. They'd left it as it was when he went. His clothes were hanging in the wardrobe, his music system in the corner, his posters – I felt as if I was only just getting to know him. Gemma and I sat on his bed.

"Were you, like, actually his girlfriend?" she asked me.

"Yes," I said, and felt pleased.

She gave me an appraising look. "I can see why he fancied you. Look, when all this is over you must let me do your hair. I could make it look really wicked. I'm good with hair."

"OK," I said. Gemma lifted my hair and looked at it. It was a tender gesture, it was Joe's sister doing it and it made me happy.

It was two or three hours later when we heard Joe's dad's car return and come to a halt in the drive. We all ran to the hall and opened the door. He was alone.

"There was no bloody answer," he said. "I knocked hard enough to wake the dead. I walked round, looked in all the windows, but it was pitch black. I knocked on every door I found. Either no one was there or they didn't want to answer. There was nothing I could do, short of breaking in. But I'm going there tomorrow, with the police, and we're going to get him."

"I'm sure if you explain to them you think your son's in danger..." said Beverley.

"Can I come?" I asked.

Joe's dad looked at me and thought.

"Yes," he said. "You could be very useful."

21

The light was still on in the Portakabin. Jacob left me at the steps and I pushed the door open. I was counting on Fletcher to get me out of this mess.

He was there, but he wasn't alone. Laban was with him. They were facing each other on the two beds, and each was holding a bottle of spirits and drinking from it. The sight made no sense. It completely disorientated me. Fletcher lifted his bottle in greeting with a drunken attempt at a smile.

"Joe," he said, his speech slurred.

I was as shocked as if someone had slapped me round the face. Fletcher and alcohol did not go together. The way he sprawled on the bed, the stupid look on his face had no relation to the Fletcher I knew.

"'sOK," he said. "They give you a dispensation here. Laban said 'sOK."

Laban seemed less under the influence than Fletch. He screwed the top back on his bottle. I could hear the thin rasp of the metal on glass through the sound of Fletcher's heavy breathing. Laban's movements were sharp, purposeful. In fact he hardly seemed drunk at all. I noticed that *his* bottle was still almost full.

"Maybe I shouldn't have brought the whisky round, but it's something of a Carbister tradition. We do things differently here. I'd forgotten Fletcher's history, Joe. But now you're here you can look after him. I daresay he'll be a bit rough in the morning."

"Joe," Fletcher repeated brokenly.

"I'm going now," Laban said. "But if you need to speak to me,

Joe, and I think you do, you'll find me in the morning. I'll be in the Croft. May it be your lot to achieve..." He paused. "Total inebriation?" Laban chuckled to himself and left.

"Joe," Fletcher continued. "I'm not as drunk as you think I am." He pronounced his words with concentrated deliberation.

"Shall I take the bottle?" I asked.

"Soon," he said.

Fletcher tried to sit up on my bed. The features of his face looked blurred and I could see his struggle to regain control. It sickened me to look at him, despite everything he'd done for me. I recognised the tables were turned now. Fletcher was my responsibility. The fact was, the one person I thought would help me was in no state to help himself.

"I'll get you some water," I said, and went to the bathroom, where there were two glasses. I filled one from the tap and returned to find Fletch still drinking from the bottle. He attempted to put it down on the floor but it toppled over and the honey-coloured liquid trickled on to the green carpet tiles. I let it spill.

"Here," I said, offering Fletch the water.

He started crying with big, gulping sobs.

"I've let you down, Joe. I never meant to do this. Please forgive me, forgive me for my sins. I'm not worthy. May the Light and the Perfection and the Light... the Light..."

I'd seen blokes in his state before. I knew he was going to throw up. I screamed at him to get to the bathroom, and he staggered towards it and just got there in time. I put my fingers in my ears so I didn't have to listen to the noise. Eventually he emerged, looking pale and gaunt.

"Joe, listen, I'm sorry. I thought it would be all right now, but..."

He saw the whisky bottle lying on its side. He gave it a ferocious kick and it spun to the door, shattering on collision. Great, I thought. I'll have to clear that up.

"I owe you an explanation," Fletcher said.

"It's OK," I cut in. "I can see what happened. It was Laban's idea. Look, I don't like it here, Fletch. They want me to do full SD to prove I'm a Perfect. I want to go back. Let's make a run for it – tomorrow, when you've sobered up."

"I owe you an explanation, Joe. I want to explain."

Fletch was like a stuck record. He hadn't heard anything I'd said. Even though he was slightly more coherent after he'd thrown up, he still wasn't with it. I thought it best to let him have his way for now, to let him give me his explanation. Then I'd return to my idea of leaving.

"Come here, Joe." He wanted me to sit with him on the bed. I shook my head. The thought of being close to him repelled me.

"Let me explain," he said again. "I don't want to keep anything back. Only you can save me."

I wish he wouldn't talk like that but I was scared to cross him while he was in this state. I decided it was best to let him have his way. I thought all he was going to do was tell me why he decided to drink whisky, so I was quite unprepared for what happened next. He started by trying to pray.

"May the Light... The Light is strong, stronger than antimatter. It can overcome everything. I must trust the Light. I..."

And then it was like someone had catapulted him back in time.

"I used to live in Stoke," he said. "I was a plasterer but I couldn't... I didn't... I used to drink a lot; there'd be days I couldn't get to work on time, so the firm finished with me. I couldn't blame them. It seems a long time ago, like a different world. I didn't live for the Light then. I was messed up, a drunk. I lived on the dole and just went from one binge to another. I had no life, nothing. My friends – they weren't my friends – they were just men I drank with. Bastards, all of them.

"Until Keiran came along. He was a street artist, he had a gang – a graffiti gang. His signature was everywhere those days. I watched him work. He needed somewhere to stay and I had my bedsit. His mother had thrown him out as he was trouble. But he was good for me, Joe. I could stand being sober when I was around him. He painted the walls of my bedsit, he painted the bathroom. It all looked different, everything. He had talent but it wasn't being recognised. I wanted him to go to Art School or something, I said I'd pay for him, support him. I said I'd give up the booze. I was the only person who looked out for him. I put him first, put him before me. You've got to understand that. Keiran McDermott. Keiran."

It spooked me, the way he pronounced his name, like it was a prayer.

"He went out at night, to do his work. Sometimes I went with him. Other times he'd go alone. I didn't know everything that he got up to, but he knew everything about me. When it happened, I hadn't seen him for a bit. He said he'd been visiting his family, making it up to them. But Joe, he was lying to me. Black lies. That night, he said he had some money, he'd take me to the Potter's Arms. They were all there, John, Mike, the others, getting drinks in,

234

lining them up. I was tense, I knew something was going to happen. I have a sixth sense. I drank to blot it out, this sense of doom. When he first said it, I thought I was hearing things.

"Keiran says, I'm moving in with my girlfriend, Terry, I might even get married. You're fucking what? Thinking of getting wed, he says. Tying the knot. I tell him, Keiran, you can't support a wife, not even a tart. You've got no money, I say to him, you're throwing your life away. I've seen it happen time and time and again. He says to me, it's no good, I love her. I tell him, you're too young, you don't know what love is. I know what love is, I told him. It's what I feel for you. It's why I don't want you to waste yourself. She'll eat you alive, Keiran. She won't let you paint – she'll make you go out and get a job. You'll be finished, I said to him. Stay with me. He says, lay off me, Terry, and then he accused me, he accused me, of being one of *them,* one of those perverts. You think I'm a fairy, I say? So can a fairy do this? I punch him hard, a right hook, flatten him. He's out cold. John and Mike pick him up and we get thrown out. Keiran's in the middle, in between John and Mike, they're supporting him.

"Keiran comes round in the cold air. He says, I don't want to see you again, Terry. You're a poof. I'm sick to my stomach, how can he think that? That's filthy, disgusting antimatter. I'm blind with anger that anyone should say it, but most of all that Keiran says it, Keiran who I love. I want to hurt him. I want to make him feel how much I'm hurting.

"I always carried a knife with me, you had to, living in Stoke. I didn't mean to do any more than shock him, make him feel my pain. I meant to cut his arm, only his arm.

"But John loses his balance, Keiran slips, my knife goes in, through his shirt. I can see the blood seeping out steadily, it doesn't spurt out or anything – it's like it's overflowing – it's a relief, to see that blood flowing. Then John and Mike, they start shouting. I know I haven't really hurt him but I decide to run anyway, just to get away, to work out what happened.

"I hid out for a fortnight. I hitched lifts, moved around the country. I was in a lorry cab when I heard the radio and learned that he'd died. I didn't mean that to happen, it wasn't my fault, it was an accident. Antimatter. It was antimatter. Rendall said so. Keiran was the lucky one. *I* was living in hell. Then one day I walked into a police station and gave myself up.

"I ended up inside. That was where I met Laban. He belonged to a charity that visited prisoners. He told me about the Light, I gave up booze and until this day I've never touched a drop. I got parole for good behaviour, but when I got out, Keiran's family vowed to get me. Laban brought me to Carbister where I would be safe. I prayed, I studied and bit by bit it all made sense. Everyone has a destiny. I am the Servant. I am a path to the Light. But drink clouded my judgement and I mistook Kieran. His death was not a mistake. Oh no. He is now one of the band of Angels. He is with the Light. His Light shines on me. He has reached his Perfection, and I was the means to that end. Rendall spoke those words to me. He said it was meant to be. But I mistook Keiran. I mistook him. I mistook him for you. I can see that now."

"I'm not Keiran," I said. "Fletch, listen, I'm just me. Joe. I'm not a Perfect."

He ignored me and continued. "I came to Lower Fold and Laban gave me a job to do. My task is to obey orders, to be the

Servant. I obeyed orders. I owed the White Ones my life, I owed Laban my life. I was glad to do what I was told. I was glad to be able to study. I learned the Light is the Sun, and the Sun is a Circle. We start where we began. I started with Keiran, and I end with you. My destiny is to serve you, Joe. You know everything now. May there never be a secret between us."

He finished talking, slipped off the bed, and got to his knees and embraced my ankles. I saw his head below me, the dandruff in his hair, his scalp beneath it. I saw the throb of an artery by his ear. I was paralysed. I had to defuse the situation, normalise it.

"OK, OK," I said. "Get up. Have some more water. Drink as much as you can. I don't want you to have a hangover in the morning."

Fletcher got up. He finished his water.

"I'm tired," he said.

I told him to sleep and he got into my bed with his clothes on. Soon he was snoring.

When I sat down again I found I was trembling. My thoughts were a jumble. I knew I had to decide what to do next, but fear immobilised me. Everything I had seen and heard that evening jostled in my mind, clamouring for attention. Fletcher had killed a man. He wasn't safe to be around. And in me he thought he had this Keiran all over again. Keiran McDermott. His name was on the memorial board. Along with others, all young men. And who were Anil and Simon?

Rendall. He was mad too. Or just a hypocrite, swilling whisky, creating fictions but pretending they were all true. The White Ones were dangerous and I'd been taken in. I'd brought this on myself.

Fletcher. He killed a man because he loved a woman, like I loved Bea. Then, for the first time, I thought how could I have been so stupid? *I only had Fletcher's word for the fact that Bea had left me*. What if Bea hadn't left me? What if Fletcher had been lying? As everyone else was lying: Rendall, Kate, Auriel – no, not Auriel. All she had told me was true.

Anil Khatri. Simon McConnell. What if they were the other Potentials? What if they hadn't managed the SD? Like Nick. My skin pricked with fear.

So now what do I do? Run? I weighed up my chances. Assuming I could take some things and go, would they be watching me? Almost certainly, yes. If they had been willing to risk my death under SD, they'd be prepared to stop me running, by any methods. If I escaped, they'd know I'd blow the whistle on them. They'd be watching me for sure. I thought of Laban then. He said to meet him in the morning. I didn't like Laban and yet now my instinct told me he was the only one who wasn't entirely brainwashed. I *knew* he didn't believe any of that pack of lies, the Book, the Commentaries – all that rubbish. Laban saw through it, I was sure. He might represent my only chance of getting out of this mess.

I looked at Fletcher again. I didn't understand how I could have trusted him. I didn't understand how I had taught myself to believe half the stuff I did believe. I realised how powerful the human mind was, how it could create reality. I prayed that one day I would have the time to unravel the whole mess and work out how this had happened to me. Now what I had to do was get away. I couldn't afford to allow any weak thoughts in. If the White Ones had taught me anything, it was how to endure – a lesson that would come in useful now.

But the pain deep inside, the one made by Bea's going, that had stopped aching. I felt certain again she hadn't abandoned me. For all I knew, she could have left to rescue me. I even smiled then. The idea of a girl rescuing a bloke, a real role-reversal. The smile went. I had to acknowledge I was in serious danger now, but a part of me couldn't actually take that on board, couldn't believe that I could die like the others. Maybe that was my sixth sense, or just naïvety. Maybe no one ever believes they're going to die, else how could you go to war? But worst of all are the people who know they are going to die and *want to*, because they believe something better is waiting for them on the other side. They're the most dangerous of all.

Funny how clear my head was then. I told myself I needed to rest. I lay on Fletcher's bed, my hands folded under my head, trying not to inhale the stink of whisky. I watched the ceiling of the Portakabin change shade as the dawn came. A lurid procession of images peopled my mind, Nick, Auriel's face, Manchester city centre, the Gathering Place, my home, my mum and dad. And Bea. I think I must have drifted off because I remember waking instantly when I heard Fletcher mutter in his sleep.

It was light now, and I was gripped by a feverish energy.

This was the day when I was going to get out of here.

22.

Bea's Story

Joe's parents picked me up from Beverley's house at nine o'clock in the morning. Apart from a grim look on his dad's face, you wouldn't have guessed what we were going to do. His mum was quite chatty, saying how Gemma had kicked up a fuss and wanted to come with us, or at least have the day off school. They didn't relent and dropped her off as usual.

I couldn't have done what Joe's mum did – just chat about this and that, comment on the weather and suchlike. It's a thing older people do, pretend everything is all right when it isn't. It's quite brave, when you come to think of it. Joe's dad said we were going to insist on seeing Joe, and if they refused us permission, then we'd get the police. I hoped it wouldn't come to that.

As for me, I was terrified and excited all at once. I wanted to see Joe so badly but the prospect of facing Kate and Fletcher again made my stomach somersault. I don't know if I could have gone there again if it wasn't for having Joe's parents with me.

We were all silent as we approached the rutted track that led to the farm.

"It's a dump," Joe's dad said.

Seeing it through his eyes, I realised that it was. Now it made me think of concentration camps. When we arrived we all got out of the car and Joe's dad knocked on the door. Will answered.

"Bea!" he said. He was clearly surprised and confused. He glanced at Joe's parents and then back at me.

"I want to see Joe," I said.

"That's not going to be possible," he replied, flushing.

"And why is that?" Joe's dad demanded.

"Well, basically, he's not here."

I didn't believe him for one minute. A fury possessed me and I pushed my way past him. I looked in the Reading Room, the kitchen, the Gathering Place, I ran out to the dormitory shouting his name. Soon a group of White Ones surrounded me. One was Kate. She grabbed me.

"Bea!" she cried. "You've come back to us. Thanks to the Light!" Then she saw Joe's parents, and her hands, which had been holding mine, fell to her side.

"We've come to see Joe," I said.

"He's not here."

"I want to see for myself."

She stood to one side. I took Joe's parents to the dormitory – Joe wasn't there. I looked around the allotments, peered into the new chapel. We went back inside. I climbed the stairs to Fletcher's room, knocked, entered and saw it was empty. The bed was stripped. The air was cold and the room smelt of emptiness. Kate was behind me.

"Where's Fletcher?" I asked.

"Gone. With Joe," she said. "To achieve his Perfection."

"Gone where?" asked Joe's mum.

I supplied the answer. "To Orkney." Briefly, I filled them in on Fletcher's conviction that Joe was a Perfect, and that I was certain now that Kate and Will were telling the truth. Joe himself had told me about the projected trip to Orkney.

"Joe being Perfect? I'd laugh," said Joe's dad, "if it wasn't so bloody serious."

I begged Kate to tell me where in Orkney they were. Carbister, she replied. None of us had heard of it and Kate herself had never been there. Nor, apparently, had Will. There was no way of contacting them by telephone, they said, and swore the number was ex-directory. That struck me as the truth. They didn't know how long Joe and Fletcher had gone for, nor when they were coming back. We had a drawn a blank.

I asked Joe's parents if we could go back to the car. I hated being back on the farm. It made me feel as if I couldn't breathe. They agreed and we sat there, trying to formulate a plan.

Joe's mum thought of ringing the police in Orkney, or maybe a local church. I knew what I thought we should do, and when Joe's dad suggested that very thing, I was relieved.

"We'll go to Orkney ourselves," he said.

It was decided. But nothing is ever that simple. Joe's mum pointed out that there was Gemma – she couldn't come with us, and we would have to wait until we saw her after school. Then there was the awkwardness about me. I offered to stay with Gemma as I could hardly expect the Woods to pay for me to go. Joe's mum asked me if I wanted to go, I said I didn't, but I think I must have been unconvincing. Joe's dad said they would take me, and that was the end of it.

The next twenty-four hours crawled by. Joe's parents were busy getting the tickets, making arrangements for Gemma to stay with her friend Vicky and sorting things out at their workplaces. I was with Beverley, talking to her about my hopes and fears. I couldn't imagine that Joe had gone there willingly, not after what he said to me that night in Manchester. Beverley said she wasn't so sure. That made me scared he'd changed his mind about leaving the White Ones. Only that was better than thinking he was in danger. I couldn't find anything to think that made me feel better. Waiting was sheer torment.

Joe's parents came to collect me early Wednesday morning. I wanted to pray that we would find Joe safe, but I discovered I didn't know who to pray to any more. Beverley was a churchgoer and she said Jesus was probably as good as anyone. It made me smile, the way she was so casual about him. And then I thought, maybe that was how you had to be about religion, not take it too seriously.

It was such a relief as the plane gathered speed on the runway and lifted with a rush into the waiting blue sky.

I got out of bed as quietly as I could, hoping not to disturb Fletcher. In a few moments I was out of the Portakabin and in the stinging cold air of the Orkney morning. I was glad of it as it woke me fully. It was a clear day with just fingers of cloud streaking the sky. I looked around me and saw the main bungalow with its white roof, some other Portakabins, a building that looked like a garage, and the Croft – the chapel where Laban said he would be waiting for me. I could see now that all around the grounds of Carbister was a high wall topped with barbed wire. It was lucky I didn't try to escape last night. However, beyond the Portakabin where I slept, there was no wall, but what seemed to be a drop, and in the distance was the sea, curving to the horizon.

Then I was aware of movement. People were making their way to the Croft for the Morning Service. It seemed wise to join them. Within a few moments I was out of the cold and in the slightly less cold chapel. Men gave me curious glances, and some nodded. Laban was among them. In fact it was him who went out to the front and started conducting the familiar Service in his faint Scottish accent. I knew the routine and the responses by heart.

I counted five other men there apart from me. Rendall was not among them. Presumably the Morning Service was too early for him – it was something else he no longer had any need for. Jacob was absent too. The Croft felt damp and smelt of mould. Laban intoned the Service perfectly, never missed a beat. I looked at him from time to time but he was not giving anything away. I wondered how much I ought to trust him. I certainly wasn't going to beg him for help – one thing I'd learnt was to be far more sparing of my faith. But I wanted to hear what he had to say to me and find out whether I could use it to my advantage.

We greeted each other as we left the Service. I noticed Laban had stayed behind to collect the service books. I offered my help, which he accepted. When we were alone, Laban went to sit at the foot of the dais where the lectern was placed. I joined him.

"How's your friend this morning?" he asked me, with dry amusement.

"He's not up yet," I said.

"Once an alcoholic, always an alcoholic."

"If you knew that," I countered, "why did you give him a bottle of whisky?"

"You've got me there," Laban said.

In other words, he wasn't going to tell me.

There was silence. Laban was a powerfully built man, all muscle. His hair was thinning and cut close to his head. His skin was rough, pitted with craters from acne. He was an ugly bloke, not the sort I'd normally have anything to do with. He didn't look like a typical White One, either.

"What's your position here?" I asked him. I knew very little about him.

"There are no positions as such at Carbister. There's Rendall, and there's the rest of us. I manage things, if you like. See to the running of the place, the provisions, the finance, all those mundane, worldly affairs that take care of themselves if you believe in the Light."

"But you believe in the Light?"

"Of course! Every bit as much as you do." His voice dripped with cynicism. "But I forget myself. You're a Perfect, Joe. An Immortal."

"I'm not," I said.

He gave me a sharp glance, then turned away and spoke the rest of his words into the distance.

"Silly boy. Tell them you're a Perfect. Then you can stay here and flatter Rendall like the rest of them do. And in time he'll pass everything on to you. You've got it made. The idiots here will do your every bidding."

"If you feel like that," I asked him, "why haven't you left?"

"How much do you know about Carbister?" he asked. I told him, very little. "Let me fill you in," Laban said. "But I'll have to start at the beginning."

"It was the late 1960s. Three students came to Stromness for their Easter vac, typical upper-class Oxbridge sorts. Colin Rendall, Matthew Chalmers and Trevor Norrington-Smith. They told their families they hired the cottage up here to start revising for their exams. Well, if you believe that, you'll believe anything. They'd stashed away enough dope and LSD to take them to eternity and back. Which was, come to think of it, what happened. One night all three of them get high as kites on acid and take the boat out for a midnight row. It's not hard to guess what happens next. The boat capsizes. Chalmers and Norrington-Smith drown, Rendall splashes about, and is just going down for the final time when my grandad picks him up."

"Your grandad?"

"Angus Middleton. It was one of his boats they nicked. He was after them. He got Rendall back to the shore and resuscitated him, called the ambulance etcetera, but lost the boat. The other bodies were recovered later. The official story was that no one was to blame – it turns out Rendall's father was a local magistrate. But I know who my money is on."

"Why do you say that?"

"Rendall's always been able to twist the truth to serve himself, and he can talk the hind legs off a donkey. I was only a kid when the accident happened, but I can still remember the day he came to our cottage with his parents to thank us – I thought he was a member of the royal family, he was so bloody gracious. One slight omission – he forgot to recompense us for the loss of the boat. My granddad was loath to mention it as it seemed mean under the circumstances.

"Then, about eight years later, Rendall turns up again. We found him walking along the shore with some more mates, more impressionable young men, saying, this is where it happened, this is where I had the revelation."

"Where he had his near-death experience and saw the angels."

"That very one. So they all fall to their knees and start praying. They couldn't see me and my mates. Lucky, as we were killing ourselves laughing. Then Viking ran over barking and broke up the prayer meeting. I went over and apologised about the dog, and Rendall said it didn't matter, there was meaning in everything. Rendall told me they were looking for some property to buy or rent, and could I help him. I said I couldn't – I knew nothing about property then. I'd only just left school, earning what I could through casual labour, waiting for the day when I could leave the bloody island.

"He didn't settle in Stromness. He found a house in Kirkwall and his friends came and stayed with him. I got curious about them. The rumour was they were starting a new religion – we're used to nutters like that up here. But I noticed how more and more people turned up, and I began to think, this is interesting, maybe there's something in this for me.

"Then Rendall came into some money when his parents died. That decided me. I was out of work again and asked if I could join them. Rendall was keen on me coming on board, very keen. I even wondered if he was a queer, but when I saw the women leave his quarters early in the morning, I changed my mind about that.

"I played along. I flattered Rendall and managed his affairs. Despite all his learning he's wet round the ears when it comes to finance. He needs me. Carbister grew and grew. I was astonished at how simple some people are, how easily they believe utter rubbish, as long as it sounds good. I've worked here since then, either travelling and recruiting, or looking after things on the estate. You might say I'm Rendall's right-hand man, except he doesn't know it."

"He doesn't know it?"

"No. Which is why he's got this crazy idea of finding a successor who's a Perfect. It's his way of cutting me out. By rights, I should be the next in line. This place would collapse if it wasn't for me. The men look up to me here. They do what I tell them. I can make it work. I've put my life into this place."

"Listen, Laban. You can have it all. The last thing I want is to stay here. I'm not a Perfect. I just want to go home."

"The others weren't like you," he mused.

"What happened to them?"

"They've gone to join the Light," he said. "They live at peace in the kingdom of eternal refulgence."

"You mean they're dead?"

"Couldn't manage the full SD. One blacked out and his heart stopped beating. The other was sick with fear and choked on his own vomit."

"But how can Rendall let that happen? What about their families?"

"Khatri's family is in India. McConnell was more of a problem. We said he ran away and we showed them an empty boat. Even the police agreed his body could be anywhere."

What chilled me was the matter-of-fact way Laban was talking. Life seemed cheap to him. By extension, my life would be cheap too.

"Is Rendall aware these boys died?" I asked.

"Died? Come on – you mean Elevated. They're in a better place. Rendall actually believes all the rubbish he spews out. When he was younger he used to be quite impressive. I could see why so many people flocked to him. Even I, for a time... He'd look at you like you were his long-lost son. He could even read a shopping list and make it sound like gospel. But now, he's a spent force, a wreck. His health's not so good – prostate trouble, I believe. Unless he hands over the reins soon, the White Ones will collapse."

I had heard enough. If all Laban had said was true, it would be in his interest to let me go. I decided to take a risk.

"Can you help me escape?" I asked. "As soon as possible?"

He thought for a while.

"Not so easy. Rendall's interest in you means they'll all be watching you constantly." He took a deep breath. "Not to mention lover boy – sorry – Fletcher. But what about this? Say you agree to take on the SD, play along with them. I'll stay with you. Fletcher might not like that, but if I was to mention his little escapade last night, that will put paid to him as far as Rendall's concerned. Then, when the time is right, I'll untie you and get you away. I'll let Jacob in on this – I know he can be trusted. Simple bloke, not much between the ears, I'm afraid. Your best bet is to take a boat from the jetty. We have our own landing place beyond the Portakabins. Can you row?"

"Yes," I said.

"Then row for dear life. If you go down the coast you can get to the village. I'll give you some money and arrange for someone to pick up the boat. Then you can get the early morning bus on the main road. What do you think?"

"Are there any other ways I can get out?"

"No."

It was the hardest decision I ever had to make. I honestly didn't know if I could trust Laban or not. I could see what he had to gain from getting rid of me – leadership of the White Ones. I could also see that my death might not profit anyone – my family didn't live in India, and one more death in Carbister would be extremely suspicious. Laban's best hope was in assisting me to escape. And yet. And yet. Why was he so keen to help me? Why did it all seem so easy?

I couldn't answer those questions. My other doubt was whether I could bear to even commence full SD. The prospect was terrifying.

"What if I can't even manage ten minutes of SD?"

"You will. It'll be me fitting your shroud. There'll be space for you to breathe."

"Are you sure you'll be in attendance?"

"I give you my word. So will you do it?"

It didn't seem as if I had any other choice. Suddenly I was overcome with tiredness and a kind of despair. The whole thing was impossible. I was weak anyway. I had to undergo the SD whatever happened, and then row in the middle of the night on the open sea, when the last time I had rowed was on a boating lake in Heaton Park! Just then I felt as if it was all beyond me. But still I said, "I'll try."

"You'll need some rest," Laban said. "We'll clear Fletcher out of your quarters and get you some shuteye."

I was truly grateful for that.

24.
Bea's Story

We had to change planes at Edinburgh. That was when the first piece of bad luck hit us. The connection to Kirkwall was delayed. It triggered the feeling in me that fate was against us and that Joe must be in some kind of trouble. Joe's mum tried to calm me down, but I reasoned the two of us had been so close, I could tune into him and I was certain something was wrong. Meanwhile Joe's dad was pacing up and down, up and down, looking out of the windows of the departure lounge as if he could make the plane materialise by force of will alone. We didn't get to Kirkwall until six-thirty in the evening.

Joe's dad had booked us a hotel so we went there first, but none of us wanted to lose any time in finding Joe. I knew that the White Ones' headquarters were at Carbister so we began by asking the receptionist where that was. Not far, she said, smiling. She directed us out of Kirkwall, to a farmhouse on the coast about seven miles away. We didn't even stop to have dinner but drove straight there in the hired car Joe's dad had arranged yesterday.

The receptionist gave us the name of the village the farm was close to and we found that easily enough. Now my earlier fear changed into excitement, a feverish excitement. The farmhouse was exactly where the receptionist said it would be, standing back from the road, painted pale blue with a collection of windmills in the front.

When I saw it I began to wonder, why the windmills? They

didn't go with White One philosophy. The farmhouse looked well-maintained and inviting. I think I hoped this was Carbister because, if it was, then Joe was quite obviously safe. No harm could come to you in a place like that. We all three left the car and Joe's mum knocked on the front door.

It was opened by a small, neat elderly woman. I knew then we were in the wrong place. But Joe's dad asked anyway, explaining he was looking for his son, Joe Woods. The lady looked baffled, and called for her husband. We lost valuable time in apologising for being in the wrong place and disturbing them. They were slow people – slow in the way they talked, I mean. They chewed over everything we said. The old man stroked his chin.

"Carbister is quite a common name in these parts. There's been the odd time we've had letters misdirected. Let me see if I can remember. About six months ago. Yes, a letter came and the handwriting wasn't clear. The postman brought it here thinking it might be for me, but I could see immediately it wasn't. The name on the envelope began with Ren-something – I'm Graeme McDonald – and it read Carbister, near Finstown. Other end of the island, that is. To tell you the truth, I was surprised the postman –"

"How do you get there?" Joe's dad interrupted.

"Aye, well, you'd be better going back into Kirkwall and follow the coast round – what's the name of the road, Bessie? Take the road that goes to Tingwall. That should get you there. Aye, that's the one. The postman took the letter back to the post office – young man, new to the job. I hope it arrived safely. You might like to…"

We explained were in a big hurry and thanked him for his help. Once back in the car we pored over the map we had of the island. We found Tingwall and Joe's dad revved up the car engine.

But all the time the sense I had that Joe was in danger grew and grew.

25.

When we got back to the Portakabin Fletcher was dressed. He was sitting on the edge of the bed, which he had made with blankets tucked in tightly, army style. His face was white. His eyes locked with Laban's.

Laban broke into the silence. "We need to speak, Fletcher, about a multitude of things."

Fletcher jumped to his feet. I noticed that he must have cleared away the whisky bottle although there was still the aroma of alcohol in the air.

"Joe needs to rest," Laban continued.

Now Fletcher looked at me pleadingly. I found it hard to meet his eyes — I was scared of him, sickened by him, and yet had to acknowledge his devotion to me. It was with massive relief that I watched him leave the Portakabin with Laban. I locked the door from the inside and got on to a bed.

There was no way sleep would come. I kept replaying everything Laban had told me, and decided that it all made sense. Rendall was a con artist. Or, he had persuaded himself of the absolute veracity of his near-death experience to absolve his guilt for the accident. If his friends were still alive somewhere, then he was innocent. If his friends were in a better place, then he wasn't just free of blame, but had done something good, something praiseworthy. His self-conviction was clearly so strong others had come under its spell. Even me, I was part of that chain.

For nine months I had believed in the Light. Now my belief

had been savagely ripped from me there was a gaping chasm. I was facing the fact that my religion – that all religions – might be wish fulfilment and self-delusion. I didn't want to think that. Then it struck me that what mattered wasn't what someone believed or didn't believe, but how they lived. How you treat other people is more important than how you treat yourself, or even puzzling out the meaning of life. You make your own meaning. By what you choose to do.

I could feel my thoughts going round in circles and knew that was a precursor to sleep. I wanted the oblivion of sleep. I knew it would make me feel better. I turned on to my side, foetal position, and tried to visualise my bedroom back home. It wouldn't come into view.

I woke after a dreamless sleep and couldn't move for a while. I lay there, recalling all I had learned and what was ahead for me. I knew that the one thing I couldn't afford to do now was have any doubt. I told myself it was in Laban's interests to let me escape, which meant he would make sure I survived the SD. Also he wouldn't have suggested me rowing to safety if he didn't know it was possible. He wanted me off the island. My freedom would profit him more than my death.

There was a rap at the door and I heard Laban's voice calling me softly.

"I'm up," I said, getting off the bed to let him in.

His eyes roved round the Portakabin, and then settled on me.

"Rendall's decided to start your full SD tonight," he said.

A surge of nausea almost overwhelmed me.

"There'll be a feast first. Take my advice, eat little and drink water sparingly. That was where McConnell went wrong. I'll stay with you and when it's safe, I'll let you go. One thing you must promise me. When you get out, say nothing about Carbister except we're a bunch of deluded freaks. Nothing else. Say nothing of what you've seen here. If you do, I'll know. Do you understand?"

"I understand," I said.

"Good." His tone changed from menacing to affable.

"And now I'll take you for a walk to freshen up. You might like to see the landing place where the boat will be, as you'll have to find it yourself in the dark."

I agreed, and in a few moments we were out of the Portakabin and into the grounds of Carbister. I could tell by the light in the sky it was late afternoon. Not many people were about.

"How's Fletcher?" I asked Laban.

"I took him to Rendall. He's doing double ASD as a penance for his drunkenness. Rendall wasn't best pleased. Men hate worst of all to see their own sins in others. You needn't worry about Fletcher."

Laban took me beyond the Portakabins towards some rough scrubby land that sloped downwards. There was a track that led down towards the shoreline. We walked about 200 yards or so until we had a clear view of the coast. There was the landing place – a fairly large, well maintained jetty with several boats tied to it. I wondered what they were used for. Did the White Ones at Carbister row for exercise? Or pleasure? Or even fish? But I guessed it wouldn't be wise to ask too many questions.

"Take the smallest boat," Laban instructed me. "The one at the end on the right."

"OK."

I was beginning to feel more hopeful. The fact Laban had brought me out here testified to the fact he really intended to help me escape. I looked out to the open sea and saw the way the coast curved round.

"Stay within the bay," Laban warned me, "and head south. There's a jetty in the village. I'll leave a torch in the boat. You'll need it. There'll be a rucksack with some provisions and cash."

"Thanks."

"We'd better head back." Laban turned and I followed him.

We were greeted when we arrived back by Jacob and a couple of others. I was told I had to prepare myself for the SD by cleansing myself and changing into the clothes Rendall had provided, which were now laid out for me in the bungalow. Once changed, I was to attend the Evening Service, and then be taken to the feast. Laban assented to this.

Rendall greeted me at the door of the bungalow. He pressed me to him. I felt the jut of his stomach and smelt again the aroma of fragrant tobacco. He let me go.

"You are, to me, this night, as a son. The good father, Joseph, nurtures his son, but at the same time prepares to let him go. Letting go is that hardest part. Yet the loving son returns to the father, and I look forward to your return, trailing clouds of glory. Both the Father and the Son will be exalted."

I would not let myself get drawn into his rhetoric.

Jacob then took me to a large bathroom with a freestanding

bath. Someone had filled it. Over a chair were laid some white clothes. I was instructed to change into them once I had cleansed myself. To my relief Jacob left me, and I was alone.

I was quite glad of the bath. It warmed and relaxed me. Lying there, I saw how thin I had become. My legs were pale and sinewy and my stomach almost cavernous. I hoped there was enough strength in my body to carry me through. The bruises on my chest hadn't yet healed. But men had survived worse than I was about to endure. I wasn't going to think negatively. Instead, I tried to imagine what would happen once I was out of here. I'd get that bus to the nearest village and the first thing I'd do, I'd phone Mum and Dad. Somehow I'd get off the island, take the ferry back, get a train maybe. Mum and Dad would meet me at the station. I smiled at the thought. And then I would track down Bea. I realised that despite all the terrible things that had happened, and my wish never to have anything to do with the White Ones again, I still wanted Bea. I no longer believed she had turned from me. And yet, when I tried to see her face in my mind, I couldn't. I couldn't bring her into view. Funny, that.

When the bath had cooled I got out, dried myself and put on the clothes they had left me. White pants and vest, baggy white linen trousers, a white kaftan and a white robe. I thought, how the hell am I going to row in that lot? I hoped Laban had thought to provide me with something warm to wear.

Jacob was waiting for me outside the bathroom. Laban was right – I wasn't going to be left unattended for one moment. Jacob led me to the Croft for the Service. It was almost a repeat of the previous night, except for two things. It was longer because of the addition of prayers relating to me, and Fletcher wasn't there. At the end, Jacob and Laban escorted me to the feast.

We entered a large dining room with a long table running down the middle. Everyone was already assembled. Someone lit the candelabras that were positioned at intervals on the table, and then the lights were turned off. Shadows danced on the walls. I was shown a place to the right of Rendall, who was seated at the end of the table.

There were more prayers, and then food was brought in. Not the kind of rank stuff we had at Lower Fold, but a rich beef stew, and there was red wine on the table.

"You must eat and drink," Rendall said. "It symbolises Contrast. Just as the Light and Dark are separate, Feasting is distinct from Fasting, from full SD. First you must feast, then you must fast."

I nodded. However, I recalled Laban's advice and asked Rendall for water. He raised his eyebrows and insisted I had at least a sip of wine. I thought it best to do so. Its richness reminded me of earlier times, before the White Ones. The memory heartened me. I played around with my dinner, protesting loss of appetite. Rendall noticed but did not make a fuss. He was happy to orate to me and Laban, but the way he was talking while his mouth was full was gross.

Time passed slowly. I tried to block out thoughts of the forthcoming SD, or rather, think of it as a means to an end – my passport out of here. I guess I was a little hysterical – I was chattier than usual, in the way I remember being before my A2s. Always when I faced some test, I seemed to get high – maybe it was the adrenaline. All well and good, I thought. I needed all the adrenaline I could muster.

I gave up trying to work out what time it was. And then, out of the blue, Rendall rose for the Grace After Meals. Now I felt sick. My earlier bravado drained away. I wondered what would happen if I just ran for it. I glanced at Laban and saw him give me a tight smile. That made me feel a little better.

At the end of Grace everyone present left their seats, came over to me, and muttered a prayer. Fingers were kissed and pressed to my forehead. I told myself, it was like an operation, really. Like going under with anaesthetic. When I was a kid I broke my arm in a game of footie in the park. Dad took me to casualty and I had anaesthetic then. I had to count to twenty but I never got there, and the next second woke up groggily in a hospital bed with Mum by my side.

Rendall, Laban and Jacob led me out of the dining hall, along a corridor and down some steps.

"You must prepare for your immersion," Rendall said.

We arrived in the basement. It was cold down there. The brick walls had been painted white. In one corner was what looked like a large vat and in another was a bed, and on it was the paraphernalia for my SD, a blindfold, ropes, a shroud. Pure terror took hold of me. I felt sobs rising that I couldn't suppress. No, I couldn't go through with it. I was retching, I was going to throw up.

Laban, who was watching me closely, took my arm and got me to a corner of the room where I was sick. He handed me a handkerchief and I wiped my mouth.

"I won't leave you," he said.

"I've changed my mind," I told him. "I don't want to do it."

"Don't be silly."

"I've changed my mind," I shouted. Rendall and Jacob turned. "I'm not a Perfect. Let me go, OK?"

"They all did this," Rendall remarked to Jacob.

I began to babble. "Let me go. Look, I won't say anything. I just want to go. The whole thing's been a mistake. I'm scared, OK? Let me go. You won't get away with it."

"You know what to do," Rendall said to Jacob. Jacob went over to a table and got a syringe. I realised it must contain some kind of sedative, and if it did, bang goes my chance of escape. I'd be out cold. I knew I had to get hold of myself and seem to submit of my own free will.

"I'm sorry," I said. "I'm sorry. I'm OK now. It was the antimatter. But I'm back in control. I won't need that." I pointed to the syringe. Jacob questioned Rendall with his eyes. Rendall shook his head and Jacob replaced the syringe on the table.

"You must now divest yourself of your clothing," they said. Jacob handed me a large towel, and I was glad to see they all turned away from me. I did as they said. Once undressed, I wrapped the towel round me. I was naked except for the shell Bea had given me, that I still wore round my neck.

Then Rendall put on a white cloak with a hood, like a figure of Death. He read some more prayers. As he did so Jacob and Laban led me to the vat. There were steps by the side and I climbed them. The vat was filled with water. I passed them the towel and stepped inside. At least the water was warm. I stood there up to my chest while Rendall concluded the prayers. Now I wanted to laugh. Maybe it was hysteria, I don't know. Then Rendall gave a signal, Laban told me to immerse and I did so, holding my breath as I did on my initiation, counting, eyes screwed shut, twelve-thirteen-fourteen-fifteen-sixteen, as long as I could manage. Then I rose out of the water choking and spluttering. Jacob passed me the towel and I rubbed myself dry, dressing as quickly as I could.

My fear had gone. I was completely blank. A sort of numbing fatalism settled on me. I had no choice. Maybe it wouldn't be as bad as I thought. And so far, Laban had not let me down. Since he was my only hope, I had to give him all my trust.

They led me to the bed. First they plugged my ears with something solid, far more effective than the wax we used at Lower Fold. Then they blindfolded me, tying the blindfold with a tight knot at the back of my head. I could feel the knot against my scalp. With the blindfold over my ears too I could make out no sound at all. Next they inserted cotton wool in my nostrils. All this I had experienced before.

Then they guided me on to the bed, and made me lie down. They took the ropes and bound my arms to my body and tied my legs together. The terror came back, accompanied by more nausea, and I wet myself. I hoped they didn't notice. Stupid thought, at a time like this. Next came the sheet, which they wrapped tightly round me. I could feel my heart thumping in my body and I was scared I was going to be sick again.

But the worst was yet to come. It was this.

Nothingness.

I couldn't move, couldn't see, couldn't hear. I didn't know if

Rendall, Jacob and Laban had gone, or not. I didn't know if one second had passed, or one minute, or an hour. It was like I was dead, but fully conscious.

The panic came in spasms. There were moments when I thought I was going to stop breathing and pass out. Then they receded and I was able to think very calmly. I told myself that it was too early for Laban to rescue me. Or that I would survive this anyway. Then I thought of the other two, of Khatri and McConnell, and of Nick, and the panic came again. I tried moving my limbs, but I was tightly bound. I tried jackknifing my body, but realised I was tied down to the table. I sobbed, but couldn't hear my own sobs.

Then I calmed again and told myself I mustn't lose it. I mustn't panic, mustn't lose consciousness either. I had to think of something that would keep me sane. I tried visualising Bea again and as I did so I felt her love and concern wash over me. But it didn't work for me, it made me feel sorry for myself. A voice inside me said, you mustn't feel sorry for yourself. If you're going to survive you must stay cool and calm. Detach yourself.

I thought I'd give myself a memory test. So I tried going through the stuff I'd learned for my A2s. Amazing how much of it was still there. The British Constitution. The American Constitution. Never thought it would come in useful, but there you go. Congress. House of Representatives. I wanted to laugh as the absurdity struck me. But I couldn't move my mouth, my throat had seized up, and my left leg was itching and I couldn't scratch.

And I thought, I'm going to die here, but a voice inside me said, you're not.

I tried to count inside my head to help regulate my breathing. In two three four. Out two three four. In two three four. Out two three four. In, out. In, out. No, I didn't think I would make it. Another wave of panic hit me and I blacked out.

26.

Bea's Story

Joe's dad insisted we stop in Kirkwall to have something to eat, as we needed the energy. I knew he was right but I resented every minute we weren't on the move. We quizzed the owners of the restaurant we ate in, but they didn't know the side of the island we were bound for. They recommended we wait until the morning when we could buy an ordnance survey map – they didn't have one.

For ten minutes or so we decided we would do that. Then Joe's mum said, "I don't feel at all tired."

Joe's dad said, "Nor do I. I haven't done that much driving today."

"I could help you," Joe's mum added.

They looked at me and I smiled at them. We could all read each other's minds. We wanted to find Joe, and tomorrow was too late. They paid the bill, we got back in the car, and found the road to Tingwall.

We were on the road for what seemed like ages. Ten miles or so from Tingwall we slowed down to read the names on the farms and cottages we passed. We had already learned there were few towns and villages. There was hardly any street lighting either. And it was late. I hadn't wanted to check my watch to see how late it was, or even look at the clock in the car. When I did, I discovered it was midnight. I mentioned that fact.

"I know," said Joe's dad. "We can't go on like this all

night. It's like looking for a needle in a haystack."

The fact we all three knew we were being foolish united us. It made us even more reluctant to give up. I noticed a road on our right.

"That must lead somewhere," I said.

"If only there was someone to ask," Joe's mum said, not for the first time.

Joe's dad took the right turning and we drove for ten minutes or so, encountering no buildings whatsoever. The road curved, climbed, then descended. There in front of us was a bungalow with a white roof, surrounded by other, lower buildings and some Portakabins. It was because the place reminded me of Lower Fold that I knew we were in the right place.

"This will be Carbister," I said.

We pulled up in front of the gate. It was locked. Around the building was a wall with barbed wire on the top. Joe's dad noticed a panel by the gate with metal buttons. He pressed one and tried speaking into the grille by its side.

"Hello? Is this Carbister? Is anyone there?"

There was no indication that the button was working. He tried pressing every one in turn. Either the entryphone was inactive or they'd all gone to bed. Or we were being ignored.

After ten minutes or so of this we tried walking round the perimeter of the building. The wall extended right down to what looked like some rocks that led down to the sea. Carbister was cut off from the world. I was more and more sure that this was where Joe was, and I made sure Joe's parents believed me. They did. But this didn't change the fact there was absolutely no way of getting in.

"What shall we do?" Joe's mum asked.

"We could drive back to Kirkwall and come again in the morning, now we know where it is." But Joe's dad's voice didn't have any conviction in it.

"You can," I told him. "But I'll stay here."

"Don't be silly," Joe's mum said. "You'll freeze to death."

"I'm not going," I said. "Joe's in there somewhere and I'm not leaving him."

Joe's parents exchanged glances. I wasn't going to give in. I was staying put.

"It's quarter to one," Joe's dad said. "I think I'd better ring the hotel on my mobile and tell them we're not coming back until tomorrow. We can stay in the car until the morning."

I breathed a sight of relief.

"I think everyone is asleep," he said, his voice level. "But people wake up early here. A lot of them are probably fishermen," he said.

I could tell he was tired. We all settled in the car, Joe's parents insisting I stretch out on the back seat. I refused and said they ought to get in the back – I was smaller than them and would be better off in the front. After a while they agreed. It was a little uncomfortable lying out over the two seats because of the gear stick, but I could cope. Joe's mum covered me with her coat, then she cuddled up to Joe's dad, who had his arm around her.

I never thought I'd get to sleep, but eventually I did.

And then I woke with a start because I knew something was dreadfully, dreadfully wrong.

27

The next thing I knew, someone was shaking me.

There was a moment of sheer terror as I tried to work out where the hell I was. I thought, I'm suffocating, they're killing me. Then I remembered what was going on – this was full SD – but I was still alive, and I could feel the pressure of someone's hands – was it Laban's? I guessed and hoped I was being untied. Then the shroud I was wrapped in was loosened and I could breathe better. I sat up and removed my earplugs while my blindfold was taken off.

"You've got to get out of here as quickly as you can," Laban whispered.

"OK," I said.

"Follow me to the front door. I'll let you out. Remember – go straight to the jetty. Everything you need is there."

Still in my white garb I ran barefoot across the stone cellar floor. We climbed the steps into the darkened hall of the bungalow. I saw Laban pause and listen. Then his eyes did a quick survey and I saw him frown.

"There's a light coming from Rendall's room," he said. "And the door's ajar. Go now. I'll have to raise an alarm and say you've escaped. You want to get away well before they send out a search party."

"Thanks for this," I said, helping myself to some boots I found by the door. They were way too big. Someone's parka was hanging on a coatstand and I took that too.

"Strange," Laban said. "The door's not locked from the

inside." He laughed. "I daresay Rendall's drunk again. Good luck."

Next thing I knew, I was out in the freezing cold. It was less dark than I imagined it would be. I reckoned it must be nearly dawn – I had obviously been asleep. That was good. I would have the strength I needed for my flight.

I darted silently through the Portakabins, noticing that in mine the light was off. I was at the back of Carbister, running down the track towards the shore. Every part of my concentration was focused on escape. What Laban had said about the search party worried me. There was no time to lose. I realised I would have to untie the boat from the moorings and hoped that wouldn't take too long. I also trusted that Laban had remembered the money. I would need that. Dimly at the back of mind I thought, I've survived SD. The worst is over. And I was filled with a wild exhilaration. I was nearly there. Nearly free.

The landing place came into view. There were three boats, two larger ones, as yesterday and the smaller one on the right, which was mine. All was going according to plan. I moved carefully along the jetty as it was still dark and I didn't want to lose my footing. There was my boat, and – yes (I could see the dark shape of a rucksack lying in it. Good old Laban! I stepped inside and the boat rocked gently. The oars were lying on the bottom of the boat. So far, so good. I saw the rucksack was open, so I checked its contents. Immediately I found the torch. There were also some clothes, a sandwich, a flask of something, and an envelope. I didn't have time to check if that was my cash, but guessed that it must be.

I switched on the torch and was glad to see it was pretty powerful. I used it to see where the boat was tied to the moorings. I knelt in the boat so I felt secure, and leaned over to unhitch it. It was simply a matter of lifting a loop of rope over the post. I got a firm hold of the rope and eased it up.

That was when I saw him. He must have been hiding in the boat opposite. At first I didn't know who he was and I thought, it's the search party, but that didn't make sense, because I would have heard and seen a search party coming. As he approached me, I did recognise him, all too well.

"Joe," Fletcher said, "I'm coming with you." And before I had a chance to react, he jumped into the boat and was facing me.

Now what? I couldn't go back. But I couldn't take Fletcher with me either. Only I had to do one of them. My mind raced through the possible outcomes of whatever decision I made, and I reckoned there was just a chance I could talk Fletcher into submission and escape with him. Anything but go back, anything but face more SD.

I continued unhitching the boat, and when I had finished, took the oars. Fletcher settled opposite, his eyes on me. The torch was lying on the bottom of the boat, and as the boat rocked, the light swung from side to side.

"They tried to keep me away from you," Fletcher said.

"Did they?" I tried to make my voice sound as normal as possible.

"I got out. I went to the cellar to find you but I heard Laban talking to you. So I decided to get here first."

"OK," I said. Although Fletcher scared me, his explanation

seemed innocent enough. If he was being kept prisoner too, he'd also want to escape. As long as he didn't prevent me from getting home, it wasn't a problem having him on board. In fact, he might even be useful, if I got tired, say, or—

"I'll never leave you again, Joe. As long as I live."

I rowed gently, keeping fairly close to the shoreline. Fletcher picked up the torch and pointed it at me.

"I'm never going back there, Joe. Laban is a false prophet. antimatter incarnate. He wouldn't let you complete your SD because he knew you were a Perfect. He wanted to stop you being revealed. Any action you take against such a man is justified by the Light."

I said nothing, just carried on rowing.

"We can go wherever you want, Joe. Anywhere. We can go to another country. Look what I have here."

He put down the torch and took two large Jiffy bags from the pockets of his parka. I was curious.

"What's in those?"

"Good quality junk."

"Junk?" My brain wouldn't engage. Junk. Did he mean what I thought he meant? "Junk. Like, heroin?"

The rolling torch lit Fletcher's face up momentarily. It illuminated his grin. "That's right. For years Laban's been trading in it. We have to have an income, Joe. I did my bit. I passed the stuff on at Lower Fold. I owed Laban my duty because he saved my life. But in trying to separate me from you, he's lost my loyalty. We can sell these and start over."

I was trying to piece this together. Laban had been using

Carbister for drug dealing? Impossible. But maybe not so impossible. The place was on the coast, quite cut off, and all the inmates would have been labelled by the locals as religious freaks. Then there were cells all over the country where the stuff could be sold on – I remembered Will and the shop in Hebden Bridge. No wonder Laban wanted me out of it as quickly as possible. Using Carbister as the hub of a drug dealing empire was his revenge on Rendall, who I know he loathed. Everything was far, far worse than I could have ever imagined. The boat began to move further out to sea as I had stopped rowing. The immensity of all of this was dawning on me. And I was implicated in it.

"Did Rendall know?" I asked Fletcher. "About the drugs?"

"He will never know," Fletcher said. "He has finally been Elevated. He is with the Light. O Light, that shines on us all, glory in your new child, Colin Rendall, and beatify his soul so that He is one with the Light, so that He is the Light, and the Light is Him."

"Fletcher, what are you on about? Is Rendall dead?"

"I had to do it, Joe. For your sake. He kept us apart and we have to be together. He fell asleep and I untied myself. Then he woke. I had no choice. I used the blindfold. I tied it tight around his neck. I'm sure he felt no pain. There is only joy in Elevation. Rendall himself taught us not to fear it. I am the Servant and my job is to clear the path to Perfection."

What was this? He had killed Rendall? The pieces rapidly fell into place. Rendall had him under double SD. Say Rendall had fallen into a whisky-assisted sleep. Then Fletcher freed himself,

Rendall woke, Fletcher killed him then went in search of me. He heard Laban talking to me and ran ahead – which was why the light was on in Rendall's room and why the door was unbolted. My heart was knocking at my ribs with fear. Should I just jump overboard to get away? Or what? What should I do? Fletcher was a psychopath, and still believed every word of Rendall's cult.

The voice in my head, the sensible one, which had been telling me what to do, came to my aid now.

Just carry on rowing, it said. *Keep him calm. Get to the shore near a house. Get help as soon as possible. It's your only chance.*

So I carried on rowing.

"Where are we going, Joe?" Fletcher asked me.

"To the shore," I said. My mouth was dry and sticky. My voice rasped with fear.

"No. Let's go to another island. There are lots of small islands. We need to stop for the Morning Service. I want to pray."

"Later on," I said, trying to stall him.

"I want to pray," he said.

"Look, you can pray here. In the boat. While I row."

Fletcher fell to his knees and while he mumbled to himself I took the opportunity to row as fast as I could. My arms were aching with the effort. The current was strong and it took every ounce of my strength to prevent us going too far out to sea. A breeze set in again, and thankfully it pushed us towards the shore. The first habitation I come to, I thought, I'll jump and run for it.

Fletcher got up and the boat rocked. He stood and clumsily made his way towards me. He remained upright, barely maintaining his balance.

"Let me take the oars now, Joe," he said.

"No. It's OK. I'm fine."

"I am the Servant. To me is the labour."

He advanced. There was going to be no way I could prevent him from taking the oars from me. He was bigger and stronger, and if we struggled we'd capsize the boat. I looked out to the shore. I reckoned I could swim the distance. If Fletcher took the oars, I'd be entirely in his power.

"All I want to do is serve you," he said.

I jumped. The shock of the icy water took my breath away. For a second I dipped under the surface of the water, but then I was out again and began to swim. I hadn't taken off my parka and the white robes I still had on clung to me and impeded my movement. The water was paralysingly cold. I thought, I've made the wrong decision, I'll drown. But that voice in my head said, *swim, swim*!

I tried an overarm crawl. Then I heard a splash and next thing I knew, Fletcher was swimming with me, catching up. I could hear his heavy breathing and knew he was gaining on me. I couldn't swim any faster. The shore was still some way off.

"Joe," he panted, put an arm over me and I lost the rhythm of my stroke. I struggled in the water, spluttering and splashing.

"Get away from me!" I tried to scream. I'm not sure he heard me.

"Joe," Fletcher said, panting. "I'm going to prove it to you. You're a Perfect. An Immortal. When you know this, you'll see your place is with me."

He pressed his hands on my shoulders and pushed me down

below the surface of the water. I thought, he wants me to drown, so I held my breath and then pushed upwards, although I was numb with cold. When I burst through into the air again, I swam as fast as I could, redoubling my efforts to get to the shore. I could feel seaweed tangling itself around my legs. Then Fletcher got hold of me once more.

"You cannot die," he said, and pushed me again below the water, his hands pressing down on my head. I couldn't hold my breath and gulped in seawater. But my feet came into contact with the seabed. I was nearer to the shore than I thought. I righted myself and pushed upwards, escaping Fletcher and I was breathing in lungfuls of cold air. Dawn was breaking and I registered that the sky was streaked with pink. I managed a few more strokes before Fletcher got me in a bear hug this time. He pushed me over and was on top of me. There was no way I could escape. He was saying something. I could no longer hear, or see. And then his mouth made contact deliberately with mine, and the loathing and fear I felt gave me the strength I needed. I kicked and pushed him off me and struggled free.

I came up for air, then tried to run through the sea to the shore. Fletcher got me by the legs, and I lost my balance. I breathed, but instead of air I took in water. Fletcher let go of me and I was free again, floating free and I found I didn't have the strength to move another inch, so I thought, I'll float for a bit, just above the seabed, and regain my strength.

It wasn't cold any more down there. It was a relief to float, to let the water enfold me. I wondered how long it would take to rise to the surface again. One, two, three, four, six, seven, eighteen, nineteen, eleven, eleven...

The pain and struggle ceased. I was travelling without effort, moving towards the Light. Where there had been terror, there was now beauty and peace beyond all understanding. An angel swathed in brightness...

28.

Bea's Story

Joe's mum and dad were still asleep. Quietly, so as not to disturb them, I got out of the car and realised I was fully awake, every sense was alert. There was a blush of pink in the sky. I put on Joe's mum's coat and crept around the side of Carbister, close to the wall, down towards the shore. The wall went right down to the rocks. There was no way I could get in.

I tried to quell my rising panic. Joe was in trouble and I couldn't reach him. A path went away from Carbister just above the shore and I thought I would walk along there, to calm myself and to decide what to do. Maybe I was creating my own fear. Maybe the tension I'd been through was playing tricks with my mind.

As the sky lightened, I looked out to sea. It should have been beautiful, the rising sun revealing the horizon, but then it spelt menace. I saw a boat. It was quite near. But it was empty. Strange.

And then I saw the struggle. Two men in the sea, flailing about. Quick as a flash I was running down the slope to the water, tripping, falling, sliding down. I got to the shore – they were closer, but now I could only see one of them. Just one. Someone had drowned.

I waded into the water. I had never been a good swimmer but I thought, if I believed I could swim, maybe I could. Then the figure I saw disappeared from view. *Now,*

Bea! I told myself. I swam a bit and saw the figure, just below the surface of the water. So I lifted him up, I lifted Joe up and wailed my grief.

In a moment Joe's dad was in the water with me, and his mum wasn't far behind. We got Joe back to the shore, not knowing if he was dead or alive. Next thing I knew, his dad was on his mobile calling for an ambulance. Joe's mum cradled his head in her arms.

"Let me," I said. "I learned first aid once."

I tilted his head back and lifted his chin to open his airways and I thought, he's not breathing. I glanced down at his chest and it wasn't rising. I listened at his mouth – nothing. I put my cheek to his mouth. My cheek remained cold. I knew what to do. I couldn't afford to panic or give way to my emotions. I knelt by him and pinched his nose closed. I checked his chin was still lifted which meant his airway was open. I breathed in deeply, put my mouth over Joe's mouth, and gave him my breath. I counted to two. And I saw his chest rise. I removed my mouth and watched his chest fall. Again, I thought. So I breathed in, covered his mouth, and breathed once more into him. Please, please, I thought. Breathe by yourself. For me, Joe. You can't leave me. I won't let you. I put my fingers to his neck to check for a pulse. And I could feel the beat of his blood. He was alive. Joe was alive. I breathed into him one more time, my hope rising. When I moved away I could see a faint movement in his chest. He was breathing by himself.

"He's OK," I said to Joe's parents.

We got him into the recovery position and stayed with him until the paramedics arrived.

29

We stayed together in the hospital. They let Bea sit by my side and while I was holding her hand, I felt better.

They said I nearly drowned. And I remember that feeling I had, of being at peace, of wanting to drift away and never come back. But unlike Rendall, I was glad I came back, because I had Bea.

When I first saw my parents I couldn't look at them. The guilt was unbearable. What a shit I'd been, so arrogant about my beliefs, so stupid, so selfish. But Mum said it was all right and there wasn't anything to forgive. Mum, Dad and Bea by my bedside. All of us – my real family.

It took me a long time to begin to feel normal again. The start was when I noticed odd little things – the way all the nurses had Scottish accents. One morning I imitated them for Bea and she laughed. The next stage was the first time I felt hungry. There's no better sensation than being hungry and eating. Just toast and tea – there's nothing better.

When I was ready they brought the police to me. I'd already told my parents all I remembered happening and they advised me to repeat what Fletcher had said. The officers didn't seem surprised. Rendall's body had been discovered – someone at Carbister had raised the alarm. Laban had been caught and was being questioned – the drugs squad had found hundreds of thousands of pounds worth of heroin. And Fletcher? The officers consulted with each other, and then one of them told me he'd drowned. He was dead. This is dreadful to admit, but I was relieved he had gone. Still, I hoped Fletcher's death was as peaceful as my almost-death had been.

I wanted Bea, and she lay on the bed with me, and we hugged, not saying anything. I think I slept for a bit. Then I ate again. Mum and Dad came over with the hospital telephone trolley and some coins.

"Here you are," they said. "Ring your sister."

I did.

"Gemma?" I said. "It's me. Joe."

"Joe?" There was silence. For the first time, Gemma was lost for words. But not for long. "Joe? Joe – you fucking idiot!" What could I say – I agreed with her assessment. Then she burst into tears. So did I. Pathetic, isn't it?

But speaking to Gem was a turning point. Reality re-asserted itself. I began to think about getting out of hospital and back home. We made plans to leave. Bea and Mum went to buy me some new clothes, some Gap jeans and a couple of sweatshirts. They were cool. It surprised me that I could feel pleasure in having them, but I did.

The night before I left the hospital, Bea came to sit with me, and we were by ourselves for some time. We talked and talked. We raked it all over, how we could have got so taken in by the White Ones and why we had laid ourselves open to being brainwashed like that. We examined every little thing and thought we'd got it sorted, that we'd laid the ghosts to rest.

But later that night, when Bea, Mum and Dad had gone and I pulled the shroud-like white sheet over me, I shuddered. At that moment I knew our complete recovery would take a very long time. I didn't even know what good we'd be able to salvage out of the wreck.

But, hey, I was alive, I had Bea, and the future beckoned.

DISCONNECTED

SHERRY ASHWORTH

"It's hard to know where to begin. I'm not even sure who I want to talk to. Or what I want to say. But maybe if I try to put all the different parts together it will make some sort of sense. So here's my story, and it's for each of you to whom I owe an explanation. But remember, I'm not sorry."

Catherine Margaret Holmes
Loving and dutiful daughter.

Cathy Holmes
A-level, A-grade student.

Cath Holmes
Friend and confidante.

Cat
Risk taker, thrill seeker, rebel.

Will that do as an introduction?

"It's not often that a book makes me think I must go out and find some more of this author's work now, but that's the effect *Disconnected* had on me. I was well and truly blown away."
Fiona McKinlay, teenage reviewer for whsonline.co.uk

An imprint of HarperCollinsPublishers